An I-TEAM Novel

# DEADLY INTENT

*USA TODAY* BESTSELLING AUTHOR
# PAMELA CLARE

**Deadly Intent**

An I-TEAM Novel

Published by Pamela Clare, 2018

Cover Design by © Carrie Divine/Seductive Designs
Image: Perfect Lazybones/Shutterstock
Image: MRBIG_PHOTOGRAPHY/iStockphoto

ISBN-10: 0-9987491-6-8

ISBN-13: 978-0-9987491-6-7

*This story is dedicated to women in uniform, who too often face sexism, sexual harassment, and sexual violence while serving their country.*

*No one should have to battle her fellow service members or her chain of command while also fighting the enemies of her nation.*

# ACKNOWLEDGMENTS

Thank you to Michelle White, Benjamin Alexander, Jackie Turner, Pat Egan Fordyce, and Shell Ryan for their unfailing support. Thanks to Shell, too, for the very handy list of Joaquin facts she wrote years ago. It was incredibly helpful. Where would I be without you guys?

Special thanks to Sarah Whitenight, for sharing her expertise from her years serving in the US Army; and to the Colorado Bureau of Investigation for answering my questions relating to ballistics and DNA analysis.

Additional thanks to Esmeralda Mijangos, Roxana Marmolejo, and Monica Flores-Rojo for lending me their expertise on Mexican Spanish so that Joaquin could have an authentic Mexican-American voice.

A hug and many thanks to author Jessica Scott, a real-life Army captain and badass, for her friendship and support and for helping to inspire this story.

More hugs and thanks to author Kaylea Cross for her friendship, support, and help in brainstorming Joaquin and Mia's story.

Thanks to all of you who love the I-Team characters so much and keep this series alive. I'm so very grateful.

# 1

---

Joaquin Ramirez parked behind a squad car, its lights flashing red, blue, and white in the twilight. He checked the Glock 27 he carried concealed in a pocket holster. It was loaded, a round in the chamber. After what had happened at the holiday party last month, he would never leave home unarmed again. Satisfied, he holstered the firearm, grabbed his camera bag, and climbed out of his truck, icy wind hitting him in the face.

A possible homicide.

That's all he'd been told. It was his weekend on call, and so far, he'd shot a protest at the State Capitol, a minor house fire, and a hit-and-run bicycle accident just off the 16th Street Mall. He'd thought his Pulitzer would free him from this kind of shit and enable him to focus on more significant assignments, but the *Denver Independent* was a small paper with only four photographers, one of whom covered sports exclusively.

Maybe it was time for him to leave, get out of Denver, and go to work for a more prominent publication, like the *New York Times* or *National Geographic*. He could travel, see the world through the lens of his camera, put his skills to the test. There would never be a better time than now. He was young, no woman in his life, no kids, not even a pet.

*Then why are you still here, working this same job?*

Matt Harker, a reporter on the paper's I-Team and Joaquin's best friend, had asked him that question last night. Joaquin had given him the answer he always gave himself. The people he loved—his friends and his family—lived here.

He hurried down the street, pulling out his camera as he went, snapping the wide-angle lens and flash into place. Just ahead, gawkers stood outside the barricade tape, their curiosity drawing them outside in sub-zero January temps.

A woman stepped out of the crowd and waved to him, huddled in a heavy parka. "Hey, Joaquin!"

"Hey, Cate, what's going on?"

Catherine Warner was the newest—and at twenty-five the youngest—member of the newspaper's elite I-Team, or Investigative Team. She had replaced Laura Nilsson on the cops and courts beat. She might look like a kid with blond hair and freckles, but she'd landed on her feet with an exposé about a couple of sheriff's deputies dealing drugs out of the evidence room.

She brought Joaquin up to speed. "A guy heard shouting and then gunshots coming from downstairs. He went down to check on his neighbor—a guy named Andrew Meyer—and found the door open. He walked in—"

"What an idiot."

"Yeah, well, the idiot found bullet holes in the shower stall along with shell casings. That's when he called the cops."

"He's lucky he wasn't shot, too. No body?"

"Nope."

"What are the cops saying?"

"Not a word."

"Did anyone else hear shots?" Discharging a firearm in a small apartment would make one *hell* of a racket—unless the shooter had a suppressor.

Cate nodded. "A couple of neighbors heard gunfire, too, but they didn't call it in. This isn't the kind of neighborhood where people are on good terms with the police."

"Any chance this guy accidentally shot himself and rushed off to the ER?" Joaquin had a decade of experience on Cate and was doing his best to mentor her, to help her curb her impulsiveness and mature as a reporter.

Cate shook her head. "I overheard one of the detectives say there was no John Doe or Andrew Meyer in any Denver-metro ERs. Also, the guy's vehicle is still here, parked in its space."

She pointed toward an old, brown Toyota Camry.

"Bullet holes, but no body. That's *loco*." Joaquin took in the scene, assessing the possibilities. It was his job to tell this story in a single image—not easy when it was dark and all he had to work with were bystanders, police tape, and squad cars.

A man he recognized as Detective Wu stepped out of the apartment.

"Detective Wu, can I ask you a few questions?" Cate hurried off to do her job, leaving Joaquin to do his.

He walked out into the street, looking for an angle that captured the scene with its tension and unknowns—the apartment with its open door, the barricade tape, bystanders, and at least a portion of a police cruiser. He adjusted the camera's ISO to 1600, snapped a few shots, then checked to see how they'd turned out.

The exposure was okay, but the image felt static. A man

might have lost his life here tonight. Neighbors, friends, and family were surely desperate and afraid for him. Joaquin could do better.

He shifted a few feet to his left, reworking the composition in his mind, then dropped to one knee and raised the camera again.

Someone stepped in front of his lens.

"Do you know what's going on?" a woman asked.

He lowered the camera and found himself looking up into a pair of big, angry blue eyes set in a strikingly beautiful face—high cheekbones, a little, upturned nose, a full mouth. "I'm with the Denver Independ—"

"Did something happen to Andy?" Red hair ruffled in the wind.

Joaquin got to his feet. "You know the guy who lives in that apartment?"

"Please answer my question."

Her abruptness surprised Joaquin, but he could see the fear in her eyes. It wasn't the first time someone had given him shit while he'd been on the job. People hated the media —until the moment they needed something.

"There's nothing official yet. A neighbor heard gunshots and found the door open but no one at home. He thinks he saw bullet holes and shell casings in the shower stall. They're calling it a possible homicide. I'm sorry."

The anger on her face melted into worry. "Thanks."

She turned away from him, walked up to the barricade tape, and stood there watching, delicate fingers from one hand raised to her lips, distress obvious on her face. Beyond her, a member of the crime-scene investigation team stepped out onto the porch and began to dust for prints.

Joaquin saw his shot.

He dropped to his knee once more, focused on the

woman, letting the CSI guy blur in the background, blue and red light from the police overheads bouncing off the apartment's windows, yellow tape cutting through the center. He took a dozen shots, checked them, then shot a few more to be confident he'd gotten it. He stood, scrolled through the images, and found a few that would work.

Now all he needed was the woman's name.

He walked up to her, reluctant to intrude into her personal space when she was clearly upset. "Hey, I'm really sorry. I hope this is all a big misunderstanding and they find your friend safe and sound."

Stranger things had happened.

She didn't bother to look at him. "Thanks."

"Can I get your name?"

Her head snapped around, surprise and fury on her face. "Did you photograph me? I didn't give you permission to do that."

"I don't need permission. You're on a public street, so—"

"God, I hate photojournalists. You show up at the scene of other people's misery looking for the shot that will land your name on the front page. You don't really care what's happening to people."

"Whoa! You don't know how I feel or what I'm thinking." Joaquin knew she was upset, but that didn't mean he had to take this. "It's my job to report news. You can give me your name or not, but the photo will still run."

She looked as if she were about to tell him to go to hell. Then the anger seemed to drain from her. "Mia Starr. S-T-A-R-R."

Joaquin jotted that down in his notebook. "Thanks, Ms. Starr. Despite what you think, I am sorry that—"

"It was her! I saw her walk up to Andy's door just a few hours ago."

A shout interrupted Joaquin, and he looked over to see a man in jeans and a T-shirt—the upstairs neighbor?—standing next to a cop, his finger pointed at Ms. Starr.

"She's the one! I heard him shouting at her!"

Every head on the street turned Mia's way.

She raised her chin. "Yes, I was here."

The police officer walked toward her and raised the barricade tape. "Ma'am, could we ask you a few questions?"

Mia had nothing to hide. "Sure."

She ducked beneath the tape, glancing back at the photographer, who watched her through dark eyes, an unreadable expression on his handsome face.

Yes, she had noticed his looks. A woman would have to be dead not to.

She followed the officer toward Andy's front porch, where they were met by a man who introduced himself as Detective Wu. "Is it true that Andy is missing? Someone said the neighbor heard gunshots and found bullet holes in his shower."

"Where did you hear that?" Wu asked.

"The photographer told me."

Wu frowned, clearly not happy about that. "We're not sharing information with the public at this time, but I do need to ask you some questions."

Mia decided to make it easy for him. "Yes, I was here tonight. Andy and I served together in Iraq. We've known each other for almost ten years. He was wounded during my first tour of duty and discharged. I was his company XO—executive officer—and I check on him when I can."

She did her best to stay in touch with everyone from

Bravo Company and to visit the ones who still lived in the Denver-metro area.

"What time did you get here?"

"It must have been around five-thirty. I stayed for about thirty minutes. Andy was sitting on his sofa watching sports on TV when I left. He was alone."

Wu wrote down her answers in a notebook. "Did the two of you argue?"

"Yes." The neighbor who'd pointed her out must have heard Andy shouting. "He wants me to help him get VA disability benefits, but there's nothing I can do."

It was the truth, if not the whole truth.

Wu pressed on, asking question after question. Did anyone call or come by while she was here? Did Andy give any indication that something was wrong or that he might be in danger? Did Andy have a history of drug abuse or any criminal associations of which she was aware? Did she know of anyone who wished him harm? Had she seen anyone hanging around his apartment this afternoon? Did Andy seem suicidal?

Mia answered "no" and "I don't know" again and again.

"Do you own firearms?"

"Yes—a SIG P320 and a twelve-gauge shotgun." Then it hit her. "Am I a suspect?"

"You are likely the last person to have seen him, so you're certainly a person of interest."

*Great.*

"Do you have any firearms with you in your vehicle or on your person?"

"No. They're at home, locked in a gun safe. I haven't fired them since the last time I cleaned them—about three years ago."

Wu asked to see her driver's license, calling in her info

over his radio before handing it back to her. "Are you still at this address?"

"Yes."

He wrote her address down, along with her work address and phone. "You say you left at roughly six. Where did you go?"

"I was hungry, so I drove to the taco place over on Federal—Tacos Azteca is the name, I think."

The detective nodded. "I know the place. They've got great burritos, too. So, you grabbed a bite to eat there. Why did you come back?"

"I was pretty sure I'd left my sunglasses here."

"Wouldn't it make more sense to call and find out for sure before coming over?"

"I did call. When Andy didn't answer, I drove over and found all of this."

Wu pressed a finger to his earpiece, listening, then took his hand mic. "Seven thirty-six. Copy."

He handed Mia her driver's license. "Thanks for your cooperation. You'll hear from us again."

*They're going to check out your story.*

The thought startled her. She'd told them the truth, but what if they couldn't corroborate it? What if there were no street cams? What if no one at Tacos Azteca remembered her?

"Is there any way I can get my sunglasses?"

Wu turned toward the front door. "You guys find a pair of women's shades?"

A man wearing white forensic coveralls stepped outside and held up a plastic evidence bag with a gloved hand. "Is this what you're looking for?"

Inside the bag were Mia's sunglasses, but they were smashed.

She took a step forward, reached for them.

Wu shook his head. "Sorry, Ms. Starr, but the sunglasses are evidence."

Mia supposed it didn't matter. She wouldn't be wearing them again. "When will you know whether Andy is ...?"

She couldn't bring herself to say it.

"We won't know anything for certain until we find him alive—or find his body."

"God. Right." She swallowed. "Am I free to go?"

"Yes, ma'am," Wu answered. "Please don't discuss this case or anything you might have heard or seen here with the media."

*As if.*

"No problem."

"I'm sorry about your friend."

"Thanks." Mia turned and, ignoring people's stares, crossed the lawn, ducked under the tape, and walked back to her car, a dull ache settling in her chest.

*Damn it, Andy!*

Who had done this? Whoever they were, they must have arrived right after she'd left. She hadn't been gone that long —an hour tops.

"Ms. Starr, hey, are you okay to drive?" The photographer had followed her, camera bag slung over his shoulder. "If there's someone I can call or if you need a lift..."

She clicked the fob that unlocked her Mazda and opened the door. She was used to taking care of herself. "I'll be fine."

She climbed into her vehicle, shut the door, and slid her key into the ignition, but it was a good five minutes before she drove away.

∾

*FUCK*, it was cold.

Huddled in his down parka, he watched from a safe distance while the cops finished up and turned the mess he'd made over to a crime scene cleanup crew. "Poor Andy. You never saw it coming."

He chuckled to himself, ignoring the pain in his skull. It had been more exhilarating than he'd imagined, and this was just the beginning.

One by one, he would get them all.

If he'd planned this better, he might have been able to pin it on Mia. It was clear the police considered the bitch a suspect. Oh, it would be sweet to see Mia Starr locked up forever. The stupid cunt. She more than deserved it.

Needles jabbed against his temples, his eyes, the inside of his skull.

Nothing made it stop. Nothing. Narcotics and marijuana dulled the pain, but it was with him even in his sleep.

He drew a breath, reached into his pocket for an Oxy, popped it into his mouth, and chewed. When this kicked in, he'd have to rethink his plans. Maybe there was still a way to make her seem guilty. Or maybe that didn't matter.

In the end, the Iron Maiden would die just like the others, and he would be free to end his pain once and for all with a bullet to the brain.

JOAQUIN LET himself into the newspaper and took the elevator up to the newsroom on the third floor. Most of the desks were empty, the newsroom quiet, the editor's office dark, its door shut. But, hey, there was still coffee.

Over at the news desk, Cate was talking with Syd Wilson, the managing editor, bringing her up to speed on the possible homicide. "As of two minutes ago, they hadn't found a body, so we can't say it's a homicide."

"It sounds like we can't say much of anything for certain."

Cate defended her story, eager as all new reporters were to get her byline on the front page. "I *do* have the interview with the neighbor. He told police he saw bullet holes in the guy's shower, but DPDs public information person won't confirm that."

"Do you think you can fill ten inches?"

"Absolutely."

Syd shouted to Joaquin from across the room. "Ramirez, did you get anything that could run on the front page?"

Joaquin studied the images on his screen, his gaze falling on Mia Starr, the distress on her face giving the photograph emotional weight. "You bet. I'll have them to you in a few minutes."

He worked his way through the assignments, picking a shot from the protest, then one each from the fire and the hit-and-run accident. They probably wouldn't have room for all of them, but that was life as a photojournalist. The vast majority of the photos he took were never published.

He wrote a cutline for each image and saved the files on the news server. "You've got it, Syd."

She nodded without glancing up from her computer screen.

Cate hurried over to Syd's desk and bent down, clearly eager to see what he'd shot for her story. "That's fantastic. That woman is a person of interest in the case."

"She didn't do it." The words were out before Joaquin realized he'd spoken.

Both Cate and Syd looked up from the screen.

"What makes you say that?" Cate asked.

"She walked up when I was shooting, blocked my view, and started asking questions. She was torn up about what had happened, really worried."

Syd laughed. "Maybe she's worried they'll catch her."

Joaquin shook his head. "Nah, man, I don't think so. If she'd killed the guy herself, she would have stayed in the shadows somewhere, kept out of sight, not stepped in front of my camera."

"But she is a person of interest, correct?" Syd asked.

Cate nodded. "I heard Detective Wu say she might be the last person to have seen Andrew Meyer before he disappeared."

"Make sure you mention her in your story and include the fact that she's a person of interest in the investigation. Let's run the story and photo on the front page."

Well, this would make Ms. Starr love the media that much more.

*Shit.*

Not sure why it bothered him—they were only publishing facts—Joaquin shut down his computer, slipped into his parka, and grabbed his camera bag. He was about to head out when he remembered. "Hey, Syd, Chris is covering for me tomorrow night."

"You got a hot date?"

Didn't Joaquin just wish?

He hadn't been on a hot date in a couple of months now. It wasn't that he couldn't find women who wanted to spend time with him. He could have gotten laid every night if that's all he'd wanted. There were plenty of women in the bars and clubs and online who were willing to do almost anything with anyone. But he was looking for a relationship, a true connection with one special woman, not just a quick fuck.

He had already told Syd about tomorrow night, but she had apparently forgotten. "My cousin just got back from a nine-month deployment in Iraq, and my family is throwing a party. I'm always the designated photographer. I told you about it last—"

"Right. Okay. Have fun."

Joaquin left the newsroom, walked down three flights of stairs, and stepped out into the frigid night, his thoughts drifting back to the photograph and Mia Starr.

**2**
_____

M ia hurried up the sidewalk toward the address Ramirez had given her, wishing she'd worn a warmer coat and sensible shoes instead of these damned heels. She'd never been any good at the girly stuff. She'd always been a tomboy—more at home in jeans and hiking boots than dresses and heels. Why had she put herself through the effort?

It was wishful thinking. That's what it was. Ramirez wanted her to meet her cousin, the one who'd taught her how to dance salsa when she was a kid, and Mia, in a fit of stupidity or insanity, had tried to make herself look pretty just in case this guy turned out to be The One.

_What are the chances of that happening?_

Unless it was snowing in hell—and it was cold enough that it might be—the chances were slim.

"The destination is on your right," Siri chirped from her coat pocket.

"Gee, thanks." Mia fished out her smartphone and turned off the directions app.

She was running late, but then it had been one hell of a

day. Thanks to that article in the *Denver Independent*, which had identified her by name as a person of interest, she'd spent her afternoon hanging up on reporters from other news outlets. She'd also gotten an angry call from Andy's sister, who'd demanded to know what she'd done with her brother's body. Mia had spent an hour trying to convince the poor woman that she wasn't a lying murderer.

If it weren't for the fact that she'd be letting Ramirez down, Mia would have stayed home. Andy was missing, maybe dead. She didn't have the heart to party. But Ramirez had just gotten back from a tough deployment, and Mia didn't want to disappoint her.

Mia tried to set aside her anger, following the rhythm of Latin music to a house in the middle of the block. She made her way up the front walk to the porch. Red chili pepper lights adorned the windows, small US and Mexican flags hanging side by side on the front door. She knocked hard, certain no one would be able to hear her.

The door opened, spilling warmth and music into the street.

Ramirez stood there in a little beaded black dress, a bright smile on her face. She opened the screen door. "You came!"

"Of course." Mia stepped inside, Ramirez's smile infectious. "You think I'd miss this? Welcome home, Ramirez."

Ramirez caught her up in a hug. "It is *so* good to be back, ma'am."

"Don't call me ma'am. Mia is fine."

She knew from experience how it felt to come home from a deployment. She'd been deployed twice—both times to Iraq—and had had enough MREs, camel spiders, sand, filthy latrines, and heat to last several lifetimes.

"Then you call me Elena." Ramirez—Elena—stepped

back. "Let me take your coat. You look so pretty. I love the color. Blue really makes your eyes stand out. I don't think I've ever seen you in a dress."

Yeah, well, there was a reason for that.

Mia handed her coat to Elena. "Thanks."

Elena was the beautiful one. With her big brown eyes, long dark hair, and curves, she exuded femininity. She turned heads even when she wore ACUs and combat boots. As an officer in her chain of command, Mia had worried about the impact of male attention on Elena's career, but it turned out that she was more than capable of putting horny soldiers in their place without Mia's help.

Elena hung Mia's coat in a crowded closet, then turned and introduced Mia to the people who stood talking with one another in the living room, raising her voice to be heard. "Everyone, this is Mia Starr. She was my captain my first year in the Army."

"Welcome!"

"Nice to meet you!"

"We've heard a lot about you."

Elena motioned for Mia to follow her. "I want you to meet my grandma and my parents. My cousin Quino is here, too."

Mia forced a smile onto her face. "Great."

She was happy to meet Elena's family, but she hated being set up. It only led to awkwardness and embarrassment.

Elena shepherded her through the party to a back room away from the music, where a tiny old woman sat in a recliner, a crocheted shawl around her shoulders. She spoke to the woman in Spanish, gesturing toward Mia.

The old woman's face lit up, and she reached out with a bony hand.

Mia understood only a few words—*abuelita*, *capitán*, *Irak*. She took the old woman's hand, held it between her own. "Your granddaughter is an excellent soldier. You must be so happy to have her home."

Elena repeated what Mia had said in Spanish.

"*Sí, sí.*" The old woman nodded, brown eyes shining. Then she said something Mia couldn't understand.

Elena translated. "She thanks you for training me well and watching over me."

"It was my honor." Mia had helped Elena get her boots solidly on the ground before resigning her commission and leaving the Army.

The conversation was repeated with Elena's parents, who came in from the kitchen when they saw Mia.

Aleta, Elena's mother, hugged Mia and thanked her. "I know what you taught her helped keep her safe. You are always welcome in our home."

"Thank you, ma'am."

"Come and get something to eat." Aleta gestured toward the kitchen.

But Elena tugged on Mia's arm. "I want her to meet Quino."

There was no rush as far as Mia was concerned, but Elena was clearly set on making this introduction. Mia followed her through a laundry room and down some stairs into what must have once been a garage but was now an extra living room. Young people danced, laughed, talked, some in English, some in Spanish.

Then Mia saw him.

Out in the middle of the floor, a man danced salsa with a young woman, his body moving with a sensuality that made it impossible for Mia to look away.

Just... *Wow.*

Mia's mouth watered.

"Quino!" Elena shouted out for him. "Joaquin!"

*That* was her cousin?

Good grief!

Mia felt an impulse to run, but stayed, as if rooted to the floor.

The man turned, a smile on his face, and blood rushed to Mia's head.

*Oh, God.*

The damned photographer.

JOAQUIN LEFT his cousin María on the dance floor, confused to see *her* here at his aunt and uncle's place. "Ms. Starr."

She stared at him with wide blue eyes, color rushing into her cheeks. It wasn't a blush. She was pissed. "*You.*"

He'd thought her striking last night, but tonight...

*Madre de Dios.*

She wore a pretty dress of royal blue that hugged her willowy body, her slender legs in sheer blue hose, black pumps on her feet, red hair hanging past her shoulders, thick and shining.

Elena looked from Joaquin to Mia and back again. "You know each other?"

"We've met." Joaquin left it up to Mia to reveal exactly *how* they'd met. "How are you doing?"

"Fine." Mia's gaze shifted to Elena, and Joaquin could tell she was trying for Elena's sake not to lose her temper.

She must have seen the paper. Well, he'd known she would.

Then it hit him. "You're *Captain* Starr, the officer who helped my cousin through her first year."

Mia nodded. "I resigned my commission three years ago."

Elena beamed, oblivious to the tension between them. "How fun that you already knew each other."

"Elena!" Tío Danilo yelled. "There's someone at the door!"

"I'll be right back." Elena hurried away.

For a moment, neither Joaquín nor Mia spoke, an awkward silence stretching between them.

Mia lowered her voice. "Thanks to your paper, I got a half dozen calls from reporters wanting to know if I was a murderer. Andy's sister called, too, and asked where I'd hidden her brother's body."

"I'm sorry." What else could he say? "That must have been tough. You should know that the reporters who called probably got your name from the police report, not from our newspaper."

"The police report is already available to the media?"

"It's a public document." He could see on her face that she hadn't known that. "Would you like a drink?"

*Amigo, you are the last man on earth she wants to have a drink with.*

She fought back her irritation with visible effort. "Sure. But just to be clear, I don't like you."

"Yeah, I noticed." He led her toward the kitchen. "Wine? Beer? Soda? My cousin David here makes a wicked paloma."

"White wine, please."

"A beer for me and white wine for her," Joaquín called to David, quickly telling him who Mia was.

David handed the wine glass to Mia. "Thanks for what you've done for our country and for supporting my cousin."

Mia took the wine and gave David a tight smile, as if the

attention made her uncomfortable. Or maybe it was just being with Joaquin that bothered her. "Thank you."

Joaquin led her to a quiet spot in the dining room. "Any news on your friend?"

She gave him a wary look. "Is this on or off the record?"

"Tonight, we're just two people who care about Elena having a conversation at a party in her honor."

She seemed to measure him through those blue eyes of hers, worry chasing the irritation from her face. "They still don't know anything."

"I'm sorry. Are you two close?"

She shook her head. "I was his XO for a time. He was injured on one of our deployments and discharged. I did my best to stay in touch with him."

"I'm sure he appreciated that."

Mia took a sip of wine. "He was bitter about how the Army had treated him."

"I know how hard this is—worrying and not knowing where he is or what happened to him."

She gave him a look. "Do you really?"

"Yeah, I do." He told her how *sicarios* from a drug cartel had kidnapped Natalie Benoit, a friend and former co-worker, while they were on a job-related trip to Mexico. "They killed all the Mexican reporters on the bus, shot them right in front of us. She was afraid they'd think I was Mexican and kill me, too. She didn't know that they were there for *her*. They tore her from my arms, ripped her away from me. For more than a week, I had no idea whether she was dead or alive."

Mia stared at him through wide eyes. "God, I'm sorry. Is she...?"

"It turns out the cartel had taken Zach McBride, a deputy US marshal and former Navy SEAL, captive, too.

Natalie broke him out of his little cell, and the two of them escaped. He got her safely back to the US, but the cartel came after her here. There was a big shootout, and some of my friends were caught up in that and wounded. Natalie married the marshal."

There was last month's holiday party, too, when terrorists had taken over the hotel, but that was still too raw. Once again, assholes had attacked his friends, and he'd been powerless to do anything about it.

"Tell me they at least got the bastards."

"They did. That's the story that won me my Pulitzer. I'm sure Elena told you about that. She tells everyone."

Mia's eyes went wide. "A Pulitzer. Wow. Congrats. She didn't tell me, but then she probably knows how I feel about photojournalists."

"Isn't it bigotry to dislike an entire group of people? You're judging all of us based on the actions of a few."

Mia took another sip of wine, her gaze shifting to the window and the darkness beyond. "During my two deployments, we had plenty of journalists and photographers who came over. Some of them were ethical, but too many of them were there for the glory. Once, when one of our guys was wounded by an IED, a photographer got right in his face. The soldier was screaming in pain and in danger of bleeding out, but the photographer got in the way of the medics, making it hard for them to do their job. I literally had to push him aside, knock him on his ass. He didn't care about LeBron's suffering. All he wanted was a chance to make money off gore and misery."

Joaquin had met shooters who'd let ambition twist them. He'd felt nothing but disgust for them. "I hate guys like that. They give everyone else a bad name."

She arched an eyebrow. "Is this when you tell me that you're different, that you're one of the good ones?"

Joaquin took a chance. "I think you already know that. That's why you're standing here talking to me."

"Oh, you are smooth." Mia laughed. "Elena is the reason I'm standing here talking to you."

"Ouch!" Joaquin supposed that was fair, given the day she'd had. He changed the subject. "Elena admires the hell out of you."

"She's tough, a good soldier."

"What does an Army captain do when she leaves the service?"

"Any damned thing she wants." Mia laughed again, a sweet sound. "I went back to school and got a master's degree in horticulture. Spending almost two years in the desert made me long to see anything flowering, anything green. I discovered that I love watching things grow. I work for the Botanic Gardens now as one of their—"

"Quino, where did you put your camera?" Elena interrupted. "Can you get it? I want a picture of me with my favorite officer."

"Favorite *former* officer," Mia corrected her.

"Anything for you, *chula*." Joaquin went in search of his camera bag.

MIA STOOD in the doorway while Joaquin led Elena onto a bit of open wood floor to cheers from their relatives.

"Quino taught Elena to dance when she was only four and he was fourteen," said a woman standing beside Mia.

So, Joaquin was thirty-four—three years older than Mia.

Not that it mattered or meant anything at all.

"He's a photographer," the woman said. "He's the artist of the family. I'm Isabel, his mother."

"Nice to meet you." Mia really ought to head home, but having seen him dance once tonight, she couldn't get herself to move toward the door.

He and Elena stood there debating something in Spanish.

Isabel leaned close to Mia. "My son wants *salsa dura*— the classic salsa—but Elena wants *salsa romantica*. They've agreed on Marc Anthony."

None of that meant anything to Mia. She knew nothing about salsa, apart from the kind that went on tacos.

Finally, the music started and Joaquin and Elena began to move. People cheered, the noise bringing people who'd been in other parts of the house and wanted to watch, too. They pushed past Mia, but she barely noticed them, her gaze fixed on Joaquin.

He moved with natural grace, every step, every motion of his hips, even the way he held Elena radiating masculine sensuality. The two of them seemed to be connected, mirroring each other with their steps as if they practiced this together all the time. Elena—down-to-business Corporal Ramirez—had transformed into a dance goddess, her short dress barely enough to cover her butt. She twirled and tossed her hair, never missing a step, a bright smile on her face. How could anyone dance like that in three-inch heels? Mia could barely walk.

Then Elena turned in Joaquin's arms, thrusting her ass backward toward him, her hips moving in a way that was blatantly sexual. He laughed, answering with thrusts of his own, their hips grinding in sync.

Whistles. Cheers.

Mia's pulse skipped.

If she had danced like this with a cousin... Well, let's just say her conservative Baptist parents would've asked questions. But there was Elena's mother, Aleta, and Joaquin's mother, Isabel, and their little old grandma, laughing, their feet moving to the rhythm. None of them seemed bothered by this at all.

Then another thought struck Mia.

If Joaquin moved like that on the dance floor, what would he be like in bed?

*God in heaven.*

No. No, no. She couldn't think about that.

She couldn't help but think about that.

Elena had begun to sing along to the music, even her ribcage undulating as she turned in his arms once again, their feet keeping a perfect rhythm as they moved around the room. Although Elena was the showier of the two of them, Mia could tell it was Joaquin who was in control, his dominance clear—a touch here, his hand catching Elena's there, his arms supporting her while she arched backward.

More cheers.

When the song ended, the room exploded into applause.

Joaquin hugged Elena close. "Welcome home, *prima.*"

"Joaquin is a good man," Isabel said.

Mia looked over to find the older woman watching her. "I ... um..."

Then Joaquin was there, hand out. "Dance with me."

Mia shook her head. "I ... I can't dance. I've never—"

"Quino is the best teacher." Elena looked at Mia, expectation on her face.

"Come on, Captain Starr," Isabel said. "Give it a try."

Her words were picked up by the others in the room.

"At least try it."

"Quino can teach you."

"You can do it, Captain."

She glanced around at them. "Only if you all promise not to laugh."

For some reason, they found this funny.

Joaquin looked into her eyes, the intensity of his gaze pinning her to the spot. "I won't laugh. I promise."

Against her better judgment, Mia took his hand. "I'm warning you. I'm probably no good at this."

"The basic step is easy. Elena, come show her."

Elena walked over to stand at Mia's right side. "Just listen to Quino."

"Step back with your right, step in place with the left, then step slightly forward with your right again. Then back with your left, step in place with the right foot, slightly forward with the left. Rock back, replace, step forward. Rock back, replace, step forward. That's it. You've got it."

They repeated that several times, Mia watching Elena's feet.

"Now, try doing it without looking at your feet. Look at me, and follow my lead."

Mia looked into Joaquin's brown eyes, felt her pulse spike—and her step faltered.

"Relax," he said in a silky voice that made relaxing impossible.

"I'd rather be taking enemy fire." She blurted the words —but it was the truth.

The room exploded into laughter—and somehow that helped. No one here wanted to humiliate her. No one wanted to embarrass her. They were just having fun, and they wanted her to have fun, too.

"It will be easier for you to follow if we're a little closer together." Joaquin drew her closer—not so close that their bodies touched, but close enough that she could feel the warmth emanating from him and smell his skin.

She inhaled deeper, savoring the scent of him, the male feel of him.

"Let's try again. One, two, three, rest. Five, six, seven, rest. You've got it. You're doing it. Now let's try turning."

The next time she stepped back with her right foot, Joaquin turned her to the right—and she lost the step.

That's okay. This is new. You'll get the hang of it." Joaquin coached her until she'd managed to get through a few turns, not once losing his patience with her. "Let's try it with music."

Someone put on the same Marc Anthony song, Joaquin counting out the rhythm for her. "One, two, three, rest. Five, six, seven, rest. Look at me, not your feet."

To her surprise, Mia found herself dancing, the rhythm of the music showing her feet what to do. At first, they moved forward and backward. Then Joaquin led her through a few turns, putting a hand on her hip to guide her. The contact startled her, his touch seeming to burn through the fabric of her dress. Again, her step faltered.

"Hey, no one gets it right the first time," he said. "Just keep dancing."

Mia tried to concentrate. *One, two, three, rest. Five, six, seven, rest.*

"You're overthinking it. Let go."

She gave in, looked into his eyes once more, the rhythm taking over.

"You've got it." Joaquin grinned, his face stunningly handsome.

Mia found herself smiling, too. She knew she must look stiff and awkward, especially compared to Elena, but she didn't care. "This is fun!"

"More fun than dodging incoming fire?"

She couldn't help but laugh. "Yes."

Too soon the song ended.

Cheers and applause.

Joaquin stepped back, raised one of her hands to his lips, kissed it, the contact alarming. "Thanks."

Heat rushed into her cheeks. "Thank you."

All at once, Mia needed to be somewhere else, anywhere else. "I should go."

"So soon?" Elena looked disappointed. "It's not even ten."

"I'm an early riser, so this is late for me." Mia gave Elena another hug. "It's great to see you again."

"It's good to see you, too. Thanks for coming. I'll get your coat."

Mia thanked her hosts, accepting hugs from Elena's mother and a kiss on her cheek from Elena's father.

"Thank you so much for what you did for our daughter."

When Elena returned with Mia's coat, Joaquin took it and helped Mia into it. "I'll walk you to your car."

She was about to tell him there was no need for that, but the look in his eyes said that would be pointless. "Goodnight, Elena. Welcome home."

Joaquin grabbed his jacket and followed her outside, and for a time they walked without speaking. He broke the silence. "Thanks again for coming tonight. I know it meant a lot to Elena."

"I try to stay in touch with all of my soldiers. Well, they're not really my soldiers, not anymore."

"Like Andrew Meyer."

"Yes." Mia's mood plummeted.

"I'm really sorry about your friend—and the news article."

"You just have a job to do. Nothing personal, right?" Mia clicked the fob on her keychain, unlocking her car door, her headlights flashing.

Was she being unfair to Joaquin? It *was* his job. And she *was* a person of interest—at least at the moment. The police would clear her.

He opened the door for her. "I hope you get good news soon."

"Thanks." She stood there for a moment, caught between anger and attraction. "Thanks for the dance lesson, too."

"My pleasure." He waited for her to climb in and shut her door.

As she drove down the street, she saw in the rearview mirror that he was still standing there, watching her.

## 3

J oaquin got to work Monday morning to find Sophie
Alton-Hunter, one of the I-Team's best reporters, at her
desk in tears, Alex Carmichael sitting beside her,
trying to comfort her, the two of them speaking quietly.

Matt Harker met Joaquin at his desk. "I think the
Christmas party might have turned Carmichael into a
human being."

"Yeah?" That was a strange thought.

Then again, it *had* been one hell of a party.

Sophie had been struggling since then, and no one
who'd been there could blame her. The terrorist leader—
that *hijueputa* Moreno—had held a pistol to her head,
threatening to kill her unless her husband turned himself
over to his men to be murdered. Marc Hunter, a SWAT
officer and certified badass, had put down his weapon and
given himself up to save her life.

*"It's going to be okay, Sophie. You'll be okay."*

*"I love you, Hunt. I am so proud of the man you are. Chase
and Addy are going to grow up so proud of their father."*

*"You're everything to me."*

Joaquin didn't think he would ever forget Sophie and Marc saying goodbye to each other before Moreno's men dragged Hunter away—or the shattered expression on Sophie's face at the gunshot that had followed.

A person didn't just get over something like that.

Joaquin put his camera bag down and booted up his computer, then made his way over to Sophie's desk. He bent down beside her. "Hey, are you okay?"

She shook her head, sniffed, the strawberry blond hair she usually braided hanging loose. "Not really. I can't sleep at night. When I do, I have nightmares."

"I think we've all had nightmares." Joaquin certainly had.

Sophie went on. "I feel sick all day, like something terrible is about to happen. I can't focus. I'm going to ask Tom for a leave of absence."

Joaquin met Alex's gaze, saw that Alex was as surprised as he was. Sophie was a consummate journalist. She'd been on the I-Team longer than the rest of them. But maybe that was part of it. A person could only take so much.

Joaquin nodded. "That's good. You need to take care of yourself and your kids."

"Do you think Tom will get angry? Kat is on maternity leave for another few weeks, so you'll be understaffed."

Kat James, who'd had a baby in the middle of the terrorist stand-off last month, job-shared with Sophie, but she was recovering at her family's home on the Navajo reservation with her husband Gabe Rossiter right now.

Carmichael gave a snort. "Who gives a shit what Tom thinks?"

"Don't worry about Tom, and don't worry about us. We'll manage. Your job will be waiting for you when you're ready to come back."

"You think so?" Sophie looked at Joaquin, shadows in her eyes, dark circles beneath them. "You think Tom will let me come back?"

Joaquin rested a hand on hers, found that she was shaking. "Of course, he will. You're one of the best, and he knows it."

"If he doesn't, he's a fucking idiot," Carmichael said.

Behind them, Tom's office door opened, and Cate stepped out. There hadn't been any shouting, and Cate didn't look like Tom had raked her over the coals.

A good start to the day.

Tom was as big as a bear and had the disposition of a junkyard dog. "I-Team meeting now. Deadline is six hours away, people."

Tom Trent was a *pendejo*—no doubt about it—but he was also an old-school journalist who worked as hard as his reporters. Joaquin respected him and his editorial judgment, even if he didn't like the way Tom treated the staff.

"Hey, it's going to be okay." Joaquin gave her hand a squeeze. "You just tell Tom how it is, and we'll be right there."

"We've got your back," Alex said.

Yeah, Alex was a different guy since the party. Weren't they all?

Joaquin walked back to his desk, grabbed a pad of paper and a pen, and followed the other I-Team members down the hallway toward the conference room. He took a seat at the table, his gaze on Sophie, who had managed to stop her tears but was visibly upset.

"Alton," said Tom, ignoring her hyphenated married name. "You've got something on your mind."

"I'm going to take a leave of absence." Sophie's voice quavered. "I am not able to function the way I should here at work. I can barely keep things together at home. I need to focus on my health and my family."

Tom frowned, tapped his notepad with a pencil. "I'm sorry to hear this. You've worked long and hard for this newspaper, and we'll stand by you."

Joaquin stared, wondering whether the man sitting at the end of the conference table was, in fact, Tom Trent. He glanced over at Harker and Carmichael and saw surprise on their faces, too.

"When were you thinking of starting your leave?"

"Today." Sophie's eyes filled with tears. "I don't imagine I'll be ready to come back for a while."

Tom nodded. "You and I will head down to HR after the meeting and see what we can work out."

"Thank you." Sophie seemed to melt with relief.

Tom turned to Cate. "Warner, you're in the hot seat."

Cate sat up straight. "I'm doing a follow-up piece on Andrew Meyer, the missing man from Aurora. Police found bullet holes in his shower stall and shell casings but no body. They pulled out some slugs, but they're not saying what caliber they are. There's one person of interest in the case—a woman who was the last person to see this guy. The neighbor said he heard some kind of argument. She was Meyer's executive officer when he was in the Army. Police are looking into her. I thought I'd pull her military record and that of the missing guy and see if anything pops."

Joaquin's body tensed. "Have the police been able to verify her story yet—where she was and when?"

Cate shook her head. "I'll ask about that again today."

"Any chance you can get an interview with the woman?" Tom asked.

"I tried. She hung up on me."

Joaquin didn't mention that he'd spoken with Mia last

night or that his cousin had served with her. He knew they would push him to get an interview with her or to meet with her himself. He couldn't say why exactly, but he was certain she hadn't killed anyone. Part of it was the way she'd acted when she'd arrived on the scene Friday night. Part of it was the fact that she was too brutally honest to make much of a liar.

*You're attracted to her.*

Yeah, he was.

His cousin David had said Mia was too skinny for his tastes, but Joaquin was intrigued by her. Her delicate face. Her willowy figure. Those expressive eyes. The vulnerability she kept hidden beneath that controlled exterior. He'd seen it when he'd looked at her through his lens, and his camera never lied.

Tom moved on. "Harker, what's going on at City Hall?"

MIA SAT in the greenhouse reviewing internship applications and ranking them in order from most promising to *please, God, no.* She didn't make the hiring decisions—she was the newest member of the horticultural staff —but she appreciated being given a voice in the selection process. If only she could concentrate.

Instead of seeing the words on the page, she saw Joaquin. Joaquin smiling as he tried to teach her the steps to salsa. Joaquin dancing with Elena, his body moving in a way that made Mia's thoughts go all X-rated. Joaquin's dark eyes looking into hers. His naked body moving over hers. His bare chest beneath her palms.

Yeah, like that was going to happen.

*Get your mind back on the job.*

Right. Internship applications.

This applicant had almost completed her coursework at Colorado State University and was most interested in the research side of things—tissue cultivation, the propagation of rare and endangered species. Would she be open to ,weeding and shoveling compost in the hot summer sun?

The next one had three years' experience working in community-supported agriculture and wanted to be a part of the community gardening program. That seemed like a better fit.

Kevin, Mia's boss, stepped inside the greenhouse. "Do you have a few minutes?"

"Sure." She set the applications aside.

Kevin sat on a stool across from her, his expression telling her something was up. "I saw the piece in the Denver Independent about that man's disappearance and read that you're a person of interest in that case."

*Fantastic.*

"Yes."

"This morning, human resources got a call from the Denver Police Department asking for your employment information—how long you'd worked here, whether you had a good record with us and so on. They wanted access to phone records from your work phone if you had one—which you don't. They also wanted to know if you drove a company vehicle or were authorized to use the wood chipper, the bobcat, or any other large equipment."

"Why would they want to know that?" The moment she asked the question, the answer hit her. "Oh, for God's sake. Seriously?"

They thought she might have used the equipment to get rid of Andy's body.

She fought back an impulse to laugh, the seriousness on Kevin's face telling her he found this anything but amusing.

"We cooperated with them, of course, and told them about the outstanding work you've done. We want to stand behind you, but we also have a responsibility to this institution. Is there anything I ought to know?"

Mia understood why he was asking this, but she couldn't help feeling hurt. "No, sir. I'm a person of interest only because I was the last person to see him before he disappeared. He and I served together and were deployed together in Iraq. He was wounded and disabled. I was his executive officer. He has problems with anxiety and depression, so I check on him from time to time. As soon as they look into where I was that night, they will clear me."

Kevin nodded, a frown on his face. "They've asked for our surveillance footage from Friday afternoon onward."

As much as this surprised her, it was also reassuring. If she'd been out there burying bodies among the rose bushes, it would have been captured by the surveillance cameras. Still, it was a lot of hassle for the security staff.

"I'm so sorry about this. Don't they realize that someone would notice if I were dragging around a body or digging holes somewhere?"

"I said something to that effect. I agreed to give them our surveillance footage. I even checked security records, which show that you didn't use your key card this weekend. If you were here, you would have had to come through a public entrance."

"That would have made carrying a dead body awkward. And for the record—no, I didn't come in this weekend."

"Right. Good. Well, I guess that's it." Kevin got to his feet. "I'm really sorry about this."

"Don't apologize. It's more of a disruption to your life

than ours." He stood and turned to leave the greenhouse, when Sharon, the office manager, hurried in.

"Can I talk to you?" Her gaze flitted to Mia.

The two of them stepped outside for a moment, Sharon leaning close to him as if she didn't want to be overheard. Then Kevin took out his cell phone and made a call.

Mia did her best to focus once again on internship applications, but she couldn't stop glancing out the window. Once when she did, she found both Kevin and Sharon looking at her. She let out a breath.

*You're imagining things.*

Kevin came inside again. "Mia, this is difficult, but I'm going to have to ask you to come with me to the front office."

"What's going on?"

"We can talk about it when we get there."

*Shit.*

This couldn't be good.

She slipped into her parka and followed him outside, her stomach knotting. Two of the security staff—Beth and Michael—were headed straight toward her.

*You have no reason to be afraid.*

Maybe not, but her pulse spiked anyway.

"They're just going to walk with us," Kevin said.

"Why? What's going on?"

"We'll talk about that in my office."

*Damn it.*

Beth and Michael fell in beside Mia, flanking her, as if they thought she might try to bolt. But she had no reason to run. She hadn't done anything.

The walk back to the office building seemed to take forever, her co-workers watching her with furtive glances until her cheeks burned with frustration and fury. One of the guards held the door open for her, and she walked into the warmth.

"This way." Kevin motioned her into his office, then spoke quietly to the two guards, who planted themselves outside Kevin's door.

Mia was at the end of her patience. "What the hell is going on?"

Kevin looked at her as if he'd never seen her before. "One of the grounds crew went to run branches through the wood chipper, but it jammed. Inside, he found a plastic bag filled with bloody towels and a bath mat. There was also a driver's license. It belonged to Andrew Meyer."

"What?" Mia gaped at him, unable to believe what she'd just heard. "You can't possibly believe that I—"

"We can talk about that when the police arrive."

"REVIEW THE SECURITY FOOTAGE NOW," Mia urged Wu. "It will prove that I was nowhere near the mulch yard today."

"There are no cameras in the mulch yard," Kevin told Wu.

"No, but there are cameras everywhere that I've been today." Mia could see that Wu was listening. "You'll be able to account for every moment of my day and know for certain that I didn't go there. I rarely go there. The footage will also show that I haven't been at the gardens since last Friday afternoon."

"We did check her key card," Kevin said. "She didn't come in through any of the staff entryways after clocking out Friday night. Surveillance would show whether she came in through any of the public gates."

"If you would check out what I told you Friday and

review this security footage, you'll see that I couldn't have done this."

Wu's gaze was inscrutable. "I've already followed up with the restaurant. The manager remembers seeing you there. We got your credit card and cell phone records this afternoon. They corroborate your story."

"Oh. Good." She let out a relieved breath.

"We'll look at this footage, see what we find. There's a backlog at CBI's lab, so it's going to take time to get the DNA back on the blood. The driver's license is valid, however, so I suspect we'll find that the blood is Meyer's."

Mia couldn't believe this. "Why would I bring incriminating evidence to my workplace?"

"I don't know. Maybe you were going to take it somewhere else and had to ditch it. Maybe you didn't realize it would jam the machine and hoped it would get mulched." Wu looked straight into her eyes. "Ms. Starr, I'd like you to come down to the station to answer some questions and give an official statement."

Mia gaped at him, stunned. "You still think I did it. I was across town when he disappeared. You know that."

"I don't know anything at this point. I'm still investigating."

How could he say that when he'd verified her whereabouts and corroborated what she'd already told him?

She shook her head. "This is crazy. So, I'm supposed to follow you down to the station now—in the middle of the workday?"

Kevin cleared his throat. "We've placed you on administrative leave for the time being. Until this situation is resolved—"

"You don't believe me." The realization put an ache in Mia's chest.

It wasn't the first time a supervisor had let her down.

"Mia, I don't know what to think. Try to see this from my point of view. Evidence that ties you to a possible homicide was found on our premises. I can't let negative publicity surrounding this case hurt this institution. People aren't going to want to bring their grandmas and their children here if they think we hire criminals. When you're cleared, you're free to return. I'll even give you back pay for the days you miss."

Mia supposed what he'd just said sounded fair to him, but to her, it meant temporary loss of income, embarrassment, shame. "It could take months for the police to resolve this, especially if they keep looking into the wrong people."

"We'll hold your job for you as we can—unless you're guilty."

Mia turned to Wu. "Am I under arrest?"

Hell, did she need a lawyer?

Wu shook his head. "I just want to ask you some questions. I need your help to make sense of this."

Kevin stood, held out his hand.

For a moment, Mia thought he wanted to shake her hand and wish her luck.

"I need your key card," he said, his expression hard.

Dear God.

"Right." Unable to believe this was happening, Mia stood, lifted the chain that held her key card and ID from around her neck and placed it in Kevin's upturned palm. "I didn't have anything to do with this. I love my job here. I'll be back."

Kevin said nothing.

Sharon stepped into Kevin's office, carrying Mia's backpack and parka. She handed them to Mia. "Here you go."

They didn't even want her walking back to the employee break room.

Mia took her belongings, slipped into her parka. She turned to Wu. "Can you give me a lift to the station? I'm not sure I can drive right now."

Wu nodded. "Sure."

Mia followed him out the office building and the front entrance to an unmarked police car, too numb to notice the staff staring at her.

## 4

J oaquin walked up to the front desk at the Denver Police Department's main station. "I need to pick up a mug shot."

The DPD hadn't yet entered the twentieth century, to say nothing of the twenty-first. They still required newspapers to fill out actual paperwork for this shit.

Without a word, the uniformed staffer, a young woman whose brown hair was pulled back in a tight bun, handed him a clipboard and a pen.

Some guy had beaten his wife, locked her in the trunk of her car, and tried to drive the vehicle into Sloan Lake, apparently not realizing it would be frozen. Fortunately, an early morning jogger had seen and called the police. The husband had run off, and the jogger, who'd heard the woman's screams, had broken the window and popped the trunk to free her moments before the ice broke. The cops had caught the husband an hour later when he'd used his credit card to pay for a cab to the airport.

*Pendejo.*

Joaquin had just handed the clipboard back to the staffer when Mia walked through the front door with Wu, a troubled expression on her face.

Joaquin stared. "Mia?"

His first thought was that she'd been arrested, but that couldn't be true. She wasn't in cuffs, and they'd brought her in through the main entrance, not through the rear doors that led to the holding cells.

She glanced over at him, clearly surprised to see him, then shook her head, letting him know that she didn't want to talk.

He watched her pass, his mind racing. Wu must have brought her in for questioning, which meant something had happened.

Had they found a body?

To hell with this.

He drew his smartphone out of his pocket and typed a text message to Julian Darcangelo and Marc Hunter. Darcangelo headed the DPD's vice unit, while Hunter was captain of the SWAT team. Both men were good friends of his. They were also Joaquin's shooting buddies. They'd taught him how to use firearms, and now the three of them trained together at the police range once a week.

A FRIEND OF MINE IS HERE FOR QUESTIONING. I WANT TO KNOW WHAT'S GOING ON. I'M OUT FRONT.

He hit send and waited. They would probably tell him to get lost, and he couldn't blame them. He had no right to get involved in Mia's business—or a police investigation, for that matter.

After a few minutes, Darcangelo stepped through the security door, a frown on his face. At six-foot-three, he stood a little taller than Joaquin, his dark hair pulled back in a ponytail, a shoulder holster resting against his black T-shirt. Before joining the DPD, he'd worked as a deep-cover agent for the FBI, bringing sex traffickers to justice. Last month, he'd helped storm the Christmas party, working with the FBI's Hostage Rescue Team to free all of them from terrorists at considerable risk to himself. Joaquin respected the hell out of him.

He glared at Joaquin. "You have to be fucking kidding me."

Trying not to be overheard, Joaquin explained. "She's my friend. I think she's in trouble, but she didn't do anything."

Could you be any less articulate, *cabrón*?

Joaquin tried again. "I just want to know what's going on so I can help her."

"You know I can't tell you anything, right?"

Joaquin let out a frustrated breath. "I know. I'm not trying to presume on our friendship, man."

"Sure, you are. That's okay." Darcangelo gestured with his head. "Come on."

Darcangelo led him to the security door, swiped his keycard, and held the door open for Joaquin. Hunter stood in the hallway, wearing a black SWAT sweater, hands on his hips. Tall like Darcangelo, he'd served as an SFO sniper then worked for the DEA, before landing in prison for a murder he didn't commit. It was Sophie's investigative work that had exposed the truth and set Hunter free. The two had gotten married and had two kids. Hunter had saved God knew how many lives at last month's holiday party and had taken a round to the side doing it. "What the hell's going on, Ramirez?"

"That's what I want to know." Now that Joaquin wasn't in

a public part of the building, he could tell them the whole story. "Mia Starr was just brought in for questioning, I think. She's a person of interest in the disappearance of Andrew Meyer, but she had nothing to do with whatever happened to him."

"You're certain of that?" Darcangelo asked.

How could Joaquin explain? Would they be able to understand if he told them that viewing the world through his camera had taught him to see things other people missed, to look beneath the surface, to read the emotions people tried to hide?

Nah, probably not.

He answered with a question of his own. "If there were circumstantial evidence against me in a homicide, would you believe it?"

The two men's gazes met again, and they shook their heads.

Hunter's eyes narrowed. "How well do you know this woman?"

Joaquin wouldn't lie to them. "We've danced together. She was my cousin Elena's commanding officer during Elena's first year in the Army."

"Huh." Hunter sounded unimpressed.

"You *danced* with her?" Darcangelo crossed his arms over his chest. "Is this about your sex life?"

Didn't Joaquin wish? "Nah, man, I told you. She was Elena's CO."

Hunter exchanged another glance with Darcangelo. "You can sit in my office for now. We'll try to find out what's going on."

"This is off the record. Understood?" Darcangelo leaned in close, lowered his voice. "If one word of what we tell you ends up in the newspaper, Old Man Irving will have our balls for breakfast."

"Got it. Thanks, man."

"A<small>NDY WAS DEPRESSED</small>—<small>ABOUT</small> being disabled, about the way the government treated him." Mia was fighting a losing battle against her temper. "Seriously, how long can it take to review six hours of security footage? I've told you where I was all day. You ought to be able to corrob—"

"I've gone over your military record." Wu pulled a file folder out of a stack that sat on the table beside him. "You were decorated twice. No disciplinary actions against you. An honorable discharge. It says here, 'an exemplary officer.'"

"I did my best, sir."

Wu nodded. "Thank you for that."

He reached for another, thicker file and opened it. "Andrew Meyer, on the other hand, was Uncle Sam's problem child. His file says that he 'demonstrated a pattern of behavior that consistently fell short of the Army's expectations for its soldiers.' He was discharged under 'other than honorable conditions.' What does that mean?"

"His service was not exemplary, but it wasn't serious enough for a court-martial and a dishonorable discharge."

"He sounds like a total fuck-up." Wu watched her.

Mia chose her words carefully. "He was a disappointment."

Wu looked down at Andy's file. "I see here that you were the officer who reported him on a number of occasions."

"I was the XO of his company."

"I thought an executive officer was in charge of paperwork, food supplies, and toilet paper, not disciplining soldiers."

"I was second in command. It was my job to deal with paperwork, to keep our company supplied and running, and to supervise certain staff."

Wu nodded. "So, all of these documents with your signature—they don't represent a grudge against Meyer?"

"A grudge?" Heat rushed into Mia's face. "No. Of course not."

"Did he have a grudge against you?"

That was closer to the truth.

"He blamed me in part for the nature of his discharge. He thinks that I'm the reason he can't get disability benefits."

"Did he have cause to believe that?"

"Do the crooks you put in prison believe their time behind bars is your fault?" Mia could see that her words had hit home. "Some people have a hard time taking responsibility for their own actions."

"Isn't that the truth?" Wu glanced at the documents again, flipping through them. "I searched his file for some documentation—how he was wounded, when and why he was discharged. There's nothing here. Do you want to fill me in?"

Mia's pulse skipped. "He was discharged after—"

A knock at the door cut her off, gave her a reprieve, the door opening to reveal a man with a dark ponytail. "Hey, Wu, you got a minute?"

"Sure thing." Wu stood, leaving Mia alone, giving her time to think.

What the hell was she supposed to say? The conditions

of Andy's discharge were classified. The whole catastrophe was classified. She had been ordered not to talk about it with anyone. She didn't agree with how the Army had handled the situation. If she'd had any say, Andy and the others would have been court-martialed. Instead, Army brass had buried everything—and ordered her to keep her mouth shut.

Mia had always followed lawful orders, and she wasn't going to stop now. She would tell the detective the truth, but not the whole truth, and hope he was satisfied. He would have to go up the flagpole if he wanted more information.

The door opened, and Wu entered, shutting the door behind him and returning to his seat, his gaze fixed on her. "It seems you have friends here."

She did?

"One of them is waiting for you in the lobby."

*Joaquin.*

He was waiting for her?

The idea both irritated her—and lifted her spirits. Her friends from work had stared at her with suspicion. Her boss, a man she trusted, had put her on leave. But Joaquin was here. He barely knew her, but somehow, he believed her.

She wasn't alone.

"He's got a couple of buddies in the department, high-ranking cops who are also friends of mine, and they're breathing down my neck to know why you're here." Wu said this as if this were her fault, part of some conspiracy or something.

That was news to Mia, and it raised her spirits even more.

"How long are you going to keep me here? I've answered

every question you asked me, some of them more than once."

"Not that last question. We got interrupted."

Oh, right.

*Shit.*

"Andy was discharged after being wounded when he left our forward operations base without authorization."

Wu's eyebrows rose. "You mean he went AWOL?"

How could Mia explain this and maintain the secrecy that the government demanded? "Not AWOL exactly. He left the post without authorization along with others from the company, including our CO, and came under attack. This is what led to his being injured and discharge."

"Why is there nothing in the file?"

"I can't answer that question." She truly could not answer it—but she misled Wu as to the reason for that. "I wasn't in charge of his service record."

Wu nodded, his gaze dropping to the files in front of him, a thoughtful frown on his face. "Thanks for your cooperation. Don't leave Denver."

"When will you finish reviewing the security footage?"

"Hard to say." He stood. "This isn't the only case we're working on."

Joaquin was standing near the door in the lobby when Mia walked out, looking exhausted and more than a little shaken. "Hey."

She didn't seem surprised to see him. "What are you doing here?"

"I had to pick up a mug shot for the paper. I saw you

come in and thought I'd wait around to make sure you're okay."

"Thanks." Her gaze went soft, then fell to the floor.

"Do you need a lift?"

She nodded. "I need a ride back to the Botanic Gardens. My car is parked there. Would you mind?"

"How about I take you out for a quick bite to eat first?"

She seemed to hesitate, then nodded. "Okay."

So, dinner with him wasn't on her bucket list.

They walked outside together, cold wind hitting Joaquin in the face.

*¡Carajo!* It was damned cold.

Denver's streets were busy with rush-hour traffic, so it took a few minutes to make it two blocks to his truck. He opened her door, shut it behind her, then walked around to the driver's side and climbed in.

Mia was huddled in her parka and shivering. "I spent two years in Iraq and can't seem to get acclimated to the cold again."

"They say it's dropping to ten below tonight." He started the engine. "Do you like Mexican food?"

She nodded. "Love it."

He pulled into traffic, heading down 13th Avenue. "My cousin Mateo owns a place not far from here. He serves the best chile verde in Denver."

"Oh, really?" Mia arched a delicate red eyebrow. "That's quite a claim."

"You'll see." Joaquin drew to a stop at a red light. "I have to stop by the paper first to drop off the mug shot. You can wait in the truck. I'm just going to leave this at the front security desk."

"That's fine."

It took a few minutes to reach the newspaper. Joaquin left the truck running, doors locked, and hurried through the paper's front door. He dropped the envelope with the mug shot on the security desk, sent a text message to Syd to tell her where the photo was, and then hurried back out to his vehicle.

"I'm starving. How about you?"

Mia nodded. "Hungry."

He drove toward Speer, the conversation lapsing into silence.

Joaquin decided to come out with it. "I heard they found bloody towels and a bath mat along with this Meyer guy's driver's license in a wood chipper—and, no, this isn't for the newspaper."

Mia watched him, doubt in her eyes. "Yes. That's what they told me. I didn't put it there. I didn't have anything to do with this."

He reached over, gave her hand a squeeze. "That's what I said."

She shook her head, her brow furrowing. "You barely know me. How can you be sure? I could be a serial killer for all you know."

Joaquin didn't talk about the spiritual side of his work with most people. Too many wouldn't under-stand. But he didn't want Mia thinking he was just saying this because he wanted to get into her pants or some shit.

"Elena trusts you, and she's a good judge of people. More than that, I've been a photographer all of my adult life. I've shot politicians and rock stars and killers. My camera taught me to see beyond what people show on the outside to what they are beneath their skin. That probably sounds strange."

She seemed to measure his words. "I guess you'd have to

be perceptive about human emotions if you want to take good photographs of people."

"When I shot you standing next to the barricade tape, your emotions were right there on your face. You were angry at me and afraid for your friend—not for yourself, but for him. I knew right away that you care about what happens to him. If you had kidnapped or killed him, you'd have been self-conscious, afraid of being seen, closed off. The last person you would have confronted was a photojournalist."

Mia seemed to relax. "It's nice to know someone believes me."

Then he told her what he'd been thinking ever since Darcangelo and Hunter had told him about the wood chipper. "The way all of this has gone down—him disappearing right after you were at his place, the bloody towels, bath mat, and driver's license turning up where you work. What if someone wanted to get rid of Andy and pin it on *you*?"

CHILLS SKITTERED down Mia's spine, Joaquin's words bringing the big picture into focus, making her see her situation in a way she hadn't before. "What?"

Why hadn't she thought of that?

She'd been too upset by Andy's disappearance and too distracted by the fear of possibly losing a job she loved to put the pieces together.

"Hey, I didn't mean to scare you."

"I'm not scared." That wasn't entirely true. The idea that someone might be trying to frame her was unnerving, but two deployments had taught Mia to control her fear. "I'm *angry*. Why would anyone do this?"

"In my experience, bad people don't need a reason to do

bad shit, but this seems personal to me. Did Andy have any enemies, people who'd like to see you in trouble?"

Mia thought about it. "I haven't been in close enough contact with him to know whether he has enemies."

"It would have to be someone who knows both of you."

"Well, *that* narrows it down." She couldn't keep the sarcasm out of her voice. "There were two hundred soldiers in our company at any given time and nineteen in Andy's platoon besides him. People came and went. We're talking about maybe three hundred soldiers."

"How many of them live in Colorado?"

"I don't know." Mia looked over at Joaquin. "Maybe you should be a detective. You think like one."

He grinned. "Nah, man, I think like an investigative journalist."

"What's the difference between an investigative journalist and an ordinary reporter?" Mia honestly had no clue.

"Investigative reporters don't just report the news. They get out there and find the news. While a reporter might cover the City Council meeting and tell our readers what happened, an investigative reporter is digging through City Council's paper trail, looking for anything that might expose corruption. The I-Team—the Investigative Team—they're the newspaper's rock stars."

"I've heard of the I-Team. Are you part of it?"

He nodded, the pride he felt in his work showing in his smile. "I'm their shooter, though I sometimes get stuck doing GA work—general assignment—like the other night when I met you."

Regret stabbed at Mia. "I was rude to you that night. I'm sorry."

"Apology accepted." He turned into the parking lot of a

restaurant named Aztlán. "Oh, man, this place is packed tonight."

Joaquin parked and then pulled his cell phone out of the pocket of his parka and typed in a text message. "I'm letting Mateo know we're here."

When the message was sent, they walked inside to find the front lobby crowded with people waiting for tables.

"This place must be good." Mia glanced around at the Mexican décor—rustic pottery, colorful floor tiles, adobe walls. "We should get our names on the waitlist."

Joaquin chuckled, his hand touching the small of her back as they moved through the crowd. "To hell with the waitlist."

"Quino!" A man wearing gray trousers with a white shirt, gray vest, and bright yellow tie made his way toward them, a big smile on his face. He looked so much like Joaquin that he might have been his older brother.

He embraced Joaquin, the two of them speaking in Spanish.

Then Mateo turned to Mia, still smiling. "So, it takes a date with a beautiful woman to bring you through my doors, cousin?"

A date? Beautiful woman?

Heat rushed into Mia's cheeks. "Um ... I ... Date?"

It wasn't like her to get flustered by male attention. Then again, she'd never really gotten male attention—not the kind she'd wanted anyway.

Joaquin glared at his cousin. "She didn't know it was a date. I was working up to that. Now you've ruined the surprise. This is Ms. Starr. She was Elena's commanding officer her first year. You got a table for us, man?"

"A table for you, *primo*? No. But for you, señorita... Thank you for all you've done for our Elena. Follow me."

Mia found herself seated in the back in a private alcove, golden light from luminaria flickering across the tile table-top. Not sure what to say or do, she tucked her napkin into her lap. "A date?"

"I can't tonight," Joaquin teased. "Tonight, I'm having dinner with you."

Mia laughed. But then she saw it, and her breath caught.

Attraction.

It was there in his eyes.

## 5

Joaquin could tell that Mateo's teasing had embarrassed Mia. Her cheeks had flushed pink, and she had looked away. Now she seemed unable to meet his gaze.

Joaquin pretended to read over his menu. "Everything is good here—the empanadas, the enchiladas. The tamales are an old family recipe."

A server wearing a colorful skirt and a white peasant blouse brought glasses of water, a basket of chips, and a bowl of *pico de gallo*, her long dark hair pulled back in a braid. "Can I get you any drinks to start off?"

Joaquin saw Mia studying the drink menu. "Try a paloma. It's kind of like a margarita."

Mia looked up. "Okay. Sure."

"A paloma for you, señorita. How about you, señor?"

"Make it two palomas."

The server disappeared with their drink order, leaving the two of them alone.

"Exactly how many cousins do you have?" Mia asked.

Joaquin thought about it. "Forty-one. No, forty-two."

Mia's eyes went wide. "Forty-two cousins?"

"First cousins, yeah."

"Wow." Mia gave a little laugh. "I have five cousins—three on my mother's side and two on my father's. When did your family come to the US?"

Joaquin bit back a grin. "We didn't. The United States came to us."

Mia's brow furrowed in confusion. "What do you mean?"

"My family has been living in Colorado since before this was a state or even a US territory. After the Mexican-American war, the border shifted south, making the San Luis Valley part of the United States. As my grandma likes to say, 'We didn't move. The border moved over us.'"

Mia's lips formed an embarrassed O, color rising in her cheeks. "Sorry. I just assumed... That was stupid of me."

He reached over, gave her hand a squeeze, the heat that arced between them startling him, making him reluctant to draw his hand away. "Don't worry about it. But, hey, now it's my turn to ask an awkward question."

There was a hint of amusement in her eyes. "Is that how this works—one awkward question excuses another?"

"Is there a man in your life?" He'd been wondering this since the night of Elena's party. "You're too smart and beautiful to be single."

Mia gave a little shake of her head, dismissing his compliment. "If we were in Iraq right now, I'd say you were looking through deployment goggles."

"Deployment goggles?"

The server appeared with their drinks, interrupting the conversation. "Here you go. Have you decided what you'd like to order?"

Joaquin went for the tamales with tomatillo salsa.

Mia ordered a smothered burrito. "Lots of chile verde, please. I heard a rumor that it is delicious here."

"The rumor is true. You're going to love it." The server took their menus and hurried away.

Joaquin picked up where he and Mia had left off. "Deployment goggles?"

"They're like beer goggles, except they're deployment goggles," Mia explained. "You've been deployed for a while. There aren't many women around. Suddenly the women you'd never find attractive otherwise start looking good."

Joaquin understood—and he didn't like it. He wouldn't have ignored Mia anywhere. Did she think he was just saying this, that he didn't mean it? Did she not know how beautiful she was?

He looked into her eyes. "I hate to disappoint you, *amiga,* but there's nothing clouding my vision."

She broke eye contact, a tide of pink rising in her cheeks again.

"Are you going to answer my question—or do I have to guess?"

"I just haven't found the right man yet. Then again, I haven't really been looking. My CO said I intimidate men. He told me that I come across as cold and unfeminine. Not that I asked him for his opinion, mind you." She took a sip of her drink, her eyes going wide at her first taste. "Oh, this is good."

Joaquin could understand people misjudging Mia as cold, but to say she was unfeminine... That was *loco*. What kind of CO talked to his female soldiers like that anyway? "These men you intimidate—how insecure they must be. I'm surprised they have the courage to get out of bed and put on a uniform. As for your CO, he sounds like a *pendejo*— a real asshole."

"Oh, you have no idea."

~

MIA DABBED her lips with her napkin and set it next to her almost empty plate. "I can't eat another bite. This was incredible."

Joaquin had finished his meal. "Like I said—the best chile verde in Denver."

She took the last sip of her drink, the bite of tequila and salt mixing with the tart taste of lime and grapefruit. "Thanks for this. It was nice to forget about this mess with Andy for a while."

Not that she'd truly forgotten. Worry had niggled at her throughout the meal, but good food, alcohol, and very good-looking company had blunted it. Now it was back in full force, the uncertainty of so many unknowns gnawing at her.

Joaquin leaned forward, looked into her eyes, took her hand. "They'll get to the bottom of this. Wu is a good cop. Darcangelo and Hunter trust him, and that's good enough for me. You'll get through this, Mia."

"Thanks." Mia wasn't sure how she'd managed to say even that much, Joaquin's touch and the empathy in his eyes making it hard to think.

She knew she should pull her hand away. She didn't want to give him the wrong idea. Instead, she let her fingers mingle with his, the contact intoxicating, her skin seeming to tingle. She could see in his eyes that he felt it, too, their irises almost black, his pupils dilated. Then his thumb traced a circle on her palm and another.

She tried to act like nothing earthshaking was happening. "How do you know so many cops?"

"I met Darcangelo through Tessa—a former I-Team

reporter. They met when she was investigating sex trafficking in Denver. Hunter married Sophie, who's still on the I-Team. They were sweethearts in high school. She got him released from prison. Those two guys—they saved a lot of lives when terrorists took over the Palace Hotel. Without them, we would probably all have been killed."

Joaquin's words flowed over her—except for that last part. It stuck, jolting her back. Mia stared at him. "The Palace Hotel? You were there?"

Everyone in the country knew about that. Narco-terrorists had turned the historic hotel into a combat zone, killing a handful of security guards and taking everyone at the hotel hostage in an effort to free one of their own from Supermax. They'd packed the basement with enough explosives to bring down the building and had threatened to kill every man, woman, and child unless their demands were met. The FBI's Hostage Rescue Team had managed to defuse the bomb, kill the terrorists, and free the hostages.

"Yeah, I was there." Joaquin's jaw went tight, his expression turning hard, shadows in his eyes.

Mia knew that look. She'd seen those same shadows in the eyes of young soldiers after shelling and IED attacks. She held his hand a little tighter. "I'm sorry. I'm glad you're okay. I hope all of your friends made it out safely."

He nodded. "Hunter took a round saving the rest of us, but he wasn't badly hurt. One of my co-workers, Kat, went into labor. I did my best to help her through it. She had a baby girl just after the shooting stopped."

Mia's heart melted. "You ... you helped deliver a baby?"

Come to think of it, Mia had heard something about a baby being born there.

Joaquin shook his head. "I held Kat's hand through her contractions and tried to keep her safe from that bastard

Moreno and his goons. I felt so helpless. But it was Gabe Rossiter, her husband, who caught the baby. He's the real hero."

Mia opened her mouth to say that Joaquin was a hero, too, but Mateo walked up to the table. "How was your meal, Ms. Starr?"

Mia withdrew her hand. "Joaquin was right. The chile verde is incredible."

"That's what I like to hear." Mateo chuckled, his gaze shifting to Joaquin. "This is on me tonight, *primo*."

"What? No." Joaquin reached for his wallet. "I've got it."

Mateo rested a hand on Joaquin's shoulder. "This is my house, and you're family. You don't pay. Come see me more often, Quino, and bring Ms. Starr with you."

Snow was falling when Joaquin drove out of the restaurant's parking lot a half hour later, small, icy flakes melting on his windshield.

"Your cousin is something else. It must be wonderful to have a big family."

"No family is perfect." Joaquin told her about his cousin Jesús, who'd gotten into gangs and ended up in prison on drug charges. There was also his Uncle Teddy, who'd let alcohol destroy his life, and his niece Rachel, who'd gotten pregnant and dropped out of high school. "We have our good days and bad days, but we always pull together. How about your family?"

"I'm an only child. My parents moved to Florida last year. I don't really know my cousins. I've met them, but we don't get together. Most of them live in New Jersey. My father was born there."

That sounded lonely to Joaquin, but he didn't say so. "New Jersey? How did you end up in Colorado?"

"My dad got a job at Ball Aerospace. He's an engineer. He met my mom here. She left her job as a teacher to be a homemaker. I was born in Golden." She gave a little laugh. "My family hasn't been here nearly as long as yours. We—"

The buzzing of her cell phone cut her off.

Joaquin had his eyes on the road, so he only knew something was wrong when he heard her tone of voice.

"What the...?"

"Is everything okay?"

"It's a bizarre text from someone I knew in the Army—a medic. It says, 'Mia, you are scaring me. Stop, or I'll call the cops.' But I haven't talked to him or seen him in more than a year."

Joaquin didn't like this. "Who is this guy?"

"Jason Garcia. He's a medic. He's still active duty. I'm calling him."

"I'm not sure that's a good idea."

But Mia had already dialed the guy's number. "He's not answering. The call is going straight to voicemail."

"I don't like this, Mia."

"Neither do I. God, I hope he's okay." She left a quick message, then tried to reach him four more times between Colfax and the parking lot at the Botanic Gardens, each time with no luck. She pointed to a black Mazda 3. "That's my car."

"You can stay here where it's warm." Joaquin's heater was finally blasting hot air. He reached under the seat, grabbed his snow brush. "I'll scrape off your windshield. I don't mind the cold."

"Oh, you don't have to do—"

He was outside before she could finish her objection and

made quick work of the light dusting of snow and frost on her windshield and rear window.

She climbed out of his truck. "Thanks for everything. I had a good time—which is surprising under the circumstances."

"I'm glad to hear it." Joaquin felt the impulse to kiss her, but it was too soon for that. She'd given him her cell number, and that was good enough for now. "You go home, rest, try not to worry. Call me if you need anything."

"I'm going to Garcia's place. I have to make sure he's okay."

"Mia, that's a really bad idea. What if this guy has gone off his rocker and calls the cops on you? That won't look good in the middle of all this stuff with Andy. Call Wu. Tell him what's going on. Maybe he can send some uniforms to do a welfare check."

"What would I say to him? 'Help me. I got a weird text from a friend'?"

Well, she had a point there.

She opened her car door.

Joaquin shut it. "I'll drive you there. You're upset. You're not thinking clearly. Besides, as long as you're with me, you've got an alibi."

Her eyes went wide. "Right. Shit. Okay."

They climbed back into his truck.

He stopped at the parking lot exit. "Where to?"

"Jason lives near the VA. I've got his address here." She tapped on her phone's screen, then read out the address. "Should I ask Siri for directions?"

"Nah. I know that area. When you're a news photographer, you have to learn your way around, or you miss assignments and lose your job."

It took them less than ten minutes to reach the address. It was an old tri-level, its windows dark.

Joaquin parked. "Are you armed?"

"Armed?" Mia shook her head. "You?"

"Yes." He touched a hand to his front jeans pocket. "A Glock twenty-seven."

They climbed out and walked up to the house, snow crunching beneath their feet, the neighborhood quiet apart from the distant peal of police sirens and the murmur of traffic. They'd reached the porch before Joaquin saw.

The front door was ajar.

"Mia, stop!" He caught her arm, drew her back. "You have no idea who's in there or what's going on."

She took a step backward. "Garcia! It's Starr. Are you all right?"

"Let's get back in my truck." Joaquin's gaze moved from the front door to the darkened windows, watching for movement. They were sitting ducks here. "We need to call the police and wait."

"You're right." She walked backward, her gaze shifting from the door to the windows to the dark side of the house. "I'm glad you've got a weapon."

"Yeah. Me, too." It wouldn't do him any good in its holster.

Maybe it was the adrenaline, but it took a moment for Joaquin to notice that the sirens were growing nearer. They'd just reached his truck when a police cruiser tore around the corner and came to a stop behind them, its sirens dying. The vehicle's takedown light flashed on, blinding Joaquin.

"Hands in the air! I want to see those hands!"

*¡Carajo! Damn it.*

This was going to be fun.

MIA SAT in handcuffs in the back of the police cruiser, Joaquin cuffed beside her, the two of them watching as the officer and two others walked through Jason's front door, weapons drawn.

*Please let him be safe. Let him be safe.*

"How well do you know this guy?"

"We aren't BFFs, but I like him. He's a good man. We served together." Mia glanced over at Joaquin, guilt and regret twisting inside her. "I'm sorry. This is my fault. If I had listened to you…"

"Hey, don't worry about it. If *I* had listened to me, we wouldn't be here. They'll let us go when they get control of the situation."

"They took your pistol."

"I'll get it back. Besides, I have others."

A burst of static came over the radio, followed by an officer's voice. His words were muffled and mixed with police jargon, so that Mia only understood the last part. "We need a body bag and a DBT."

"A body bag?" *God.* "What's a DBT?"

Joaquin's brow furrowed. "It means 'dead body transfer.' I'm sorry."

Mia's mind reeled, her pulse ratcheting. "I can't believe this. This can't be real. Who would want to hurt Jason? All he ever did was save lives and help people. He would never hurt anyone. This doesn't make sense. He made it through Iraq. I can't believe he could be killed like this. Damn it!"

"Breathe, Mia. It's going to be okay."

Mia shook her head, swallowed the lump in her throat. "Not for Jason it won't."

Lights went on inside Jason's house, and the three officers who'd cleared the place stepped outside again, the one who'd detained them heading their way. Joaquin had called him Petersen, and the two seemed to know each other. That hadn't stopped the officer from patting them down, confiscating Joaquin's firearm, cuffing them—and stuffing them in the back of his vehicle.

"We had reports of gunshots from this address," Petersen had said.

"We just got here and saw the door open," Joaquin had explained. "We didn't even go inside. We were about to call the police."

Petersen hadn't said a word in response.

A blast of cold air hit Mia in the face as Petersen opened the car door and took hold of her arm. "Let's go."

"Go where?" Mia looked at Joaquin, alarm trilling through her.

Joaquin gave her a nod. "It's okay. He's a good cop."

Officer Petersen hauled her out the door.

"Is Jason dead? He's my friend. We served together in the Army. I got a strange text from him, so we came to check on him and found the door open."

"You'll have time to tell your story down at the station." Petersen turned her over to another officer, who led her to his vehicle and shut her inside.

She knew what they were doing. They had separated her from Joaquin to make sure the two of them didn't make up a story before they were questioned. Well, it didn't matter because they didn't have to make up anything.

Then it hit Mia, breath leaving her lungs in a slow exhale. If she hadn't gone to dinner with Joaquin, she would have been home alone with no one to confirm her whereabouts. And if she'd come here by herself...

*You'd be knee deep in shit right now.*

The minutes ticked by. A van pulled up—the crime scene investigation unit. Then an ambulance arrived. Two EMS guys climbed out and drew an empty gurney out of the back. The sight of it made Mia's stomach knot.

They disappeared inside, only to reappear about ten minutes later, a body closed in dark plastic and strapped to the gurney.

*Jason.*

How could his life have ended like this?

Mia let rage push her grief aside. Someone was killing her soldiers.

But why?

A man appeared beside her window, and the door opened.

Detective Wu leaned down. "Why am I not surprised to find you here, Ms. Starr? Let's head downtown."

## 6

"What time did you get to the restaurant?"

"It was just after six." Joaquin had been through this once already with a different detective. He knew Wu was just being thorough. A human life had been taken, after all, and a man was still missing. Even so, the questions were getting old. At least Joaquin was no longer in handcuffs. They'd taken those off when they'd brought him in here.

"What did you order?"

"I had the tamales with tomatillo salsa." Joaquin knew what Wu's next question would be. "Ms. Starr had a smothered burrito. We both ordered palomas."

Details like these enabled detectives to shake suspects apart, exposing their lies. In this case, it was the truth.

"You told the other detective that you didn't have a receipt. Why is that?"

"My cousin, Mateo Ramirez, owns the place. He wouldn't let me pay. You can call him. He'll confirm everything I've told you."

"Would your cousin lie for you?"

"Of course—but not about something like this." Mateo would kick Joaquin's ass if he thought Joaquin had been involved in a homicide. "He's got surveillance cameras in the parking lot and on the front door. They won't lie."

Wu nodded. "We're checking on that."

"How long do you plan to detain us?"

Wu didn't give him a straight answer. "I've got a few more questions."

But Wu's definition of "a few" was different from Joaquin's. The man was relentless, pelting Joaquin with one question after another.

What time had they left the restaurant? Why had they gone to the victim's house? How long had Joaquin known Mia? Did he know the victim? Why had Joaquin come to the police station earlier today? Why had he waited for Mia? What had she told him about her relationship with the victim? How long had he had a concealed carry permit? Why had he been armed?

It was that last question that finally got the better of Joaquin's temper.

"Why was I armed? I've seen too much bad shit happen to good people. That's why. I was at the Palace Hotel last month. I watched while terrorists hurt and threatened to kill my friends. I will *never* be helpless again."

He all but shouted those last words.

Wu seemed to study him, then opened his mouth to speak but was cut off by a knock at the door. "Come."

Darcangelo stuck his head inside. "Wu, let's talk."

Wu didn't look happy. "I know this guy is a friend of yours, but—"

Police Chief Irving appeared in the hallway just outside the door, white dress shirt stretched over his big belly. "Wu. Now."

Wu got to his feet, walked out into the hallway.

"I'll be back to talk with *you* in a moment," Darcangelo said to Joaquin before closing the door.

*Well, shit.*

Joaquin waited a good ten minutes before Wu returned. This time the detective left the door open.

"Mr. Ramirez, you are free to go."

*Thank you, Darcangelo.*

Joaquin stood. "What about Mia?"

"She's free to go, too."

"And my firearm?"

"You can collect it at the front counter." Wu turned and was gone.

Joaquin stood and would have followed him through the doorway but found himself face to face with Darcangelo.

"Not so fast, *cabrón*." Darcangelo forced him to back up, stepped into the interrogation room, and shut the door behind him. "What the fuck were you thinking?"

"We didn't know we were walking into a murder scene. She got a strange text message. That's it. It's not like we heard gunshots and ran through the door."

Darcangelo glared at him. "You were all of five minutes behind the real killer. *Five minutes*, Ramirez. What if he'd still been there?"

"I was armed."

"You hadn't drawn your weapon. If he'd been inside, he'd have heard and seen you coming. He could've opened that door and lit the two of you up before you cleared your holster."

It was the truth.

Darcangelo drew a breath, some of his anger fading. "You did the right thing to stop Ms. Starr from entering the house."

Then it hit Joaquin. "Wait—how do you know this?"

"You cannot repeat what I'm about to tell you. If the killer heard about this, a woman's life might be at stake."

"Okay."

"The eighty-year-old lady across the street reported the gunshots to police and saw a man in a black hoodie run out of the house. She tried to record him with her phone but had technical difficulties and ended up making a very fine video of her own face."

"Nice."

"She had the phone figured out by the time you two got there. She has a video showing when you pulled up and everything you did until Petersen arrived. The time stamps of the two videos—the one of her face while she's watching the killer leave and the one of you and Ms. Starr—show that only five minutes had gone by."

"*Mierda*."

"Yeah. The killer stayed behind to ransack the place. He took the guy's wallet and credit cards. He went through his medical kits, too, maybe looking for drugs."

"This video—that's how you got Wu to let us go, isn't it?"

"I made sure he heard about the evidence sooner rather than later. I figured you have better things to do than hang out here."

"Thanks, man. I owe you."

"Pay me back by keeping your ass out of trouble. What's going on between you and Ms. Starr anyway?"

"Nothing." Not yet.

"She's still a person of interest in the other case. You don't want to get caught up in that, too."

Joaquin was tired of this shit. "She had nothing to do with it. Someone is trying to set her up, attacking Andrew Meyer right after she left, dumping evidence at her place of work. I'll bet the killer sent that text message tonight, too. Maybe he wanted to make Mia look bad. Or maybe he knew she'd come and hoped to get a shot at her."

Darcangelo frowned. "We can't be sure these two cases are connected."

"Oh, come on! Mia knew both men. The three of them served together in Iraq. In the span of a few days, one goes missing, and the other is murdered. And *both* situations offer evidence that implicates Mia."

Darcangelo considered this for a moment, then gave Joaquin a slap on the shoulder. "If you ever get sick of the newspaper, you'd make a good detective. Now get the hell out of here."

Joaquin started out the door and then realized he was going nowhere. "Hey, can you give us a lift? My truck is still at the murder scene."

MIA SAT in the lobby waiting for Joaquin, her gaze fixed on nothing, the anger that had gotten her through the past few hours dulled by a creeping sense of numbness. She didn't see Joaquin come out of the back or walk up to the counter to sign for his firearm, her mind stuck on the image of Jason in that body bag.

It wasn't the first time she'd seen someone she'd served with carried away like that. Far from it. But this wasn't supposed to happen here.

She'd thought it was over. She'd thought the war was behind them. They'd made it through their deployments. They'd come home. They were supposed to be safe—as safe as anyone could be in this crazy world. But now Andy was missing and probably dead somewhere, and Jason, who'd never done anything but save lives, was dead, gunned down in his own home.

It made no sense.

When Mia had been active duty, there had been briefings about terrorist leaders who had ordered their followers to find and kill American service members anywhere in the world, including here at home. But, no. This couldn't be terrorists. Terrorists always took credit for their slaughter. That was the point. They killed to get attention and sow fear. Killing earned them nothing if it was done anonymously.

This had to be something else. If only she could think straight.

Random images moved through Mia's mind. The body bag. Joaquin dancing. The lead vehicle in their convoy exploding into flames. Jason trying to tie a tourniquet on LeBron Walker's thigh while the photographer snapped photos. Blood on sand. Andy with blisters on his hands and thighs.

*Tell al-Sharruken*

Liquid ice slid into her veins.

Could this be about Tell al-Sharruken?

Andy had been part of that, but she and Jason hadn't. Though Mia hadn't gone to the ruins, she'd refused to help cover up what the others had done. But Jason had tried to help Andy and the others, doing everything he could to alleviate their pain.

"Mia?" Joaquin's voice startled her, made her jump. "Are you okay?"

"Yeah." Her heart was still racing. "I'm fine."

"This is my buddy, Julian Darcangelo. He's giving us a ride back to my truck."

Mia stood, held out her hand. "Nice to meet you."

"Ms. Starr." Julian Darcangelo looked familiar. Then she remembered she'd seen him yesterday. He didn't look much like a cop. Tall with dark blue eyes that seemed to look through her, he wore jeans and a black T-shirt, his dark hair pulled back in a ponytail. "You've had a rough time of it lately."

She walked with the two men back through the building to a rear stairway that led down to a frigid parking garage full of squad cars, then climbed into the back of Darcangelo's SUV, the men's conversation drifting over her—until Darcangelo spoke to her directly.

"I'm sorry. I was caught up in my own thoughts."

Darcangelo repeated himself. "I hear you served through two deployments. Thanks for your service."

Mia never knew how to respond to this. She wasn't a hero. She hadn't done anything particularly courageous. She'd spent two years hauling ammo, food, and toilet paper around the desert. Others had fought and died. Yes, she had given up eight years of her life, but she'd gotten a college degree out of it.

For a moment, she said nothing. Then she remembered what Joaquin had told her about this man. "Thank you for yours. Joaquin said you saved a lot of lives at the Palace Hotel last month."

"Just doing my job." Darcangelo shifted the conversation back to her. "What did you do in the Army? Ramirez says you were his cousin's CO."

"Elena joined us during my last year. We were part of a forward supply company. I did mostly clerical work." Mia didn't really feel like talking about this, but the conversation did at least take her mind off Jason. "We were close to the fighting but not part of combat operations. One of our convoys was hit by an IED, and we lost some people. LeBron

Walker almost died. Powell, my CO, got a shrapnel wound that left him with a slight limp. Apart from that, we came under mortar fire a few times."

Joaquin looked back at her from the front seat. "That must have been rough."

"The IED was terrible, but the mortars—they never came close to hitting us. We would take cover and crack jokes, waiting for the radar guys to triangulate the position of the idiots firing at us and take them out."

"Jokes?" Joaquin looked surprised. "Like what?"

"Oh, dark stuff. 'If they can't do better than that, I'm never going to get out of those truck payments.'" The memory made her smile. "Or, 'Whoever survives, remember to throw out my porn stash before they ship my shit home to my wife.' Or, 'Next time you book us a vacation, Starr, take us somewhere with a damned beach.'"

Darcangelo chuckled. "Dark humor. LEOs do that, too."

Joaquin's expression had gone serious. "So do journalists. Journalism isn't as dangerous as being a cop or a soldier, but you see a *lot* of shit."

"Hell, yeah, you do." Darcangelo shared a glance with Joaquin.

Mia felt the weight of that glance. She had worked in a mostly male environment long enough to recognize deep friendship. Joaquin and Darcangelo were close.

There were still cops at Jason's house when they arrived. Darcangelo parked, wished Mia well, told Joaquin to get lost, and walked over to talk with Petersen, the cop who had detained them.

Mia found herself staring at the open front door, the finality of the situation hitting her full force. Jason was dead. He was gone. He had survived Iraq only to be murdered in his home.

*Son of a bitch!*

Joaquin came up beside her, his hand closing around hers. "I'm so sorry, Mia."

"Elena knew him. She would want to hear about this." Mia glanced around, wondering if the killer was still nearby, watching.

"I'll stop by her place on my way home and give her the news."

"Let's get the hell out of here."

Joaquin drove her back to her car, then followed her home. He got out of his vehicle and walked with her to her front steps. "Are you sure you don't want me to come inside and check the place?"

"Why do you care? You barely know me." The words came out cold. She hadn't intended that. "I'm grateful for what you did today. I really am. I don't know what would have happened tonight without you. But I don't understand."

He ducked down and kissed her forehead. It was a fleeting kiss, and it wasn't even on her mouth, but it made her breath catch and left her pulse racing.

He stepped back. "You did a lot for Elena. I couldn't let you face all of this alone. More than that, I feel a connection to you, Mia. I can't explain it. I just know it's there. Call if you need anything."

"Goodnight." Mia hurried inside her condo, where it was warm, then watched through her front window while Joaquin drove away.

Then, without stopping to take off her parka, she went to her bedroom closet, opened her biometric safe, and took out her pistol.

～

JOAQUIN WOKE up to snow the next morning—and the realization that he was fucked. He showered and drove to work early, hoping to catch Cate before the I-Team meeting. He was at his desk cleaning the inner barrel of his zoom lens when she walked in. Her expression when she saw him told him she knew.

*Shit.*

"Hey, Cate, can we talk?"

"You know Mia Starr." She dropped her stuff on her desk, her expression hard.

"In private." He motioned with a jerk of his head toward the hallway that led to the conference room.

She followed, heels clicking on the tile floor.

Joaquin shut the door behind them. "Mia Starr was my cousin's commanding officer her first year of active duty. I met her Friday when I photographed her outside Andrew Meyer's place. I had no idea who she was then. She ripped my head off. I ran into her again Saturday night at my cousin Elena's welcome home party."

"You sat through the I-Team meeting yesterday and said nothing."

"What did you want me to say? 'Hey, my cousin served with her. I saw her at a party.'" Okay, so he'd also danced with her, talked with her, walked her to her car.

"You could have offered to connect me with her or tried to convince her to let me interview her."

"She can't stand media. If she'd wanted to do an interview, she wouldn't have hung up on you. Nothing I could have said would have changed her mind." Of that, Joaquin was certain. "I'm trying to stay out of this—for my cousin's sake."

"So, you take her to dinner and drive her to the scene of a murder? How is that staying out of it?"

*She has a point, amigo.*

"I ran into her at the police station when I went to get that mug shot of the bastard who tried to kill his wife. She looked upset. I offered to drive her back to her car—"

"And ended up at a restaurant instead. Hmm. Wrong turn?"

"I owe her a debt of gratitude for what she did for Elena."

Cate pinned him with her gaze. "Did you sleep with her?"

"That's nobody's business—but, no, I didn't."

Not that he hadn't thought about it. A *lot*.

"You need to stay away from her. It looks bad for her, Joaquin. Even if she had nothing to do with last night's homicide, they found bloody towels and Andrew Meyer's driver's license in a wood chipper at the Botanic Gardens where she works."

*Old news.* "I think someone's trying to set her up."

Cate rolled her eyes at this. "Really?"

Joaquin told her most of what he knew, leaving out any mention of the woman across the street and her videos. Darcangelo had sworn him to secrecy on that score. "If you want to be a top-notch investigative reporter, you've got to keep an open mind."

Cate balked at this, her gaze dropping slowly to her feet. When she looked up at him again, there was curiosity in her eyes instead of anger. "They didn't say anything about the strange text message at the press conference."

*Mierda.*

"Yeah? Well, don't print that." Joaquin didn't want to give away info that could ruin the cops' investigation. "They keep certain details to themselves, things they think might help them prove a suspect's guilt."

"How did they manage to clear the two of you so quickly?"

"My cousin has video surveillance outside his restaurant."

"Lucky for you." Cate frowned, crossed her arms over her chest. "I still think you should have told me that you knew her."

"It wouldn't have changed anything."

"Maybe not, but at least I wouldn't have to wonder if a co-worker is keeping secrets about one of my stories. Are you going to see her again?"

"I don't know." He had decided last night after that impulsive kiss that he would leave that up to Mia. It had only been a kiss on the forehead, the kind of kiss he'd give Elena or his *abuelita*. But she wasn't family, and he hadn't asked her first.

"Oh, Joaquin, help me out here." There was a pleading tone to Cate's voice. "What can I do to get ahead of the other papers on this story?"

"You could interview people who knew the two men. You could request their military files, though I don't know what the government will release to the general public. You might not get more than—"

Tom stepped into the hallway, a scowl on his face. "Ramirez. My office. *Now*."

"He was just bringing me up to speed on what he knows about last night's homicide. I've got a couple of new angles to go on."

Joaquin didn't need Cate to protect him. Tom intimidated a lot of people, but he didn't scare Joaquin. "I'll be there in a minute."

This was going to be a long damned day.

## 7

Mia found a table at the crowded coffee shop, sat, and took a sip of her coffee, the strong taste of dark roast bringing some life back to her brain and body.

She'd barely slept last night, her mind unable to let go, her thoughts jumping from Andy's disappearance to Jason's murder to Tell al-Sharrukin to Joaquin and back again. She'd given up trying to sleep at five, packed her backpack full of everything she'd need for the day, and hopped the light rail, which had lots of surveillance cameras. First, she'd gone to the gym and done her workout. Then she'd showered and taken the light rail downtown. She'd been careful to choose a coffee shop that had video surveillance and made sure to look directly into the camera.

Twice now it seemed that someone had tried to make her look guilty of a serious crime. She wouldn't stay at home alone where she could become a target like Andy and Jason —or find herself without an alibi.

She took another sip of coffee then slipped her tablet out of her handbag and logged onto the coffee shop's Wi-Fi. She wrote a quick email to Wu, asking him how the investigation of Andy's disappearance was progressing and reminding him that she wasn't able to work until he exonerated her. Then she wrote to Kevin, her boss, to let him know how disappointed she was that he hadn't stood by her.

She deleted that second one.

*You'll just get yourself fired.*

Damn it!

She *hated* this feeling of helplessness. She hated to have to wait, not knowing what was going on with the investigation or when it would be over. She hated having this cloud of suspicion hanging over her head, following her everywhere she went.

At least Joaquin believed her.

He was the one thing about this past weekend that didn't suck.

*I feel a connection to you, Mia. I can't explain it. I just know it's there.*

She knew what he meant because she felt it, too. It hardly seemed possible that she'd met him only last Friday.

He had kissed her. No, it hadn't been a kiss on the mouth. It had been more like a kiss you'd give your sister. But if that's what it felt like when Joaquin gave her a little peck, what would a full-on kiss with lips and teeth and tongues do to her?

Warmth that had nothing to do with caffeine zinged through her.

She probably shouldn't think about that.

*Is there a man in your life? You're too smart and beautiful to be single.*

He probably hadn't meant that. He'd seemed serious, a warmth in his brown eyes that had made it hard to breathe. But Mia knew she wasn't any man's idea of beautiful, not really. Her hair was more orange than red. Her mouth was too broad. She was too thin with small breasts that barely filled a B cup.

*You shouldn't be thinking about Joaquin anyway, not when Andy is still missing and Jason is in the morgue.*

She set her coffee down, pulled her smartphone out of her handbag, and called the one person in the world she'd hoped never to speak to again.

He answered on the second ring. "If it isn't the Iron Maiden. What do you want, Starr? Is your ice cave getting lonely?"

Bennett Powell was an asshole. He was also her former commanding officer.

"Knock it off, Powell." She refused to take the bait and got to the point. "Garcia is dead. Someone killed him last night, shot him to death in his home. Andy Meyer is missing. He disappeared from his home Friday evening. There were bullet holes in his shower stall."

For a moment, he said nothing. "So?"

"You were their commanding officer. I thought you'd want to know."

"Am I supposed to send flowers?"

And he thought *she* was cold?

"You don't care?"

"Meyer was a fuck-up. The planet is better off without him. Garcia—that's a bummer. He was okay."

"Someone is trying to make it look like I'm responsible."

Powell burst into laughter. "That's the best damned thing I've heard all day. Hey, did the cops bring you in, maybe strip search you and make you bend over? Please tell me they did."

She fought to control her anger, reminding herself that he no longer had any power over her life. "The two of them gone in four days—it made me wonder whether this might have something to do with Tell al-Sharruken."

Powell gave a snort. "You think ancient Assyrians came after them?"

"Of course not. Maybe someone is angry—"

"Lots of people are angry—at you. No one was upset with Andy or Jason. Besides, Jason wasn't part of it. He just tried to help. But you turned in the rest of us to advance your own career. You knew you'd never move up otherwise."

"All I did was tell the truth." Mia fought to keep her voice down. She was in public. She didn't want to make a scene. "You were our leader. You lied to command. You led those guys into breaking the law. It's your fault that—"

"You know what your problem is? No man wants you. You never get laid, so all of your natural womanly goodness has dried up, died. Your cunt is probably full of cobwebs. You're a cold—"

"Go to hell, you limp-dick loser." Mia ended the call, hands shaking, to find people at nearby tables staring at her. "Sorry."

"I FEEL WHAT I FEEL, man. Am I *loco*?" Joaquin took another drink of his Knockers' Glacier Stout, his stocking feet on Matt's coffee table.

He and Matt had gone out for Thai food after work and ended up here, waiting with the TV on mute for the Big 12 basketball game to start on ESPN.

"I'm fifty and divorced and look like Howdy Doody, and you're thirty-four, good-looking, and hip, and you're asking *me* for relationship advice? You must be desperate." Matt shook his head, laughed. "But I gotta say—it does sound a little strange. You two meet at a crime scene. She knows Elena. She gets you dragged in for questioning. She could be real trouble. Couldn't you feel connected to a woman with fewer problems, maybe someone with millions in the bank and an older sister who's single?"

Joaquin gave Matt a look of feigned disgust. "And end up with you as my brother-in-law or some shit?"

"The chicas love you. They love your physique. They love your dancing. They love your Pulitzer. Hell, *I* love your Pulitzer, but not enough to sleep with you."

"No woman has slept with me because of my Pulitzer." Not as far as he knew.

"The point is that you could be getting laid *twice* every night of the week if that's what you wanted. Why get involved with this Mia person?"

"I'm not *involved* with her—not really. Besides, hookups feel so empty, man. It's like jacking off using another person's body instead of your hand."

"You say that like it's a bad thing." Matt took a drink of his beer. "Right now, I'd be happy to—"

Joaquin's cell phone buzzed somewhere. He got to his feet, found the damned thing in his coat pocket. "It's her. It's Mia."

Matt frowned. "Why am I not surprised?"

Joaquin answered. "Hey, Mia."

"Joaquin? I can barely hear you." The sound of loud music and voices came from the background. "I'm going to step outside."

"Where are you?"

"A nightclub on Pearl Street." The music and voices faded. "Sorry about that."

"Are you okay?"

She seemed to hesitate. "Yes, I'm fine. I've spent the

whole day in coffee shops, restaurants, and bars where they have surveillance cameras. I'm afraid to be alone. I'm afraid to go home."

There was genuine fear in her voice.

"Has something happened?"

Matt looked pointedly at Joaquin. "No, you're not involved with her at all."

Joaquin ignored him.

"No, nothing. I ... I just ... Sorry. I shouldn't be bothering you, not after everything I put you through last night."

"Mia, it's okay. What's going on?"

Her words came out in a rush. "I'm afraid, Joaquin. It's probably all in my head, but I can't shake the feeling that someone is watching me. I'm afraid that this isn't over, that Andy and Jason are just the beginning. You probably think I'm crazy, but I'm not."

Maybe it was her fear, or maybe it was just instinct, but Joaquin knew at that moment that there was something Mia hadn't told him or the police. Whatever it was, it scared the hell out of her.

"I don't think you're crazy. You've been through a lot these past few days." He glanced at his watch, tried to gauge whether he was good to drive. Two beers in two hours. No problem. "How about I come get you, and we head to my place? You can tell me what's going on, and you won't be home alone. I've got a spare room if you decide you want to stay the night."

"Okay."

"Where are you?"

"I'm at a club called Igneous Intrusion."

"I know where that is. Stay put. Don't go anywhere alone, not even to the restroom. I'll be there in about ten minutes. I'll text you from outside."

Matt got to his feet, worry on his face. "You're leaving?"

"Sorry, man, but she's at a nightclub scared out of her mind." Joaquin grabbed his parka off the back of Matt's kitchen chair. "She thinks someone's watching her."

"Maybe she really *is* out of her mind. Are you sure you don't want me to come? Someone needs to have your back. I'm a neutral third party. Besides, then I can check her out for myself, see what kind of vibe I catch."

"I don't need a bodyguard." That's why there was a Glock in his pocket.

Joaquin picked up his camera bag—he never left it in his vehicle—and headed toward the door. "I'll see you tomorrow."

Matt walked him out. "Okay, fine. But I'm drinking what's left of your beer."

MIA SAT AT A TABLE, bass thrumming, nothing left of her Diet Coke but ice. She shouldn't have bothered Joaquin. He'd had to deal with enough already because of her. Besides, she'd never been the kind of woman who needed a man to rescue her. Still, she'd be lying if she said she hadn't felt better when he'd said he was on his way.

She felt it again—prickles on the nape of her neck. She turned to look, doing her best to make it seem casual. The place was packed, and the lighting dim, making it hard to see individual faces.

*Damn it.*

She wasn't helpless. She had her SIG in her handbag, and it was loaded. No, it wasn't legal to carry a weapon like this without a permit in Colorado, but she would rather get busted with a concealed weapon than caught by a killer without one.

There was a lull between songs, the abrupt absence of music leaving sudden quiet in its wake. The prickling sensation returned, stronger this time.

On instinct, she looked up.

A man in a black hoodie.

His face was hidden by shadows, but the moment she spotted him, he walked away and disappeared, swallowed by the crowd on the balcony.

Her cell phone buzzed, making her jump.

It was Joaquin.

I'M HERE.

She hadn't taken off her parka, so she grabbed her handbag and backpack and hurried out the door, glancing back to see if the man in the hoodie was there.

Joaquin sat double-parked in his truck, engine still running. He threw the passenger door open.

She hurried over and climbed inside, locking the door. "I didn't imagine it."

"What?"

"There was a guy on the balcony—a man in a black hoodie. I looked up and saw him watching me. The moment he realized I'd seen him, he vanished into the crowd. I didn't get a look at his face. It was shadowed."

Still, there had been something familiar about him.

Joaquin muttered something under his breath in Spanish then nudged his truck into traffic. "Where's your vehicle?"

"I took the light rail. I wanted there to be a record of everywhere I went."

"Smart." He stopped at a red light, his gaze on his rearview mirror. "You need to report this, let Wu know."

"I don't think he'd believe me. He always thinks I'm lying."

The light turned green.

"Then I'm calling Darcangelo. He's up to date on this case. He'll get Wu to listen." Joaquin's phone was plugged into the console on his dash. "Call Darcangelo."

A few seconds later, a voice Mia recognized came over the speakers.

"Hey, Ramirez, you keeping out of trouble?"

"Mia's here with me, and I've got you on speaker. We're on our way to my place. She spent the day in public because she was afraid to be alone. But just now she saw a guy in a black hoodie watching her. The moment he saw that she'd seen him, he disappeared."

There was a pause. "Tess and I are in the middle of dinner with Hunter and Sophie and their kids. Give us thirty minutes, and Hunter and I will head your way. Where can I find you?"

"We're going to my place."

"See you there."

The call ended.

Mia looked over at Joaquin. "I'm sorry to wreck your evening."

"You did the right thing calling me."

"I wish I'd gotten a look at his face."

"I hope you'll tell my buddies everything you told me. What you said about this being only the beginning—what did you mean?"

Mia looked out her window. "It's just a gut feeling."

"If you know anything, now is the time to speak up."

What could she tell them? What had happened at Tell

al-Sharruken was classified. The Army had done all it could to bury it. If the story ended up in a police report and made its way into the papers, Mia could face charges.

Was she willing to go to prison for a hunch?

She couldn't be sure that the fallout from that nightmare was behind this. Still, she had to tell them something. She didn't want anyone else to disappear or die. How much could she say? All she knew for certain was that the bastard behind this knew her, Andy, and Jason.

That meant he had once been a brother in arms.

SHE HAD SEEN HIM. She had looked *right at him*. Had she recognized him?

*Fuck. Fuck. Fuck.*

She'd been spooked and had left the bar right after that, climbing into some asshole's pickup truck. But Mia didn't have a man in her life. She was the Iron Maiden, the Ice Queen. If you touched her, she'd freeze your dick off. As far as he knew, no one had ever had the balls to try.

He'd gotten a glimpse of the guy's face through the windshield of that pickup and was sure he'd seen the bastard once before somewhere.

*Where? Where? Where?*

If only his goddamn head didn't hurt so much.

He'd been surprised to find out Mia hadn't been arrested. The papers said she'd been questioned. That was it. She wasn't even a suspect in Garcia's death. The cops must be total morons if they couldn't follow the trail of breadcrumbs he'd left for them. The bloody towels and bath mat and the driver's license. The text message.

Did he have to write her name in blood or something?

*Oh, fuck. Fuck. Fuck.*

He pressed the heels of his hands to his eyes, sagged against the concrete support of the highway underpass, the pain unbearable.

"You okay, buddy?"

He opened his eyes, found a drunk shuffling toward him, bottle in hand. He fumbled in his pocket for an Oxy, chewed it. "Fuck off."

When that didn't work, he drew his pistol, waved it in the drunk's face.

"Well, that's bad manners." The drunk shuffled away. "Asshole."

He bit back a cry. The drugs never kicked in fast enough. It wasn't going to end until he killed himself. God, he'd do it now, but this bullet was meant for someone else. And then there was Mia.

Then it came to him.

*The news photographer.*

That's who he was. The bastard driving that truck had taken the photo of Mia that had run on the front of the *Denver Independent*. His name was probably there below the photo. Even if it weren't, he wouldn't be hard to find.

*Just follow him home from work.*

That's what he'd done with Garcia. Poor, stupid Garcia.

Mia could try to hide, but he would find her.

## 8

Mia stepped out of the elevator and followed Joaquin down the hallway. He must earn decent money to have a condo in the River North Art District. RiNo was Denver's trendiest neighborhood, full of galleries, brew pubs, clubs, boutiques, and restaurants. He stopped outside number 407, unlocked the deadbolt, and stepped aside to let her enter, flicking on the lights before locking the door behind them.

"Wow." Some of her anxiety melted away. "I guess it pays to be a newspaper photographer."

This made Joaquin laugh. He took her parka and hung it with his in a closet. "Make yourself at home."

She found herself standing in a small foyer and looking into an ultra-modern kitchen with stainless steel appliances and European-style cabinetry. A row of pendant lights hung above a kitchen island, a glass bowl filled with apples and bananas sitting on the granite countertop. "Nice place."

Beyond the kitchen was a small dining area with a table of reclaimed wooden planks, a bench with a multi-colored cushion on one side, chairs of molded plastic in bright turquoise on the other. The table itself was all but buried beneath mail and newspapers, a laundry basket with folded clothes sitting on one end.

The living room had a blocky sectional sofa in soft gray and a rustic wooden coffee table that was covered with books and newspapers. Floor-to-ceiling windows looked out on a deck that faced west—toward the mountains. It was too dark to see the mountains now, but city lights glittered below.

"Sorry. The place is a mess." Joaquin gathered up the mail, shoved it into the laundry basket, and disappeared down a small side hallway.

"I think it's beautiful." Her gaze traveled over the photographs on the walls—a field of *Aquilegia caerulea*—Colorado blue columbines—a bald eagle standing on a frozen lake, a jagged mountain peak against a blue sky, ocean waves unraveling on a sandy beach. "These are yours?"

He called to her from another room. "On my days off, I try to get out to shoot. Let me show you the spare room."

She followed him down the side hallway.

"I've got my own bathroom, so this one's yours." He pointed to a small bathroom with a tub and shower stall at the end of the hallway. "My room is to the right here, and the spare room is there to your left. Let me know if you need anything."

"Thanks." Mia walked into the bedroom, flicked on the lights, and found herself surrounded once more by color.

The bed had an antique iron frame, its green paint chipped to reveal the metal beneath. A hand-pieced quilt of fabric in every color Mia could imagine—rich blues, hot pinks, vibrant reds and purples, greens, oranges, yellows—covered the bed. Photographs adorned the walls. Two older black men playing chess in a park. A rusted car frame in the middle of a lush forest, its interior filled with ferns. Sunrise through a sandstone arch somewhere in the desert.

Joaquin came up to the door behind her. "You hungry?"

"No, thanks." Stress always killed her appetite. "You're incredibly talented."

"Sometimes I get it right."

"Sometimes? Are you blind? These are beautiful."

"Thanks."

She followed him back out to the living room and sat on the sofa, more tension melting away. Being here ought to have felt awkward. She barely knew Joaquin, after all. But she felt more relaxed now than she'd been all day.

"Want something to drink? I've got beer and soda and, well ... beer and soda."

"Can I have a glass of water with ice?" Her gaze moved over the books on the coffee table, stopping when she saw his name. "You published your photos."

So *that's* how he'd been able to afford this place.

"I've got a couple of photography books and a textbook." He walked over to the sofa, handed her a glass of water. "After my Pulitzer, the paper published that. It's a 'Best of' book with photos dating back to its first edition in 1890. That gave me the idea to write an instructional book about news photography. It got picked up by Columbia as a textbook. I released a book of Colorado nature photos about six months ago."

Mia picked up the book, turned through its pages. The photographs of Denver as a cowboy town were fun. There was the state capitol, newly built and festooned with ribbons and banners. There was Pearl Street—nothing but mud and wooden walkways. "Are the photos that won you the Pulitzer in here?"

He bent down, flipped toward the back. "Here."

The photographs told a story. Armed men in body armor fast-roping onto the balcony of a building. A man doing CPR on another man who appeared to be dead, a woman with dark hair leaning over him in tears, dead bodies on the floor around them. "This is it, isn't it—that shootout with the cartel?"

"Yeah."

Mia stared, transfixed, at the next page. It was Julian Darcangelo, but he was badly wounded. Another man sat behind him, holding him and applying direct pressure to a gunshot wound in his shoulder. Mia didn't have to know anything about the two guys to know they were close friends, closer than brothers. The pain and exhaustion on Julian's face and the worry and love—yes, love—on the other man's face told the entire story of that moment in a way that words never could have.

"Powerful."

"You're going to meet him in a minute." Joaquin tapped his finger on the other man's face. "That's Marc Hunter."

Mia's stomach knotted. She closed the book, set it aside. "I saw what I saw tonight. I hope your friends don't think I'm overreacting."

He sat on the corner of the coffee table, looked into her eyes. "Trust me, Mia. They won't."

JOAQUIN STOOD off to the side, listening while Mia told Darcangelo and Hunter what had happened tonight. Darcangelo asked most of the questions. The man had once worked as a deep cover agent for the FBI, tracking down sex traffickers and freeing their victims. He had a lot of experience working with terrified, brutalized women.

Not that Mia seemed terrified. She was calm, composed, almost business-like in her responses. He had no difficulty imagining her in a uniform. Still, he could tell from the shadows in her blue eyes that she was afraid. Not for the first time, he wished he'd been there tonight. He'd have gone after the bastard.

"I left the restaurant and walked down to that nightclub —Igneous Intrusion."

Darcangelo nodded. "I know the place."

"I went there because there's a security camera on the corner. I got a Coke, sat at a table away from the dance floor, and tried to figure out what I should do next."

"What do you mean?" Hunter asked.

"I didn't know whether I should go home, go to a hotel, or call someone. I'm tired of having a cloud of suspicion over my head. I had nothing to do with Andy's disappearance or Jason's murder."

Hunter nodded. "Got it."

"I'd been there for maybe ten minutes when I got the feeling I was being watched. I tried to be casual about looking around. I moved to the other side of the table. The music ended, and something made me look up. A man was standing on the balcony, watching me. He didn't have a drink in his hand. He wasn't dancing. He was just standing there, watching me. The moment he saw me looking at him, he stepped back into the crowd. That's when I called Joaquin."

"Did you get a look at his face?"

"No, sir. It was dark, and he was wearing a black hoodie that shadowed his face."

Darcangelo and Hunter exchanged a glance.

The black hoodie. It seemed like a random detail, but given that the man who'd killed Jason Garcia had been wearing a black hoodie, it probably wasn't a coincidence.

A killer might have gotten close to Mia tonight. What sucked is that Joaquin hadn't been able to tell her that. He had promised Darcangelo not to say a word about the old woman and her video. Thank God Mia had called him.

The men waited for her to go on.

She folded her hands together in her lap, her fingers laced so tightly that her knuckles were white. "There was something familiar about him. I can't say what. I got the feeling that if I had seen his face, I would have recognized him."

"It makes sense to me," Hunter said. "If these two cases are connected—"

"If?" Joaquin blurted.

Hunter shot Joaquin a stony glance. "If these two cases are connected—and it seems to me that they are—whoever is behind this has to be someone who knew both victims and who knows you. You are the thread that brings it together, which is why the department has been so interested in you."

"Who would want to hurt you, Mia?" Darcangelo leaned in close, but Joaquin could see that he was careful not to touch her.

Mia looked away, squeezed her eyes shut, her composure crumbling, the fear she was trying to hide naked on her face for just a moment. She had something she wanted to tell them, something she was afraid to say.

"You can trust them, Mia. Tell them what you told me."

She shut her emotions down, looked over at him, nodded. "I'm afraid that the killer isn't finished. I'm afraid he's got other people in his crosshairs ... and that I'll be one of them."

Darcangelo and Hunter seemed to consider what she'd said.

"There's a missing piece here," Hunter said. "Why, Mia?"

"Any information that sheds light on this might help us save lives, including yours," Darcangelo said.

Mia glanced up at Joaquin, an almost pleading look in her eyes. "If I tell you, I could go to prison."

Okay, that is *not* what Joaquin had expected her to say.

Prison? *¡Mierda!* Fuck.

When Darcangelo spoke again, his voice was soft, soothing. "If you have information that helps catch a killer, the DA would bear that in mind when considering charges against—"

"It's not like that." Mia's lips curved in a fleeting smile as if Darcangelo had just said something funny. "I haven't done anything wrong—yet. Telling you might constitute breaking the law."

"Huh." Understanding dawned on Hunter's face. "Classified information?"

Mia nodded. "Confidential."

If Joaquin remembered correctly, "Confidential" was the lowest level of classified information. Still, operatives who had leaked classified info had gone to prison, even when that information wasn't Top Secret.

No wonder she was afraid to tell them.

He crossed the room, sat on the coffee table across from her. "I know you're scared. It must feel like you've got the weight of the world on your shoulders right now. But we have laws that protect whistleblowers, including military personnel."

"Ramirez is right," Hunter said. "I served with Special Forces and—"

"Trash detail." Darcangelo winked.

Hunter ignored him. "They can't penalize you for exposing those who break the law, as long as you disclose that information to your chain of command, the courts, or law enforcement."

Mia nodded. "I read the statute today, but I'm no longer active-duty military. I couldn't find anything that protects *former* military personnel."

Joaquin saw her dilemma. "You're in a gray area."

"If I tell you, you'll have the power to destroy my life. You have to promise me that we're off the record. If this ended up in the newspaper, I would be outside the protection of any law. You can't tell anyone, especially not that reporter."

Joaquin tried not to feel insulted by this. She barely knew him. To trust him with something of this magnitude... He should feel honored. "I promise I won't talk about what you tell me with anyone who isn't in this room."

IT SEEMED to Mia that she stood on the edge of a precipice. One more step and she'd go over that edge with no way back. But her life wasn't the only one at stake here. If what had happened at Tell al-Sharruken was at the heart of this, there could be a dozen others, maybe more, whose lives were at risk.

Could she trust these men?

She looked from Joaquin to Julian to Marc.

"We'll have to share what you tell us with Detective Wu and Old Man Irving, the chief of police, but we can keep a tight lid on it," Julian said. "We wouldn't share classified information with the press or anyone in law enforcement who didn't need to know. We might want to contact sources in the Pentagon to get whatever files exist."

"I'm not sure there are files," Mia said. "There is no official record of what happened that day. The only people who know about it are those who were there and the chain of command that responded afterward."

"That bad, huh?" Marc said. "'Do Not File.'"

"Yes. Exactly." Paper trails had been shredded, computer files purged, any mention of what had happened that day destroyed.

Joaquin leaned closer. "You can trust these guys, Mia, and you can trust me."

Did she have any other choice?

"Do you mind if I write this down?" Julian asked, notepad and pen in hand.

She shook her head—then took the plunge, her pulse ratcheting. "Tell al-Sharruken."

"Can you spell that?"

"S-H-A-R-R-U-K-E-N. It's a place in the Kurdish area of northern Iraq, an ancient Assyrian site—sand, old walls, a few stone pillars."

The men waited for her to go on.

But where should she start?

"When I joined Bravo Company, my commanding officer, Captain Bennett Powell, a West Point grad, did and said things that were ... inappropriate. I reported what was clear sexual harassment to Colonel Frank, who was in command of our brigade, and to our EO rep. They patted me on the head, thanked me for coming forward, and then did nothing." Mia had felt utterly betrayed.

"After that, things got worse. Powell called me names in front of the others—Ice Queen, Iron Maiden, bitch, whatever. I found out later that I wasn't the only woman to complain about him. Other women came to me, confided in me."

Joaquin muttered something in Spanish. "He sounds like a real asshole."

"I hope your story ends with him getting his ass kicked," Marc said.

Julian nodded. "Or better yet, his balls."

"I wish." The men's rage on her behalf came as a kind of affirmation. She hadn't gotten that from anyone, not even her own parents. They'd told her she should expect harassment working in a male-dominated field—as if succeeding at a job previously reserved for men took away a woman's right to dignity and respect.

"When we deployed to Iraq in 2013, I was company XO. I stayed at the FOB—the forward operating base—most of the time, handling administrative tasks while the rest of the company hauled around toilet paper and MREs."

Powell had used that time away to alienate others from her, degrading her behind her back until his nicknames for her had become widespread at the FOB.

"One day, I came across a couple of E-fours talking about selling something, discussing how much they thought they'd get for it. I thought it was illicit drugs. It turned out to be artifacts."

Marc gave a low whistle. "Looting."

Mia nodded. "Powell had been taking a group of a dozen soldiers off base, using the supply company as a kind of cover to look for artifacts. It's a violation of the code of conduct and international law. It could have gotten us in serious trouble with locals, destroying any goodwill we had left with the nearby communities. I reported it to Colonel Frank. I thought they'd be court-martialed."

"Let me guess—he did nothing."

"He yelled at Powell, I think, but Powell denied it and claimed that I had some kind of grudge against him. Colonel Frank buried it." Mia swallowed, a helpless sense of rage building inside her. "The rest of that deployment was misery. Powell found all kinds of creative ways to get back at me—putting camel spiders in my tent, locking all of the female sanitary supplies in his office so that I had to ask for them each month, excluding me from meetings. Someone put a coffee can full of human feces in my tent."

Joaquin muttered something in Spanish, his eyes dark with anger. "And no one did anything to stop this son of a whore?"

"No. Nothing. I told myself it didn't matter. I was there to do a job for my country, not to win a popularity contest. But, still, it was hard." She realized this wasn't part of the story she was trying to tell them. "Sorry. None of that really matters. I guess I drifted off topic."

"No, no." Joaquin touched a reassuring hand to her shoulder. "You just tell the story as it comes to you. We're listening."

Mia took a sip of her water. "It all blew up one day in September. I was in my office, and one of the men ran in to say that one of our guys was sick. I found Andy in his bunk, coughing, his nose running. I thought maybe he had the flu —and then I saw the blisters. They covered his hands and legs—huge, yellow blisters."

Mia told them how she'd called for a medic and gone with Andy to medical, only to find a half-dozen other men there with the same symptoms. "Most had blisters. Some were having difficulty breathing. The medical staff had no idea what was going on. Jason worked hard to treat their burns and relieve their pain. He was the one who called around, did the research, and figured it out. It took a few days, but he figured it out."

"Jason Garcia, the homicide victim?" Julian asked.

Mia nodded, her throat growing tight. "He was a kind and good man."

"What was it?" Joaquin asked.

"It turns out that Powell had taken his gang out to Tell al-Sharruken, where their shovels had hit a buried cache of old shells. Some of the shells were cracked. They dug the shells out, handled them. They didn't realize the shells were leaking. Andy, Powell and the others—they had all been exposed to mustard agent."

## 9

"Mustard agent?" Joaquin stared at Mia, stunned by what she'd just told them. "You mean mustard gas?"

"It can be a liquid or a gas, so mustard agent is the more accurate term," Hunter said. "But, yeah, mustard gas."

Darcangelo shot Hunter an annoyed glance. "Thanks for the chemistry lesson."

"Hey, any time."

But Mia wasn't listening to them, her body rigid, her gaze turned inward as she relived the horror of what she'd seen. "It turned out that they had been exposed three days prior. The symptoms don't show up right away. When they started to get sick, they hid it, knowing they'd get in trouble. But a few of the younger guys were so afraid that they spilled it all. Those who were badly affected, including Andy and Powell, were sent to Germany for treatment and then shipped home."

Joaquin listened while Mia described the clusterfuck that had followed as the colonel she'd warned went into full CYA—cover your ass—mode.

"I thought Powell would face a court-martial, but Colonel Frank couldn't admit that he'd been told about his troops looting. The Pentagon didn't want word about the mustard agent to get out."

"Why not? Wouldn't it be good to warn people that this shit is out there?"

"Not when the U.S. government supplied the chemicals that made it," Hunter said. "We gave Iraq the chemicals to make mustard agent and Sarin during the Iraq-Iran War. It's not a secret, not when so many U.S. and Coalition troops have been hurt by the shit since 2003. But it's not really public knowledge either. The suits in D.C. aren't in a hurry to admit to the world that the U.S. violated the Geneva Convention."

Joaquin had heard and seen a lot of fucked-up bullshit in his years at the paper, but this was in a league of its own. "So that shit is there because of *us*?"

Hunter and Mia nodded.

*Mierda.*

"I went above the colonel's head, told the brigadier general of our division that I had reported what Powell was doing. But no one cared that Powell had endangered his own men. What mattered more to them was the potential for embarrassment. 'US troops wounded by chemical weapons while looting,' doesn't make a favorable headline."

Joaquin could see that. "No, I guess it doesn't."

"I was promoted to captain and told not to discuss the matter, which was now classified. The entire incident was swept under the rug."

"What happened to the looters?" Hunter asked.

"Most of the men involved were discharged, some unfavorably. None of those who were disabled by the mustard agent—Powell, Andy, Chris Hedges, Tony Rigatti—got disability benefits. It wasn't because they'd been off base without authorization or looted artifacts. It was solely because they'd been injured by a substance the government doesn't want to acknowledge."

"Mustard agent."

"Did anyone threaten you, Mia?" Darcangelo asked.

Mia shook her head. "I didn't see Powell or Andy or any of the others again until I got back from that deployment, but they hated my guts. They all blame me for the fact that they didn't get disability benefits, though I had nothing to do with that. The last time I saw Andy, he spent the entire half hour I was there shouting at me, calling me names."

For a moment, there was silence.

Joaquin spoke first. "Thanks for trusting us, Mia. I know it must have been hard to do when everyone you ought to have been able to trust has disappointed you. But we're not like those guys. We're *not* going to let you down."

When she looked into his eyes again, he saw it—doubt and, beneath that, a fragile hope that this time would be different.

Darcangelo thanked her, too. "It's going to make a big difference to this investigation. Now we have some idea where to start looking for the killer."

Hunter nodded. "It doesn't take years of work in law enforcement to see what might motivate one of these guys to hurt you—or implicate you."

*Sí, claro.* Absolutely.

But Joaquin had questions. "Why would one of them strike out at the others? Why kill the medic? What could anyone have against him?"

"I don't know. It makes no sense. I just have a gut feeling that what happened at Tell al-Sharruken is behind this somehow."

"Can you give us a list of the soldiers who were part of the looting?" Darcangelo asked.

"Yes. There's something else you should know. I've got a loaded pistol in my handbag, and I don't have a concealed carry permit."

Joaquin jumped to her defense, not sure how Darcangelo and Hunter would react to this. "A fine is better than ending up dead."

Darcangelo looked over at Hunter. "We'll deal with that later."

Hunter nodded. "We can probably get the sheriff to issue an emergency concealed carry permit—once you're no longer a person of interest in that first case."

Mia looked relieved at this. "Thank you."

"I'm afraid we've got to ask one more thing of you, Mia." Darcangelo was using that soothing voice again. "We need you to tell Detective Wu everything you told us. He's the detective assigned to these cases. He needs to hear this from you."

MIA INSISTED that Wu come to Joaquin's place. She didn't trust the detective the way she did Julian and Marc. It took him a half hour to get there. In the meantime, Joaquin made her a cup of Mexican hot chocolate.

"What? None for me?" Julian looked hurt.

The two of them started bickering—in Spanish.

Marc leaned down and spoke for Mia's ears alone. "Darcangelo spent a lot of time as an undercover operative in Mexico."

"Ah." That explained it.

Joaquin returned with the mug of hot chocolate, set it on

the table, then took a throw out of a nearby chest and wrapped it around Mia's shoulders.

How had he known she was cold?

Wu arrived a few minutes later, and Mia went through the entire story again. It was easier this time, perhaps because she'd done it once. Or maybe having Joaquin sitting beside her made her feel safer.

Whatever the case, it was clear that Wu respected Julian and Marc. He took notes, interrupting her from time to time to ask questions. But never once did he hint that he thought she was lying as he'd done when he'd questioned her at the station.

"Why didn't you tell me this before?" he asked.

Seriously?

"Until last night when I'd heard that Jason had been killed, it didn't dawn on me that there could be a connection. I don't take the divulging of classified information lightly, and, frankly, sir, you haven't given me reason to trust you."

*That* felt good.

Wu nodded as if that made sense to him. "Just doing my job. You'll be happy to know that a K9 search of the grounds at the Botanic Gardens found no human remains. The security footage proves that you didn't go near the mulch yard at any time from the day of Mr. Meyer's disappearance through the time when the evidence was found in the wood chipper."

Relief washed over Mia. *Finally,* they were getting somewhere.

Wu went on. "Also, the only prints on the driver's license are Meyer's."

"So I'm no longer a suspect?"

"No."

Another surge of relief.

She found herself smiling. "I can go back to work."

Wu stood. "I'm going to have to talk to Irving to see how he wants us to handle this from here. Are you going to be staying here now?"

Startled by this question, Mia looked from Wu to Joaquin. "Uh... I..."

Joaquin answered for her. "She's welcome to stay here in my spare room until she feels safe at her own place."

"We need to get you that emergency concealed carry permit," Hunter said. "Call the sheriff's department tomorrow and pick up the application. Darcangelo and I will help you get whatever you need from the DPD."

"Thank you." Mia stood, reached out, shook Julian's and Marc's hands. "I appreciate all you did tonight. I know it's late."

"Happy to help."

"It's part of the job."

They turned to go, walking with Wu toward the door.

Wu stopped, turned to face her once more. "You trusted me tonight, so I'm going to trust you. If you see the man in the black hoodie again, call 911. Don't try to talk to him. Don't open the door for him. Don't follow him. That fits the general description of a man an eyewitness saw fleeing the scene of Jason Garcia's murder—and a man who showed up on the surveillance videos from the Botanic Gardens."

Mia stared after him, chills skittering down her spine as the men walked out the door and Joaquin locked it behind them. Questions sprang to her mind. How long had Wu known there was another suspect? Why had no one warned her earlier? Was the eyewitness the reason they'd been released last night?

Joaquin crossed the length of his apartment. "You were

amazing tonight, Mia. You're a true hero. I know that couldn't have been easy. How are you feeling?"

"Relieved in a way. Drained."

"I bet."

"Did you know that they had an eyewitness and another suspect?" She could see the answer on his face.

"I knew about the eyewitness, not the security footage."

"Why didn't you tell me?"

"They made me promise not to say a word. I'm sorry."

She couldn't fault him for keeping a promise. "That's why you came so quickly to get me, isn't it?"

He walked up to her, rested his hands on her shoulders. "I care about what happens to you, Mia."

His words hung in the air as Mia wondered what he meant by that.

"It's late. You must be exhausted. We should get to bed."

Mia took her handbag with her firearm to her room and changed into her nightgown and bathrobe. Then she went into the bathroom to brush her teeth and wash her face. When she had finished, she opened the door and stepped into the hallway to see Joaquin standing shirtless in the kitchen in a pair of dark blue pajama bottoms that hung perilously low on his hips. He was checking his pistol.

*Oh, my ...*

God, he was gorgeous.

His body was all lean muscle from the slabs of his pecs with their dark curls and flat nipples to his biceps, abs, and obliques. A dark trail of curls disappeared behind his waistband, drawing her gaze to a place where it had no business being.

He was saying something. "If anything happens, I don't want the two of us getting confused and shooting each other."

Okay, that was important.

She jerked her gaze back to his face, swallowed. "Right. I'll grab my weapon and run into your room."

"Perfect." He walked over to her. "Let me know if you need anything, okay?"

Being close to him like this was overwhelming. Mia could feel the heat radiating off his body, smell his skin. It was intoxicating.

She stood on her toes, pressed a kiss to his cheek. "Thanks, Joaquin, for everything. Goodnight."

"Goodnight." He stood there and watched her as she walked into his spare room and closed the door behind her.

JOAQUIN LAY in bed looking up at his ceiling in the dark, unable to sleep, what Mia had told them running through his mind.

*Ice Queen, Iron Maiden, bitch.*

Powell, that *cabrón*, hadn't gotten what he'd wanted from Mia. Rather than facing the fact that she wasn't interested in him, he'd pulled one of the oldest tricks in the book and made it seem like something was wrong with her. Yes, she was reserved, but she had passion. Joaquin had seen the glint of anger in her eyes when she'd talked about how Powell had treated her. He'd seen compassion, too, for the soldiers who'd been hurt.

Mustard gas? *¡Carajo!*

Powell's reprisals against her ought to have gotten him thrown out of the Army long before he'd had the chance to fuck up anyone else's life. Coffee cans of shit? Making her ask for tampons? Camel spiders?

Hell, Joaquin didn't even want to know what those were.

Whoever the killer was, he'd gotten close to Mia tonight. She had given Wu a list of the men who'd been a part of the looting, even those who didn't live in Colorado. Wu would be checking into them, but it would take time.

In the meantime, they needed to help Mia get that concealed carry permit and keep her safe. Whoever this guy was, he was former military, just like she was. Although Joaquin knew that Mia was tough—she'd had to be tough to make it through that living hell of a deployment—all it took was one bullet.

*Mierda.*

Joaquin closed his eyes, willed himself to relax, images running through his mind like a slideshow. Mia standing near the barricade tape the night he'd met her, her face lined with worry. Mia smiling as she danced with him. Mia in shock over the medic's murder. Mia looking at him through pleading eyes, trying to decide whether to trust him. Mia standing in a white nightgown and robe, her red hair hanging loosely around her shoulders, her gaze fixed on his chest.

Hell, yes, he'd caught that. Had that been desire in her eyes?

*And what are you going to do about it if it was?*

*Nada.* Nothing. Not yet. The last thing Joaquin wanted to be was the next man in Mia's life to let her down by putting his dick first.

But, oh, if she ever told him she wanted him...

He touched a hand to his cheek where she'd kissed him, his skin burning still.

If that day came and the two of them crossed the line into sex, he was pretty certain they would light his bed on fire.

JOAQUIN MADE huevos rancheros for breakfast while Mia showered. They lingered over their coffee, talking about her job, about the concealed carry permit, and what to do to keep her safe.

"I'll be fine." She gave him a smile that put a hitch in his chest, her red hair hanging in damp ropes around her shoulders. "I'm touched that you worry about me."

"Of course, I do." He reached out, took her hand, ran his thumb over her knuckles, her skin soft. "You're a special woman, Mia."

Color came into her cheeks, and she shifted her gaze to the window—but she didn't pull her hand away. "If it makes you feel better, we've got armed guards at the Gardens, and there are people and security cameras everywhere."

He let her hand go, instantly missing the contact. "Can you ask one of them to walk you to your car?"

She nodded. "That's a good idea. I plan to submit my application for the emergency concealed carry permit before I go in today."

That's when Joaquin saw the clock. "*Mierda*."

He was due at the paper in the I-Team meeting in ten minutes. "I've got to run, but there's a spare key in the drawer beneath the fruit bowl that you can have. You've got my number. Call if you need anything. Sorry to run out on you."

"Go. I'll be fine."

He stepped into a pair of boots, grabbed his camera bag. "See you later."

She gave a little wave. "Hasta la vista."

*That* was cute.

He grinned. "Now you're speaking my language."

He drove down alleys, through parking lots, and on the streets, making it to the paper with one minute to spare. He worked off his breakfast with a sprint up three flights of stairs to the newsroom, where he found the I-Team staff already heading toward the conference room. He set his camera bag down on his desk, grabbed a notepad and pen, and fell in with them.

"Glad you could make it," Matt said in a low voice. "What happened last night?"

Joaquin shook his head.

"Oookay." Matt let it go.

Joaquin took a seat at the conference table next to Anna Hughes, who usually worked in news for the city section. She had wanted a seat on the I-Team for a long time and had dressed for the occasion in a dark blue pantsuit with her dark hair pulled back in a tidy bun. "Hey, Anna. Good to see you here. Did you get drafted?"

She gave him an unconvincing smile that told him she was nervous. "Tom asked me to fill in for Sophie until Kat gets back from maternity leave."

"Hey, Anna." Cate waved to her from across the table, her gaze fixing on Joaquin. "Seen Mia lately?"

Joaquin didn't like the way she'd said that, something in her voice and the way she looked at him putting him on alert.

Tom walked in, pencil behind each ear, stack of newspapers in his hands. He glanced around the table. "Hughes is joining us for a few weeks until James gets back from maternity leave. I think you all know her, so we can skip the meet-and-greet."

"Thanks for having me here," Anna said.

"What do you have for us, Hughes?"

Tom was putting her in the hot seat on her first day?

Anna sat up a little straighter. "A manager at one of Brighton's Section Eight housing units invited police to practice K9 property searches and insisted that all the residents allow the police to enter their homes despite the fact that they didn't have search warrants. I have a half-dozen residents on the record saying their apartments were searched against their will and an admission from the Brighton PD that they didn't have warrants. They say they thought it was all just an exercise and voluntary."

"*Right*. Voluntary." Tom clearly approved of this scoop. "Did they find drugs, make any arrests?"

"No. No illegal drugs, no arrests."

"What does the city government have to say about it?"

"The manager of the units told me that people who have nothing to hide shouldn't object to their property being searched."

"Whoa." Alex gaped at Anna. "Okay now. That's bullshit."

Syd looked up from her control sheet. "How much room do you need?"

"I can do it in ten to twelve inches. I would love it if we could get a photo of one of these residents, maybe some shots of how the police left their apartments."

Tom looked to Joaquin. "Ramirez?"

"I'll head out to Brighton after the meeting, get a shot for the front page and something for the jump."

Tom's gaze shifted to Cate. "Warner, you look like you have something to say."

"Good job," Joaquin whispered to Anna, who looked relieved.

"I've been working on my sources inside the Denver PD, and it's paying off. I got a call this morning from a source who told me that something big is happening on the Meyer disappearance and Garcia murder, which the police believe to be connected." Cate's gaze shifted to Joaquin. "The source told me that Irving spent the morning on the phone with the Pentagon, asking for info about Mia Starr and the two men. According to Detective Wu, she's not a suspect in either case at this point. But my source says something big is about to break."

*¡Carajo! Fuck.*

Joaquin held her gaze, kept his expression neutral. If the police department had a leak and the paper published an account of what had happened at Tell al-Sharruken, Mia might think Joaquin had sold her out. Worse, she might end up in legal trouble, maybe even go to prison.

At the same time, investigative journalists depended on sources like this one. If Joaquin alerted Darcangelo and Hunter, he'd be putting Mia ahead of his job—and his obligation to the paper.

Tom frowned. "Can your source deliver proof of this or give us some idea of what's happening? 'Something big coming' doesn't work as a headline."

"Yes." Cate looked triumphant. "She said she can give me documents, so I'm meeting with her later over her lunch hour."

*Hell.*

## 10

M ia left Joaquin's place and took the light rail to the
sheriff's department on Colfax, where she filled out
the paperwork for her emergency concealed carry permit
and paid the fee. Someone at the police department—either
Julian or Marc—had already faxed over a statement docu-
menting her situation. In less than an hour, the SIG in her
handbag was legal.

She took the light rail to the stop closest to her house,
then walked home, staying acutely aware of her surround-
ings. Most people were at work, and kids were in school,
leaving the streets quiet. She found her Mazda untouched
and her condo just as she'd left it, no sign of any attempts to
break in.

She sorted through her mail, then took a quick shower
and dressed for work. It dawned on her as she was packing a
lunch that she might want to check with Kevin first to make
sure someone with the Denver police department had told
him she'd been cleared. She had her answer when Sharon
refused to put her through.

"What's this about, Mia?" the woman said in an annoyed voice.

"I've been cleared and want to get back to work as soon as possible."

"We haven't heard anything about that."

Disappointment and frustration cut through Mia. Did Sharon think she was lying?

"Tell Kevin to expect a call from the Denver police."

She hung up and called Wu's number. Her call went to voicemail. "Can you please contact the Botanic Gardens and let them know I'm no longer a suspect? I want to go back to work, and no one has gotten in touch with them yet."

She was looking at seed catalogues—and daydreaming about a certain sexy photojournalist—when Kevin called her back.

"I'm so happy to hear the good news. When would you like to start again?"

"Now would be perfect. I miss my work."

"Okay. I'll brief security and see you in my office in an hour. And for the record, Mia, I'm so relieved. You're a valuable member of our staff. We are concerned about your safety, though. Detective Wu explained that you might be one of this killer's targets. We can talk about that when you get here."

"Okay. Great. See you in an hour."

So much for having her life back. It wasn't Kevin's fault or Wu's or anyone's apart from the bastard in the black hoodie.

She drove to work, parked in the staff lot, and entered through the front gate.

"Good to see you back, Mia!" said Tori, who sold tickets at the main entrance.

No one had seemed to care about her when security had

escorted her off the property. If Mia wanted to continue working here—she loved her job—she would just have to get over that. Besides, hadn't she faced much worse?

Mia pushed a smile onto her face. "Good to see you, too."

She stepped through the gate, some of the tension she'd carried these past days leaving her. She had missed this place. She knew every square foot, every garden bed, every tree, every flowering plant. She spent the next ten minutes walking the paths, taking it all in. Dormant rose and lilac bushes that would explode into blooms in early June. Patches of bare soil that hid tulip and daffodil bulbs. Dwarf conifers in the Japanese garden that brought green to the winter landscape. *Bouteloua gracilis*, her favorite grass, jutting out of the snow in tufts, its feathery blooms now dried and full of tiny seeds.

She made her way toward the main building, hoping the horticulture team had finished sorting through the pile of internship applications. Then again, she'd only been away for a day and a half.

*Wishful thinking.*

"Mia!" Sharon motioned her toward the conference room. "Kevin's waiting for you. It's good to have you back."

"Thanks." Mia found Kevin sitting with Michael, the head of security and one of the two guards who had escorted her off the property.

The men stood, shook her hand, welcoming her back.

"Sorry about the other day," Michael said.

"Michael has just been telling me that he's concerned about our ability to protect you while you're here."

Were they going to send her home again?

She started to speak, but Michael cut her off.

"I've talked with the Denver PD. I've also given an image

of the suspect from our security footage to the front-gate staff. We can escort you to and from your vehicle and make you a part of our rounds, but we can't assign someone to accompany you all day. We just don't have the numbers. We think it's best if you stay indoors, preferably in the non-public areas of the facility, like the greenhouses or the offices."

Mia let out a relieved breath. "For a moment, I thought you were going to send me home again."

Kevin chuckled. "There's always work in the green-houses. And you can pick up where you left off with these."

He rested his hand on top of a stack of papers.

Internship applications.

Mia couldn't help but laugh. "Right."

JOAQUIN STOOD next to the gas pump, waiting for his tank to fill and watching while Anna disappeared inside to use the restroom. When the door closed behind her, he stepped away from the pump and called Darcangelo.

One ring, two...

*Cabrón, answer!*

"Hey, Ramirez, s'up?"

Joaquin knew what he was doing could land him in a load of shit, even get him fired, but he'd made a promise to Mia. "You've got a serious problem."

"I'm listening."

"This has to stay off the record. I'm risking my career by calling you."

"Let me close my office door." A moment of silence. "Okay, go ahead."

"You've got a leak. Catherine Warner told the staff at the

I-Team meeting this morning that she has a source in Irving's office who told her what's going on with the case. The source told Cate that Irving had spent the early morning on the phone with the Pentagon and that something big was about to break. Cate is supposed to meet this person at lunch to get files or some shit."

"Son of a bitch."

"Tell me about it, man. I would have called you earlier, but I wasn't alone."

Anna didn't know her way around like Joaquin did and had asked to carpool to Brighton with him.

"You have any idea who it might be?"

"It has to be someone physically close to Irving, someone he trusts or someone who can hear what he says over the phone or who sees what's on his desk. Cate is new and inexperienced. She used the pronoun 'she,' so it might be a woman."

Experienced reporters didn't give away the gender of confidential sources.

"I appreciate the tip. I'm going to run this by Old Man Irving right now."

"You can't be overheard. I could lose my job."

"I'll whisper directly into his hairy ear. Does that work?"

It might keep Joaquin's ass out of the fire, but it didn't assuage his guilt. He had betrayed a colleague. He had betrayed the paper. "Thanks. I appreciate it."

"No, thank *you*. We all made Mia a promise. Besides, we can't function as a police department if our staff is leaking shit to the papers."

Joaquin ended the call, walked back to his truck, and started washing windows.

He'd done the right thing. Mia had only talked to the

cops because she trusted him. If a leak to *his* paper landed her in prison, he would never forgive himself.

Anna walked outside again, a smile on her face. "There is nothing that improves a person's disposition quite like an empty bladder and a full cup of coffee."

"I hear that."

They talked about Anna's story on the way back to Denver and the paper, Joaquin listening, offering advice when she asked.

"Hey, try not to worry. You've got this." Joaquin meant it. Anna had good news instincts and lots of solid reporting experience.

By the time they arrived, she had worked out her lede and her nut graph.

"Thanks, Joaquin."

"*De nada.*"

Cate wasn't there when they arrived. It was just after noon, so she had probably left to meet with her source.

Had Darcangelo and Irving found the leak in time?

*Ah, shit.*

Joaquin tried to focus on editing photos and writing cutlines, his mind bouncing back and forth between wondering whether he'd reached Darcangelo in time and thinking about Mia. Had she gotten her concealed carry permit? Had she gone back to work? Would she sleep at his place or stay at her own home tonight?

He was in the middle of going over his images with Syd when Cate stepped out of the elevator and walked to her desk.

The expression on her face told him everything he needed to know.

"My source didn't show." She dropped her handbag on her desk. "I've called, but she isn't answering her phone."

Joaquin went on talking with Syd as if he hadn't heard this, while Alex and Matt coached Cate on ways to handle that situation.

"Maybe something held her up," Matt said. "Maybe she got cold feet. That happens. Try calling later."

"You might have to do some hand-holding, reassure her you won't give her identity away," Alex suggested.

Joaquin walked back to his desk, gaze on his notepad.

"How did it go in Brighton?" Matt asked him.

"I got some good shots." Joaquin gestured toward Anna. "She did a great interview with a woman whose apartment was basically trashed. It's her first day on the I-Team, and she's on the front page."

"Way to go, Hughes," Alex said.

Joaquin grabbed his camera bag. "I'm going to get some lunch and then head to LoDo to shoot an entertainment feature."

"Grungy guys in T-shirts and jeans in front of a brick wall?" Matt joked.

"God, I hope not." That described every band photo ever. "See you later."

As he left the newsroom, Joaquin noticed Cate watching him.

"I'm taking her out the north gate," Michael said into his hand mic.

The sun had just set, streetlights casting their glow over pavement and asphalt. Mia stayed alert, watching for movement in the shadows.

The whole thing felt surreal—hurrying to her car flanked by an armed security guard, her hand inside her handbag, ready to draw her SIG—but the only people they encountered were other staff members.

Mia clicked her fob, unlocking her car door. "Thanks."

"My pleasure." Michael opened the door for her. "This asshole attacked his two victims in their homes. Be careful."

The same thought had occurred to Mia. "I will. Thanks."

She headed home through rush-hour traffic, thinking through her condo from a security perspective. It had lots of windows, a sliding glass door that led to her deck, and a wide-open floor plan. The tub was plastic, so it wouldn't offer protection from bullets.

Of course, she had no idea what kind of firearm the attacker was using. A .45-caliber round could penetrate a door or wall. She'd seen AK rounds go through concrete.

God, how Mia hated this! She hated feeling afraid to go home. No one had the right to put this kind of fear in another person.

Well then, damn it, she wouldn't be afraid. Jason and Andy had most likely been taken by surprise. She wouldn't let that happen. She would be ready.

*Big words.*

She drove home, the dark windows of her condo somehow forbidding. She hadn't turned her front light on, so the porch was dark—a great place for someone to hide.

Weapon drawn, she headed up her front steps, her pulse thrumming. She cleared the porch, unlocked the door, and stepped inside, locking out the night. She let out a relieved breath, saw a shadow on the wall, and jumped.

It was just her ficus tree.

*Damn it!*

It wouldn't hurt anything if she stayed at Joaquin's place one more night, would it? The police would have another 24 hours to catch the bad guy, and she could rest a little easier.

She hurried to her bedroom and threw together an overnight bag, an idea half-formed in her mind about making dinner for Joaquin to thank him for all he'd done. She drew out her cell phone.

WHAT TIME WILL YOU BE HOME?

AM STUCK ON I-25 COMING BACK FROM AURORA.

That gave her some time. She texted back.

SEE YOU AT YOUR PLACE. I'M MAKING DINNER.

She walked out to her car, senses trained on the darkness, carrying her overnight bag in one hand and her SIG in the other. This time she left her porch light on. She drove to the grocery store, grabbed one of the small carts, and made a mental list of the things she needed to make her Chicken Breasts Diane. Chicken breasts. Lemons. Parsley. Scallions. Butter. Chicken broth. A salad to go with it, maybe some pasta.

She wasn't doing this just because she was afraid to be home alone. That's what she told herself, anyway. No, she was doing this because Joaquin had been so kind to her—okay, and because he was incredibly sexy and smart and talented and danced like a sex god and had said that he cared about her.

*Don't get your hopes up.*

He could have meant anything by that. For all Mia knew, his interest in her didn't go beyond casual friendship.

*Way to talk yourself into feeling disappointed.*

She went through the self-checkout lane and carried her bags to her car, her gaze moving over the parking lot.

There were lots of people, but no one wearing a hoodie. Once her car door was shut and locked, she let out a sigh of relief and headed northwest to RiNo and Joaquin's place.

She parked in one of the guest spots, grabbed her groceries and overnight bag, and let herself through the security door with his key. *This* was another reason Joaquin's apartment was safer. Cameras. A security door.

A few minutes later, she stood in his kitchen, feeling a lot safer—and just a little excited. She was going to spend an evening with Joaquin that wouldn't involve homicides or police interrogations.

JOAQUIN SMELLED something delicious the moment he stepped out of the elevator. Usually, that meant the couple down the hallway had just been to the Farmers Market. But tonight, someone was making *him* dinner. He couldn't remember the last time anyone besides his mother had done that.

He unlocked his door, his mouth watering at the mingled scents.

"Hey." Mia stood at the stove, wearing his barbeque apron over jeans and a white blouse.

"That smells so good." He walked over to her, resisting the urge to come up behind her and rest his hands on her hips.

She was sautéing something—chicken breasts and scallions. "Chicken Breasts Diane and pasta. I made a salad, too. It should all be done in about five minutes—if the pasta cooperates. I brought a bottle of white wine."

"That sounds perfect." Joaquin got busy setting the

table, complete with wine glasses and candles. "How did it go today? Did you get the permit?"

"Yes. Your friends had already faxed over the documentation, so it went quickly."

"I'm glad to hear it." Darcangelo and Hunter had never once let Joaquin down.

"My boss let me return to work, too." She told him how security was keeping her inside in non-public areas. "I spent the day sorting through internship applications and repotting orchids for our big orchid sale."

"I'm glad your security guys are on top of it."

While she got dinner on the table, Joaquin started some music—his contemporary piano playlist with Clara Ponty—poured the wine, and lit the candles. By the time they sat down together, he was as nervous as if this were their first date.

"Thanks for this." He looked into her eyes, saw that she was nervous, too.

"Thank you—for everything." She raised her glass, so he raised his.

They clinked, sipped.

"How was your day?" she asked—*just* as he took his first bite.

"Mmm." He moaned, chewed, swallowed. "That's good."

She smiled, picked up her fork. "It's the only fancy thing I know how to make."

"You make it well." Then he remembered her question. "Today was okay. I sat through the I-Team meeting, shot a few news photos, spent a lot of time in traffic. I took advantage of the traffic jam to check in with my parents and grandmother. My *abuelita* gets grouchy if I don't call her at least once a week."

He decided to wait until later to tell her what had

happened with Cate and the leak at the DPD. It seemed wrong to ruin her cheerful mood and the dinner she'd worked hard to make for the two of them. The situation was under control, so it wasn't urgent anyway. Darcangelo had called him while he'd been stuck in traffic to thank him. Irving had caught his administrative assistant red-handed making copies of the files and had fired her on the spot, threatening her with charges, too.

Yes, Mia needed to know, but the news could wait.

"Is that a typical day for you?"

"Yeah—except for the days when I pry into people's private tragedies or get up in their grill with my lens." He couldn't help it.

She smiled sheepishly. "I take that back."

"Don't worry about it." He didn't want to talk about himself or his job, not when there were so many things he wanted to know about Mia. "Why did you join the Army?"

"I wanted to go to college. It was really that simple."

Joaquin listened while Mia told him how she'd had automatic admission to the state schools here in Colorado because of her high GPA, but couldn't afford tuition. The candlelight played over her face as she spoke, made her features seem even more delicate, her blue eyes darker. It hit him that this was the most relaxed he'd ever seen her.

"I got an ROTC scholarship, and, four years later, I had a degree in biology and was a second lieutenant."

"Your parents must have been very proud."

She gave a little laugh. "They didn't understand any of it —why I'd wanted to go to college, why I'd gone into ROTC. Their plan for me was to marry some guy from their church, stay home, and have kids. There's nothing wrong with that if that's what a woman wants to do, but it wasn't what *I* wanted. I love learning. I wanted an education, a career. My dad still says that I'm too smart for my own good. He says men don't like smart women."

"That might be true for stupid men, but it's not true for the rest of us. Your dad sounds seriously retrograde on gender stuff."

"Oh, you have no idea. When I told him I was learning to service our fleet of vehicles, he said, 'Don't they have any men where you're posted?'"

"You know how to service vehicles?" Joaquin was impressed.

Mia nodded. "Officers who don't get their hands dirty or who act helpless lose the respect of their soldiers, so if there's anything you don't know how to operate or repair, you'd better learn right away."

That made sense to Joaquin. "But your dad stood behind you, right? When all that shit was going down with your CO, he stood behind you."

Her gaze dropped to the table. "When I was going through the sexual harassment stuff with Powell, my parents told me that women serving in male-dominated fields should expect to be harassed."

*¡Ay, carajo!*

*This* pissed Joaquin off. "That's bullshit. You know that, right?"

Something in her half-hearted nod told Joaquin that her mind knew it, but her heart wasn't so sure. He reached out, took her hand, her fingers so small compared to his. "You didn't deserve what Powell did to you, Mia. No woman deserves that."

## 11

Mia felt more relaxed than she had since all of this began. The wine had something to do with that, but so did the man who sat beside her on the sofa, his body turned toward hers, his dark eyes watching her. She'd never met a man like Joaquin, a man who wanted to know her thoughts and who listened when she spoke rather than using her answers as a springboard to talk about himself.

She wanted to kiss him. She wanted to run her hands over those muscles she'd seen this morning. She wanted him to want *her*.

Sadly, she'd never had that kind of luck with men.

"You know *all* their scientific names?" he asked.

"Most of them. Sometimes I forget something or get mixed up, but if you want to talk about plants as a horticulturalist, you have to use scientific names. Did you know that there are more than two hundred common names for the *Nymphaea alba*, the European white lily?"

"Seriously? I had no idea plant names were so complicated."

"They vary region to region, country to country. If I use

one of those common names, people in another part of the country wouldn't know what I was talking about."

"That makes sense." Those lips of his curved in a slow smile.

"What?"

"You're amazing. You're smart, brave, beautiful..."

Heat rushed into her face. "Oh, stop."

His brows drew together. "You know you're beautiful, right?"

"I'm pretty average. My mom says I have my dad's square jaw. Elena is feminine and gorgeous. I'm not."

Joaquin said nothing for a moment then pointed to the walls around them. "Which of those photographs is beautiful?"

She glanced around the room. "I think they're all beautiful."

"How can they all be beautiful? They're all different. If the columbines are pretty, how can the eagle be pretty? If the mountains are beautiful, how can the ocean be beautiful, too?"

She saw where he was going with this. "Okay. All right. I get what you're saying, but objectively speaking, some women are a lot more beautiful than others."

Joaquin shook his head. "Yes, Elena is pretty. She's curvy and sexy and has that sweet little face. But you're beautiful, too."

She shook her head. "Pretty maybe, but..."

"Your features are delicate and every bit as feminine as anything Elena has going on. These cheekbones." He reached over, ran his thumb over her cheek, leaving a trail of fire where he'd touched her. "That adorable nose. Those big blue eyes. Those full lips.

Mia didn't know what to say, this kind of intimate

perusal unlike anything she'd experienced before, in part because she didn't feel threatened by him.

He went on. "If I had to describe the two of you in plant terms—"

"Plants?" She laughed.

"Plants are your special language, right? If I had to describe the two of you as plants, I'd say Elena is a rose, but you're like that columbine on my wall. Delicate. Graceful. Beautiful."

Mia couldn't look at the photo. She could only stare at Joaquin.

Did he mean what he was saying?

He leaned in until his face was inches from hers. "I don't want to rush you, Mia. I don't want to push you into doing something you don't want to do. But right now, all I want to do is kiss you."

Mia's pulse spiked. "*Yes.*"

Before she could blink, he'd drawn her into his arms, one hand sliding into her hair to angle her head. He looked into her eyes, suddenly serious. "*Mia.*"

Some part of Mia couldn't believe this was really happening.

Then he ducked down, brushed his lips over hers, once, twice, three times. It was the softest caress, like the touch of petals, but the heat of it burned through her, made her heart pound. Then his mouth closed over hers.

Mia forgot to breathe, stunned by the intensity of it. This is how she'd always wanted to be kissed, how she'd dreamed of being kissed. She pressed herself against him, one strong arm drawing her closer, his body hard against hers.

Where had he learned to kiss like this?

He chuckled. "You gotta breathe, *hermosa*, or you're going to pass out."

She exhaled, drew in a deep breath. "I might pass out anyway."

"Did you like that?"

Was he seriously asking her that question?

"God, yes. Kiss me again."

Once more he started slowly, feather-light kisses that made her lips tingle. He drew her lower lip into his mouth, kissed the indentation above her upper lip, traced the outline of her mouth with his tongue. Then, with a moan, he took her mouth with his once more, crushing her against the hardness of his chest.

She yielded to him, parting her lips for him as his tongue sought hers. She'd never been kissed like this, and at first all she could do was savor it. But at that first, velvet touch—his tongue to hers—something ignited inside her. She began to kiss him back, challenging him for control, her fingers curling in his hair. He took up the challenge, the heat of his response making her only too glad to yield once more. She arched against him, her head falling back to offer him her throat.

He took what she offered, pressing his lips against her pulse, nipping the sensitive skin beneath her ear with his teeth, teasing her with flicks of his tongue. She felt herself sliding down the cushions, his weight coming with her, until he lay on top of her, his lips tracing fire over her skin, his erection pressing against her hip.

His mouth found her clavicle and followed it until he was pressing kisses against the base of her throat. Then he raised his head up and pressed his forehead to hers, his heart thrumming against hers. His pupils were so dilated that his irises seemed almost black, the lust on his face mirroring what she felt.

"I don't want to stop."

"Yeah, me neither." He kissed her forehead. "I don't want to risk whatever this is between us by having sex too soon. When we cross that line, I want us both to be ready for it, to want it. I want it to mean something."

His answer left her speechless. No man had ever talked to her about sex like that before. Not that she'd had many partners, but still...

"I hope that settles that question," he said after a moment's silence.

"What question?" Mia couldn't remember any questions.

"Whether or not I truly think you're beautiful, because, Mia, I do."

"WHERE DID you learn to kiss like that?"

Joaquin sat up, drew Mia with him, his heart still pounding, his cock threatening to split his jeans. The last time a kiss had affected him like this was ... Yeah, he had nothing. "That was as much you as it was me."

She gave a little shake of her head.

"I just paid attention to what you seemed to like." Was that so different from the men she'd been with before?

God, he hoped not.

"Have you been with a lot of women?" Her eyes went wide as if she hadn't meant to ask him that. "Sorry. It's one hundred percent *not* my business."

He brushed a strand of red hair from her cheek. "You can ask me anything you like. How would you define 'a lot'?"

"I don't know." She thought about this for a moment. "A dozen?"

"A *dozen*?" Joaquin laughed. "I probably come in at about

half that number, mostly from my college years. It took me a while to understand that sex isn't love. I've gotten more careful and pickier as time has gone on."

He wasn't looking only to get laid. He wanted a woman who truly cared about him, a woman who wanted to share his life. "How about you?"

"Two. I had a boyfriend my sophomore year in college and one the year I graduated. After that, everything was wrapped up in regulations, and I was moving from post to post. I just never met anyone who made me feel … "

"Safe?" he offered.

She nodded. "Yes—or attracted enough to take the risk."

Well, he liked that.

"You want to dance?" It had helped him work off sexual steam more times than he could count. "You can practice your salsa moves."

She laughed. "My salsa moves? You mean my stumbling and tripping and stepping on your feet—those moves?"

"You were not as bad as all *that*." He stood, drew her to her feet, then walked over to his sound system, taking advantage of having his back to her to adjust himself.

"But I *was* bad."

"No, *mi amor*. You were new to it." He searched his iPod for his list of current favorites—some traditional puertorriqueño salsa, a little Colombian and Cuban salsa, some Mexican boleros—then pressed play.

The sounds of guitar and congas filled the room, horns joining in as he turned to face Mia. She was smiling, but, yeah, he could see she was nervous, too.

"Relax. Do you remember the basic step?" He stood beside her, demonstrated. "One, two, three, rest. Five, six, seven, rest."

She picked it up more quickly this time, moving lightly on her stocking feet.

"See? *No problema*." He took her into his arms, led her back and forth across the floor, then tried a turn.

She lost the rhythm, and this time she did step on his foot. "Sorry!"

"Hey, you're not the first. Don't worry about it. Let's try that again. One, two, three, rest. Five, six, seven, rest. All we're going to do is go in a different direction. It's the same basic step." He tried another turn.

This time she followed without difficulty.

"You have a natural sense of rhythm." He led her through another turn and another, until they were moving around the floor.

She was laughing now. "This is so fun, but isn't your downstairs neighbor going to get irritated?"

Joaquin shook his head. "I've had a half dozen people dancing in here at once, and he has never complained. This is an old factory. There's concrete beneath this floor."

That song ended, and another began. Four songs into the playlist, she seemed to have the basic step down. "Now it's time for the fun stuff."

He ran her through a handful of beginner's steps—basic step in open hold and closed hold, inside turn, outside turn, cross body lead—and then moved on to an *enchufa*, a Cuban move. "We basically trade places, with you crossing under my arm while I turn. I'll show you."

They tried it a few times, each time going a little bit better, until Mia's feet slipped out from beneath her, her socks sliding on the wooden floor.

She shrieked. "Oh!"

Joaquin caught her, steadied her, the two of them pressed together, looking into each other's eyes, both breathless. The moment seemed to freeze, his world constricting until it held nothing but her. The light in her blue eyes. The flush in her cheeks. The feel of her against him.

Oh, he was *so* fucked.

Maybe the lyrics of the songs were getting to him, all that romantic stuff about love and sex. Maybe it was just the intimacy of dancing. Or maybe he'd been single for too damned long.

No, it wasn't any of that.

It was the kiss they'd shared—a kiss that had blown his mind.

It was Mia.

"Let's slow it down and try again." He found himself singing aloud to the next song, holding her a little closer.

"You have a nice voice. What does it mean?"

"Well..." *How are you going to get out of this one?* "I don't know if I can make it sound good translating it into English."

Now they were more or less slow dancing.

"Try."

He closed his eyes, held her, sang to her. "I've been watching you dance all night/I feel you watching me, feel the heat of your gaze on my skin until I burn/This isn't like anything I have known/I want you in my arms/I want to kiss you everywhere, to taste your sacred places..."

He stopped singing, stopped dancing, and simply stood there, looking down into those big, blue eyes, his pulse tripping. He lowered his mouth to hers, kissed her slowly, then drew back. "It's late. We should get some sleep."

Not that there was much chance of that. His entire world had just shifted, from the stars in the sky down to his DNA.

She nodded. "Thanks for tonight."

Then Joaquin remembered Cate and the leak at the

DPD. He didn't want Mia to lose a night's sleep worrying. He would tell her in the morning.

"You're welcome."

She went her way, and he went his.

But it was a long time before he fell asleep.

MIA TOSSED and turned all night, her body too aroused for sleep, erotic thoughts of Joaquin turning into erotic dreams that woke her. When her phone's alarm beeped at six, she could have sworn she hadn't slept at all, and yet she didn't feel tired. Instead, she felt revved, as if she'd already had a few cups of coffee.

*It's called hormones, Starr.*

She got up, made her bed, then hurried into the bathroom, her mind drifting back to last night as she showered and dried her hair. The entire evening had felt special, intimate. Dinner. Dancing. Their conversation. That kiss.

*I don't want to rush you, Mia. I don't want to push you into doing something you don't want to do. But right now, all I want to do is kiss you.*

Oh, my God, that kiss.

The way he'd said her name and looked into her eyes just before their lips had touched. The way he'd made her heart pound. The way he'd laughed when he'd realized she hadn't been breathing and had taken that big breath.

*You gotta breathe,* hermosa, *or you're going to pass out.*

If *that* was how the man kissed, she could only imagine what it would be like to have sex with him, to spend the night in his bed, to wake up next to him in the morning.

*I just paid attention to what you seemed to like.*

She'd never felt so connected to a man before. It wasn't

just that he'd been thoughtful. It was as if he'd truly seen her, seen who she was on the inside.

*You're amazing. You're smart, brave, beautiful...*

Somehow, he had even made her feel beautiful.

When her hair was dry, she put on a little makeup— mascara to turn her red eyelashes black and a little blush— and went back to her room to dress, slipping into a pair of jeans and a Botanic Gardens T-shirt. She found Joaquin in the kitchen wearing jeans and a dark blue dress shirt and working on breakfast.

She wondered for a split second whether things would be awkward between them now, but her fear vanished at the smile on his face when he saw her.

"Good morning, beautiful." He walked over to her and handed her a cup of coffee, kissing her on the lips. "Did you sleep well?"

"Not really."

"No?" He looked worried.

"My head was too full of you."

He grinned. "Ooh. I like that."

"How about you?"

"Nah. My mind couldn't quit thinking about a certain beautiful redhead."

Warmth rushed into Mia's cheeks. "I like that."

She helped him finish breakfast, and they sat down together to scrambled eggs, toast, and sliced grapefruit.

Mia had just sprinkled pepper and hot sauce on her eggs when she noticed the serious expression on Joaquin's face. "Is something wrong?"

"I meant to tell you this last night. The police department had a leak."

Mia listened in stunned silence as Joaquin told her how one of the reporters at his paper had gotten word from someone at the police department that big news was about to be revealed about Andy's and Jason's cases that involved Mia and the Pentagon.

"I called Darcangelo, and he warned Chief Irving, who caught the person making photocopies of the case file. He fired her and might even file charges. In the end, Cate got nothing, so you don't have to worry about any of it showing up in the paper. I think Cate suspects that I warned the police. If she were to find out ..."

Mia went from wondering why Joaquin hadn't told her all of this earlier to worrying about what would happen to him if his boss found out what he'd done. "Would you be in lots of trouble?"

"If Tom, my editor, knew that I had exposed Cate's secret source and cost her a big story, he would probably fire me on the spot—and he wouldn't be wrong. Reporters depend on sources like that for the big stories. I took something from Cate yesterday, something I can never give back."

Mia could hear the conflict he felt in his voice. "You went against the interests of your colleague and your paper for me. You put your job at risk for me."

"I made you a promise, Mia. If I lost my job, I'd be okay in the end. But if I lost your trust or put your future at risk—I couldn't live with that."

Mia's heart melted. "Thank you."

"I ought to have told you sooner. I'm sorry. I didn't want to ruin our dinner, and then... With everything last night, I just forgot."

She reached out, took his hand. "Please don't apologize. Is there any way Cate could find out from the source what happened? Are there emails or texts or phone records she could use to put this together?"

He took a sip of coffee. "Nah. No way. Darcangelo made

sure that the leak had no idea who'd turned her in. The fact that Irving caught her with the file was a stroke of good luck. Cate might suspect me, but it's nothing she could ever prove."

Mia let out a breath. "Well, that's a relief."

"Today could be an interesting day in the newsroom."

## 12

Joaquin stepped into the elevator, camera bag on his shoulder, his mind so fixed on Mia that he didn't notice Matt enter with him.

The doors closed.

"Oh, hey, Harker."

"What's that smile on your face about?" Matt leaned in, even though there was no one else there to hear. "Did you get lucky last night?"

Were Joaquin's emotions that transparent?

Joaquin opened his mouth to tell Matt that he'd had an amazing evening with Mia, when he realized he couldn't. "Nah, nothing like that."

Until the police caught the killer and Mia was no longer the potential focus of any newspaper investigation, he couldn't tell anyone that he had feelings for her, not after what he'd done yesterday. Besides, he wasn't sure how Mia would feel about him discussing their relationship, new and fragile as it was, with others.

"Oh, come on. I know you too well. What's up?"

"Can't a guy be happy?"

"At eight-thirty in the morning on a workday?" Matt shook his head. "No, absolutely not—unless he spent the night before getting laid."

"I did not get laid last night. I went dancing and had a good time."

"You and your salsa."

"I offered to teach you. As my mama says, 'A man who can dance is worth his weight in gold to women.'"

The elevator doors opened onto the newsroom, and the two of them made their way to the corner reserved for the I-Team.

Anna and Alex were already there. Tom was shouting at someone behind closed doors. Anna sat at Sophie's desk holding a copy of the paper, a dejected look on her face.

"Sorry, man," Alex was saying. "That sucks. You work hard on a story, and some nimrod of a news editor fucks it up."

"What's up?" Joaquin made his way to his desk.

"There's a typo in my headline." Anna held up the front page and read. "Crossing the line: Brighton cops search Section 8 housing without *warants*.' With one R."

So *that's* why Tom was shouting.

"So sorry, Anna." Joaquin felt for her. She wouldn't be able to enter that story or any of the follow-up pieces in any journalism contests or use it as a clip when she applied for other jobs. "You did great work. Nothing changes that."

Cate was the last to arrive. She said good morning to everyone—except Joaquin.

"Did you get in touch with the source that flaked on you yesterday?" Alex asked.

*Carajo.*

Why did he have to go there?

"I did." Cate put her handbag down on her desk. "Chief

Irving *just happened* to walk in on her while she was copying documents for me. He fired her on the spot and is consulting with the city attorney to decide whether he should file charges."

The sharp edge of guilt pressed in on Joaquin. Whatever that source was going through right now—loss of income, anxiety, possible legal troubles—was his doing.

"It sucks to be your source," Alex said. "You know what this means."

Joaquin wasn't sure he wanted to hear.

Cate answered. "It means no one at the cop shop will share information with me or any other newspaper—not for a while, anyway. My beat just got tougher."

"I'm really sorry, Cate." What Joaquin was sorry for, he could never tell her.

She shot him a cold glance. "Yeah."

Joaquin checked his voicemail and emails, saw that Syd had already sent him a couple of assignments. A photo of a blind man whose service dog had been stolen from him while he'd been walking down the street. A shot of two brothers in their nineties who had just finished climbing all fifty-three of Colorado's fourteeners—mountains with summits above 14,000 feet in elevation.

The next one hit Joaquin in the chest.

Syd wanted a photo of the widow and new baby of one of the security guards killed in the terrorist attack at the Palace Hotel last month. The man had died trying to save the lives of strangers, including everyone in this newsroom, leaving behind a wife who was about to have their first baby.

Sometimes life was so brutally unfair.

Joaquin made a few calls to set up the shots Syd had requested, then walked with the others to the conference room for the morning's I-Team meeting.

Tom was the last to arrive. "Hughes, sorry about the headline. It was a damned good story. Warner, did you hear from that source at DPD?"

"She's been fired. Irving caught her copying files and canned her on the spot. He usually doesn't come into the copy room, so she thinks he might have been tipped off." Cate looked pointedly at Joaquin. "I can't help but wonder if someone from our newsroom contacted the police to warn them—maybe someone who sympathizes with Mia Starr, someone who, say, took her to dinner."

Joaquin met Cate's gaze straight on, wondering how he was going to get out of this. But he didn't have to say a word.

"You're way over the line, Cate," Matt said. "Ramirez has been a loyal member of this team since you were in high school."

"*Ramirez*? You must be high," Alex said. "It sucks to lose a source, but—"

"Ms. Warner, if you want to accuse a member of this team of sabotaging your investigation, you'd better damned well have proof before you open your mouth." Tom jabbed a pencil at Cate. "Do I make myself clear? You owe Ramirez an apology."

Cate's gaze fell. "Sorry, Joaquin."

Joaquin was touched by their faith in him, but he didn't deserve it. "It's okay. I know you're just upset."

God, he felt like a traitor—not just to Cate, but to every person in this room who'd just stood up for him.

~

MIA CARRIED her tools to the sink, filled a small bucket with bleach and hot water, and dropped the tools in to soak. Orchids were extremely sensitive to bacteria and other diseases, and she didn't want to risk spreading pathogens. She washed her hands, then got organized, opening bags of potting medium, gathering the orchids she'd be repotting, and refilling the mister. Then she retrieved the tools, rinsing each and drying them before she carried them to the table.

She found herself humming and dancing salsa steps as she worked, the last song she and Joaquin had danced to stuck in her head. She didn't mind it. The melody was lovely, the rhythm sensual, and the lyrics sexy as hell.

*This isn't like anything I have known/I want you in my arms/I want to kiss you everywhere, to taste your sacred places...*

She wasn't sure how she'd survived having Joaquin sing those words to her last night, his body pressed against hers. He was the most sensual man she'd ever known, passionate about his work, about music and dancing, about his friends and family. But that wasn't what amazed her most about him.

He'd stood by her. He'd put his own career at risk to protect her.

No man had done that for her before.

God, she hoped he didn't get into trouble. He'd said there was no way anyone could prove that he was behind exposing the leak, but Mia knew only too well that life rarely went to plan.

"Don't worry about it," he'd said before she'd left for work, taking her into his arms, kissing her soft and slow. Then he'd invited her to stay at his place until Wu had the bad guy in custody. "We can pick up where we left off with the dance lessons."

She hoped they'd pick up where they'd left off with kissing, too, because, oh, sweet heaven.

Mia realized she'd stopped working and now stood

there, staring off into space, a *Brassolaeliocattleya* Pink Diamond in one hand, the scissors in the other.

*Get it together, Starr.*

She had hundreds of plants to repot today, and she wasn't going to get the job done by daydreaming. She washed the plant's rhizomes, then cut them to create four viable plantings, each of which got its own pot. But soon, she was humming again.

Oh, how she wished she understood Spanish. She'd be able to understand the lyrics of all the songs. She'd be able to speak with Joaquin in his mother tongue. She'd be able to understand those little terms of endearment he'd used. Okay, *mi amor*—that was simple enough. But the other one...

Why couldn't she learn a little Spanish? She could learn a few words and phrases over lunch, and then she could surprise him.

With renewed focus, she set to work propagating orchids, then grabbed a sandwich in the cafeteria and sat down in her office. She booted up her computer and searched online for Spanish language websites.

The first offered nothing but profanity and slang in Mexican Spanish. Telling Joaquin to fuck his mother was really not what she'd had in mind.

The next page had a lot of basic phrases, the kind a person might want to know on vacation. But she didn't want to ask Joaquin where she could find the restroom or how far it was to the next gas station.

She clicked the next and found a mix of basic phrases, some of which were romantic. While she ate lunch, she memorized them, copying them to a Word document, repeating them aloud. "*Te quiero.* I like you. *Te deseo.* I want you."

The phrases kept getting hotter. "*Tócame*. Touch me. *Quiero arrancarte la ropa*. I want to rip your clothes off."

Oh, hell, yes, she did.

The next one was long and a mouthful, but no truer words had ever been spoken in any language. She worked her way through it. "*Creo que eres el hombre más sexy que he conocido*. I think you're the sexiest guy I've ever met."

"Why, thank you, Mia."

Mia shrieked, jumped to her feet and dropped what was left of her sandwich onto the floor. Heat rushed into her face. "Michael. I ... um ... I'm studying Spanish."

Michael chuckled. "I heard. My wife is from Ecuador. After I met her, I did exactly what you're doing."

"Oh. Well, it must have worked." Mia tried to sound casual as she bent down and picked up the remnant of her lunch.

"It did." Michael gave a little laugh. "Sorry to startle you. I went to check the greenhouse but didn't find you there. I wanted to make sure you were okay."

"Apart from feeling utterly embarrassed, I'm fine. Thanks."

"Don't worry about it. It will be our secret. Whoever he is, he's a lucky guy." Michael left her in peace.

She printed out the phrases she wanted to memorize, whispering them while she worked on orchids. She was still practicing the phrases when she arrived at Joaquin's place more than five hours later. She parked in the guest spot and walked toward the security door and elevators, mentally rehearsing.

*Te quiero, Joaquin. Creo que eres el hombre más sexy que ...*

What was the rest of it?

She unlocked the security door and pushed the button

for the elevator, which was up on the third floor. She pulled her cheat sheet out of her handbag.

Movement caught her gaze—a reflection in the elevator's polished steel doors. She glanced over her shoulder.

A man in a black hoodie.

On a surge of adrenaline, she dropped down to a crouch, her hand thrusting into her handbag after the SIG, but it was too late.

*BAM!*

The first shot shattered the glass security door, splintering it into fragments.

*BAM! BAM! BAM! BAM! BAM!*

Bullets whined past her head, hitting the steel behind her with a thud. Something burned across her hip and ribcage. She heard the elevator ding and rolled through the open doors, then sat up and fired back just before they closed.

*BAM! BAM! BAM!*

JOAQUIN LEFT Speer heading north toward his street. He couldn't wait to see Mia and leave the workday behind. Apart from the I-Team meeting, it hadn't been a bad day.

Police had found the stolen service dog, and Joaquin had been on hand with his camera to capture the owner's relief and happiness when he and his dog had been reunited. The two nonagenarians had challenged Joaquin to an arm-wrestling match and had come close to beating him, the laughter on their faces afterward caught on camera. Joaquin hoped he was as fit as those two when he hit ninety.

The shoot with the widow and her new baby had been

just as tough as he'd thought it would be. When she'd heard he was from the *Denver Independent* and had been at the Palace Hotel that terrible night, she'd burst into tears. Joaquin had stayed with her, listened to her talk about her husband, and thanked her as one of the people her husband had tried to protect. The photo of her holding her little daughter next to a photograph of her husband had put a lump in his throat.

He turned onto his street and flipped on the signal to turn into his parking garage—then slammed on the brakes as a man ran out of the garage right in front of him.

A man in a black hoodie, pistol in hand.

The bastard raised the weapon, fired on the run, shattering Joaquin's windshield. Joaquin reflexively turned his face to shield his eyes. By the time he looked again, the man was running down the street. Joaquin let him go, only one thought on his mind.

*Mia.*

Heart slamming, he gunned it into the garage, his gaze catching Mia's Mazda in the guest parking spot. Then he saw it—the security door to the elevators. It was shattered.

*Madre de Dios, Mia.*

He jerked his truck to a stop next to a wall of shattered glass, grabbed his phone and leaped out, dialing 911, knowing he was going to find Mia there, badly wounded, maybe dying, maybe already dead.

*Jesus, no.*

He rounded his vehicle to find... no one.

Relief left him almost legless. Somehow, he gave his address to the dispatcher, his gaze raking over the devastation. Shards of glass everywhere. Indentations from bullets in the steel elevator doors. Scattered shell casings from a 9 mm and a .45 caliber.

The bastard had cornered Mia here, but she had

fired back.

Had she been hit?

There was no blood spray on the walls. Then, there on the tile floor, he saw it.

*Blood.*

Fuck.

*Mia!*

He punched the button, realized the dispatcher was asking him questions. "There's been a shooting with injuries. We need an ambulance. The shooter is running south on Walnut in a black hoodie. He had pistol in hand. The injured party is inside the building. I'm trying to find her."

"We've got her on the line, sir."

*Thank God.*

"We've toned out SWAT and an ambulance."

Joaquin could hear the sirens now. "Tell her I'm on my way up. Thanks."

He ended the call. If they were talking to Mia, they didn't need him. He sent a text to Mia, trying to keep to the essentials as bystanders began to gather.

"What happened?"

"Was someone shot?"

"Don't touch anything," Joaquin told them. "This is a crime scene."

Saw shooter. He's gone. Are you badly hurt?

The elevator doors opened. Joaquin stepped inside, found a bloody fingerprint on the button for the fourth floor.

How had the son of a whore found her?

The seconds ticked by as he waited for her response. He

was looking at his phone when it came.

Not bad. Doors locked. I'm in the bathroom.

Joaquin paced the length of the elevator, bolting the moment the doors opened onto his floor and running to his apartment. He fished his keys out of his pocket, saw blood on his front door, unlocked it. "Mia, I'm here."

He didn't want her to shoot him.

Drops of blood on his floor led him to the bathroom door. "I'm right here. I'm coming in, Mia, okay?"

"I promise not to shoot you."

But the door was locked.

Unable to remember at the moment where he'd put the key, Joaquin took a step back and kicked it in.

"He's here," Mia said into her cell phone. She lay back in his tub, still wearing her parka, pistol sitting on the floor beside her. "I got blood on your floor."

"You think I give a damn about that? God, Mia, I was afraid I was going to find you dead." Joaquin knelt beside her, resisting the urge to hold her. "Let's get you out of this parka."

She winced as the coat came off, her pain cutting at him. "I think it's just a graze. I can't tell. My ears are ringing. It was so loud."

"I bet."

Her T-shirt was ripped just below her left breast and stained with blood.

"We need to take off your T-shirt, too. Do you trust me with that?"

"Are … you … kidding?" she ground out from beneath clenched teeth, trying to pull the shirt over her head.

"Let me do it."

With the shirt out of the way, he could see that her jeans were torn, too, near her hip. Most of the blood seemed to be coming from there.

She unzipped her fly, tried to wriggle out of them, speaking into her cell phone again. "He's helping me get out of my clothes."

Joaquin had forgotten about dispatch.

"You stay still. I've got this." Joaquin took off her shoes and socks, then tugged her jeans down and tossed them aside.

Two bullet wounds marred her pale skin—one just below her left breast and a much deeper one near her left hip bone. Both were still bleeding, blood staining the white lace of her panties and bra.

He grabbed two clean washcloths, put one in her hand, and guided her hand to the wound below her breast. "Hold it there." He pressed the other against the wound near her hip. "Can you hear those sirens? The cavalry is almost here."

"Yes, I'm still here," Mia said, talking to dispatch again. "He's still here, too. He's giving me first aid."

The sirens were right below them now.

Joaquin saw that she was shivering. "Are you cold?"

She shook her head. "Just … shaky."

"It could be shock." He reached with one hand, yanked a clean towel out of his cupboard, and did his best to cover her. "You should stay warm."

She smiled, looked up at him through those killer blue eyes. "I didn't think the first time you undressed me it would be like this."

Her words pierced his adrenaline, cutting the tension.

He laughed. "If I'd known I'd be ripping your clothes off the moment I got home, I would at least have brought you flowers."

## 13

It had been a long time since Mia had felt this close to someone. Joaquin stayed with her and held her hand, leaving her side only to let the EMTs into the bathroom and to pack her things.

"I don't think you'll be coming back here," he said.

Joaquin insisted the EMTs wrap a warm blanket around her shoulders and do all they could to preserve her modesty in an apartment full of male cops. He even held off Wu, telling him that he could get their statements after Mia was discharged from the ER.

She wasn't used to having someone watch out for her like this, anticipating her needs, putting her first. It made her feel cared for, cherished. It was a balm to her shattered nerves. She closed her eyes, let him carry the weight of their situation. But images swarmed through her mind—the reflection in the steel door, a black hoodie in the shadows, shattering glass, bullets.

*BAM!*

Her eyes jerked open.

"Sorry," said one of the EMTs, who was applying pressure to the wound near her hip. "I didn't mean to hurt you."

"No, it's not that. I'm just ... jumpy."

"Do you want a sedative?"

"No. I'm fine, really."

A big man in SWAT gear walked up to where Mia lay on the gurney, M4 in one hand, Joaquin's camera bag in the other. It took her a moment to recognize him.

"Marc. Thanks for coming to the party."

He touched a gloved hand gently to her shoulder. "I only wish we'd been on time instead of fashionably late. We *are* going to find this bastard. Is there anyone you'd like us to contact on your behalf—your family?"

She shook her head. "No, I'm fine. Really."

"Those are your shell casings down there, right—the forty-five rounds?"

She nodded. "I don't think I hit him."

"Maybe not, but you fought back. You scared him and sent him running. Unfortunately, we're going to have to confiscate your firearm for now. It's part of the investigation."

"I think it's in the bathtub."

Joaquin walked up to them carrying Mia's overnight bag. "Hey, Hunter, do me a favor. Catch this son of a bitch."

"You got it." Marc handed Joaquin his camera bag. "Are you okay? I saw he fired at you, too. Your windshield is shattered."

"What?" Mia hadn't known this. "He fired at you?"

Joaquin didn't seem rattled. "He missed."

*Thank God.*

Marc walked toward the bathroom. "Ramirez, you give me gray hair."

Joaquin rode in the ambulance with Mia, carrying her

things through the door and holding her hand while the medical staff gave her IV antibiotics to prevent infection and got to work cleaning her up. The shrapnel wound on her ribcage didn't need stitches, but the deeper graze on her hip had several small bullet fragments.

The doctor shot her up with a local anesthetic, flushed the wound with saline, then prodded it with surgical tweezers, pulling out bits of metal and dropping them in a plastic basin. "Just one more ... little .. fragment."

Mia gasped, clenched Joaquin's hand, as the tweezers pressed deeper, hitting tissue that wasn't numb.

Joaquin stroked her cheek, kissed her hair. "Can't you wait and give her more Novocain?"

"Sorry." The doctor held up the last fragment. "Got it."

Mia felt a little dizzy. "That was ... a lot less fun than I'd hoped."

"Let's put on some lidocaine gel. After it sits for a while, we'll get you stitched back together." The doctor stood, stripped off his sterile gloves, and left the room.

For the first time since the police arrived, Mia was alone with Joaquin.

He stroked her hair. "I'm so sorry, Mia. I don't know why he didn't make sure you were numb first."

She looked up at him. "I'm so glad you're here."

His gaze moved over her face, as if he were trying to memorize her features. "The bastard jumped right in front of my truck. I could have hit him, but I slammed on the brakes. When he shot at me and I realized who he was, all I could think about was you. Then I saw your car and the shattered glass—God, Mia. I was sure you were dying or dead. I don't think I've ever been more afraid."

Mia wasn't used to hearing men admit that they felt fear,

and it moved her to think he'd been afraid for *her*. "How did he find me?"

"I don't know, but I'm sure as hell going to find out." He looked angry.

A knock came at the door, and Wu stuck his head inside. "Ms. Starr. Is now a good time?"

*Oh, great.* She didn't want to deal with him, not yet. "Sure."

"First, let me say how sorry I am that this happened and how relieved I am to see that you weren't badly hurt."

She held up a hand to shut him up. "Before you ask me anything, I want to know how he found me."

Joaquin wanted to hear this, too. "This time, you answer *our* questions first."

Wu didn't look happy. "The suspect used Jason Garcia's credit card to pay for an online search for your address, Mr. Ramirez. We got a pop on the card and were following up on that when your call came in, Ms. Starr. Somehow, he knew you were staying with Mr. Ramirez, and he tracked down Mr. Ramirez's address using a public records website."

"How could he know I was staying there? Maybe there's another leak in the police department."

Wu cleared his throat, clearly uncomfortable with Mia's allegation. "My best guess is that he followed you, saw the two of you together, and looked up Mr. Ramirez's license plate. Maybe he saw you when you picked her up at the nightclub."

"But you don't know for certain." Joaquin wasn't impressed.

"No, I don't."

"Mia was almost killed tonight. If you'd warned us sooner, this wouldn't have happened."

"It takes time to access credit card records, even for police detectives. We're doing everything—"

"I don't believe that." Joaquin was too shaken to hold back. "Mia is alive right now, no thanks to DPD. She could have been his third victim."

"Fourth," Wu said.

Mia's face went white. "What?"

"*Fourth?*" Joaquin asked.

"I spent most of the afternoon in Colorado Springs. Whoever this guy is, he shot and killed Brigadier General Stephen Frank. He caught him outside a pay-by-the-hour hotel and shot him in the head. No witnesses, no cameras. There was no wallet with the body, so we can only assume the killer took it, as he did with both Meyer and Garcia. I saw the report and recognized the general's name from the information you gave us. This time, the killer wrote your name on the wall in the victim's blood."

"He killed Frank, too? My name ... in blood?" Mia seemed to have trouble absorbing all of this. "Is he still trying to frame me?"

Joaquin held her hand tighter.

"Perhaps," Wu said. "Or maybe it was a warning that he was coming for you."

*That* was a comforting thought.

"Where were you last night between the hours of eight and ten?" Wu asked.

"Give me a break, man. She was at my place with me." Javier ran his thumb over her knuckles, checked in with her. "How are you doing, Mia?"

She gave a little shake of her head. "I don't even know."

Wu repeated his question as if Joaquin hadn't answered it already. "Where were you last night?"

"I thought you said I wasn't a suspect."

"It's just a routine question."

"I was at Joaquin's house. I didn't leave until this morning."

"What do you make of the fact that Brigadier General Frank is dead now?"

"I don't know. Frank is the one who let them get away with looting at first. He helped bury my report. He got a promotion for it, too. He *was* involved in the initial investigation about the mustard gas and some of the men's discharges, so I suppose someone might hold that against him."

"Do he and Powell get along?"

"They did, most of the time until ... Wait. You think Powell is behind this?"

That bastard.

Joaquin already hated him.

"He's a person of interest in the case. He has a strong motive against you. Why don't you start at the beginning and tell me what happened tonight?"

Joaquin listened while Mia told Wu the whole story, clearly doing her best to remember details.

"I didn't see his face. The glass had so many cracks in it, and the light was in my eyes. But there was something familiar. I shot back, got off a few shots. I was so pumped up on adrenaline. I doubt I hit him. After the elevator doors closed, I dialed 9-1-1. I was afraid he'd see where the elevator stopped and then follow me up to Joaquin's floor. I went into your apartment, Joaquin, and locked the door, and then shut all the bedroom doors so he wouldn't be sure which room I was in. I locked myself in the bathroom and laid down in the tub. I thought it offered the best cover."

Joaquin was impressed. "That was smart."

Wu went on. "You said you were distracted walking to the elevator. Were you on your phone or something?"

Mia's cheeks turned pink, and she glanced furtively up at Joaquin. "I was ... um... trying to memorize some phrases in Spanish."

Spanish phrases that made her blush?

They would have to talk about this later.

Wu kept up with the questions until the doctor stepped in with the nurse to stitch Mia's wound. "We can finish this later. There are pieces in motion the two of you need to hear about, and there are important decisions to make."

What the hell did Wu mean by that?

MIA PULLED the borrowed scrubs up over her hips, gritting her teeth to keep from moaning. Her bra and panties, both wet with blood, had been bagged for her, and a pair of green surgical scrubs offered to her by a caring RN.

"Just don't tell anyone," the nurse had whispered.

The scrubs top snapped down the front, which made it easier to put on.

The nurse returned, small pill in a tiny white paper cup. "It's Vicodin. The doctor has an RX for you—just a handful of pills to get you through the next couple of days."

Mia hesitated. "Will it knock me out? I've never taken a narcotic before."

"It might, but you weren't planning on driving tonight anyway, were you?"

No, she wasn't, but then she had no idea what was going

to happen next. Joaquin had gone to meet with his police friends and Wu to talk about their situation, while she dressed and got her discharge instructions.

The nurse poured the pill into her hand and gave her a plastic pitcher of water. "What it will do is dull that pain and give you a chance to rest and heal. Give it thirty or forty minutes to kick in."

"Thanks." Mia swallowed the pill, then searched for her socks and shoes, moving stiffly, every step tugging at the deep laceration near her hip.

In the end, the nurse had to put her shoes on her feet and tie them.

"I feel like a baby."

The nurse smiled. "I think you're a hero. Besides, everyone needs to be babied once in a while."

A knock came at the door, and Joaquin stuck his head inside. "Can we come in?"

"She's ready to go," the nurse said. "She's had a Vicodin, so she can't drive."

Joaquin entered with Marc and Julian, both still in body armor.

"Hey, Mia," Julian said. "Way to be a badass tonight. How do you feel?"

"Lucky." It was then she noticed the serious looks on the men's faces. *Damn.* Not good. "What's our sitrep?"

Marc went first. "This whole thing has blown up. Because of Frank's murder, the CBI and FBI have stepped in. Tonight or tomorrow at the latest, the FBI is going to want to talk to you. They're going to want to hear what you told us."

Joaquin spoke next. "The media is all over this, including my paper. Cate is sitting out there with one of our other photographers and a half-dozen other reporters, waiting for us. I left my pager in my truck with my camera, but I've got about thirty text messages from Cate and Tom, asking me where the hell I am."

"I'm sorry, Joaquin. Your life was sane before you got mixed up with me."

Julian frowned, shook his head. "Sane? No. I wouldn't go that far."

Joaquin ignored him. "Don't worry about me, Mia. I just want to keep you safe."

"We need to figure out where to take you next," Julian said. "You don't meet the criteria for WitSec. We have a few police safehouses around Denver. That's a possibility."

"There's also the Cimarron," Marc said.

"What's that?" Mia had never heard of it.

"My brother-in-law and his father have a little mountain cabin," Marc said.

Joaquin and Julian both found this funny for some reason.

Marc was grinning, too, apparently in on some joke. "If you'd like, I can call and see if they'd take you in. Jack West is a former Army Ranger, and his son served on a Marine Special Operations Team alongside Navy SEALs until he was badly burned in an IED explosion."

"How awful." Mia couldn't imagine anything more terrible.

"He recovered and married my sister, Megan. Their place is a hell of a lot nicer than a safehouse, and I guarantee you, no one will find you there."

"Thanks."

"There's something else to consider," Julian said. "Ramirez, this guy clearly knows who you are. He knows where you live. He might even come looking for you or think that Mia is still at your place. We have no idea what he'll do next. Either you need to lay low for a while, maybe head up to the Cimarron, too, or you need to stay somewhere else—and far away from Mia. You can't go back and forth between wherever she is and your job. You could lead him to her."

"You're right. *Mierda*."

Mia's stomach sank, the big picture coming into focus. "I can't go to work, can I? Not now. Not after tonight."

Julian shook his head. "I'm sorry, Mia. I know it must feel as if your world has been turned upside down, but I promise you, we *will* find him. Will you need help with your employer? DPD will be happy to give them whatever they need."

"I'm sure it will be fine. I've got some vacation days coming." She hadn't planned on using them like this.

"Let me call the Cimarron first and see what they have to say before we start making plans." Marc stepped out of the room.

Weighted down by a sense of overwhelm, Mia found a chair and sat, wincing.

Joaquin sat beside her. "I've got a lot of extra vacation hours. Why don't I take some time off? I don't want you to have to deal with all of this alone."

"You would do that?"

He nodded. "Hell, yeah."

"Won't that complicate things for you at the paper—being associated with me while this story is making headlines?"

"After tonight, it's too late to stop that. I'll deal with that later."

Marc stepped back into the room, a grin on his face. "Jack's answer was, 'What the *hell* kind of question is that? Of course, they're welcome here!'"

"That's Jack." Joaquin chuckled. "You're going to love it there."

JOAQUIN SAT in the back of Hunter's SUV, Mia all but asleep in the seat beside him, her head resting against his shoulder, his arm around her. The pill they'd given her at the hospital had all but knocked her out. Then again, it was late.

Hunter and Darcangelo had worked with hospital security to take them out a back way, sparing Mia a media onslaught and postponing the confrontation between Joaquin and Cate. With an escort of SWAT cops, they'd taken Joaquin and Mia first to his condo and then to hers, then stood back while the two of them packed for their stay at the Cimarron. By the time they'd left Denver, it was almost ten, and Mia was so loopy on Vicodin that she could barely function.

That was fine by Joaquin. She deserved a break, some time to forget, a chance to escape fear and pain and memory. She'd been strong tonight, too strong—no tears, no panic, no shock. Still, he'd been able to tell that she was overwhelmed there at the end, the horror she'd lived through catching up with her.

"I wish I'd hit the bastard." Joaquin didn't realize he'd spoken aloud until he heard his voice. "If only I'd known who he was before I slammed on the brakes, I could have ended it all *right there*."

Darcangelo looked back over his shoulder. "Stop. You reacted on instinct and did what any one of us would have done."

"You did the right thing by letting him go," Hunter said. "I meant to say something earlier. If you had chased him and shot him, you'd be in a legal mess. If he'd shot you, you might be dead. Either way, that's not what you want."

"I was afraid he'd gotten to Mia. I had to let him go to help her." He hadn't even had to think about that one.

"You made the right decision under a lot of pressure. Feel good about that." Hunter flipped on his turn signal. "Here's the turn-off."

Out of the darkness loomed the ranch's front gate—an archway constructed of big logs with a wooden sign bearing the words "Cimarron Ranch" on a crossbeam. Nate West sat there in his pickup, ready to close the heavy steel gate behind them.

Hunter flashed his brights. West did the same. Then Hunter turned off the highway and headed down the dirt road that led to the great house.

Joaquin glanced back at the highway, wanting to make sure they weren't being followed. Apart from West's truck, there was only one set of headlights behind them.

"Relax, Ramirez," Darcangelo said. "That's Wu."

Mia stirred, moaned, then lifted her head.

"We're almost there. The ranch house is just over this rise."

She sat up, glanced around, confusion on her pretty face. "The house? You mean the cabin?"

"That's what he means," Hunter said.

They reached the top of the rise, and there it was—the Cimarron's great house coming into view.

"There it is," Joaquin said.

"That's not a cabin," Mia said in a sleepy voice. "That's a hotel."

Joaquin chuckled along with Hunter and Darcangelo. The house *was* huge. It had its own two-story library, a gym, a home theater, a five-car heated garage, and a back deck that looked out on some of the most beautiful scenery in Colorado.

"My sister married into one of the wealthiest families in the state," Hunter explained. "All of this land you see outside your window is part of the ranch. Jack and Nate run Angus cattle and breed quarter horses."

"Huh." Mia still looked confused.

Yeah, the poor *chula* was gone.

From behind them, West flashed his brights.

Hunter pulled over, let West pass him, then followed. "They're putting the two of you up in their guest cabin. Jack thought Mia might want some privacy after all of this, rather than having to hang out with people she doesn't know."

Joaquin hadn't known they had a guest cabin, but then the ranch was huge.

They passed the great house, drove behind it heading south for a while, then turned up a snowy road. They came around the bend, and Joaquin saw it—a log cabin large enough to hold his condo, Mia's condo, and possibly this SUV. The porch light was on, the windows glowing with welcoming light.

Jack stepped away from a pile of firewood, ax in hand, and waved.

"There's the cabin," Mia said, still not understanding.

Hunter parked, and he and Darcangelo got out and went to say hello to Jack, who welcomed them with bear hugs and a big smile.

Joaquin helped Mia out of her seatbelt. "You wait here. Don't get out on your own. I'll come around and help you."

"Okay."

Joaquin climbed out, went around the back of the vehicle, and opened Mia's door. She slipped almost boneless into his arms. "I've got you."

Arm around her shoulders, he guided her over to their host. "Hey, Jack."

"Ramirez, good to see you again."

"This is my friend Mia Starr. She served a couple of tours of duty in Iraq and was my cousin Elena's captain during Elena's first year in the Army. She's pretty out of it on Vicodin right now."

Jack took Mia's hand. "Welcome, Mia. It's an honor to have you as our guest."

∾

*MIA. Mia. Mia, you bitch.*

He sat in the old bus he now called home, pressing gauze from an old first aid kit against the graze on his inner thigh. She had almost shot his balls off.

*Fucking cunt!*

How had she known he was there? One moment he'd been about to blow a fist-sized hole in her head with a 9 mm hollow-point round, and the next...

He squeezed his eyes shut, the pain behind them worse than the bullet wound.

*Needles. Needles. Needles in my skull.*

He ought to have killed *her* first. She was smarter than the others, smarter even than that old fart-sack Frank. It wasn't going to be easy to get close to her again. The bitch *was* involved with a guy. The bastard must be gay.

*He could have gotten you.*

Yeah, but a guy like him wouldn't be armed. Rather than chasing him like a real man, the twat had sped away. Chicken shit.

He was supposed to have finished this tonight. He'd planned to celebrate by putting a bullet through his own brain and ending this endless pain. But somehow, he'd fired six shots at five yards and hadn't managed to kill her. Maybe he was too out of it on Oxy, or maybe she had eyes in the back of her head.

Now he had to find her again and get past all her police friends—he could only imagine the lies she'd told them—so that he could kill her. That meant living, enduring this pain longer. How the fuck could he do that?

Maybe he should kill himself and forget about Mia Starr.

He thought about that for a moment, imagined how sweet oblivion would be. But then Mia would get away with all of it. She would get away with betraying them. He couldn't let that happen.

Mia Starr had to die.

## 14

Mia's first thought when she awoke was that she was terribly late for work. Then she opened her eyes to find herself staring at a cathedral ceiling of polished wooden planks with support beams of pine.

The cabin.

Kevin had given her a paid leave of absence—up to eight weeks—and Julian and Marc had brought her and Joaquin here last night. She'd met Jack, the former Army Ranger who owned this place and was letting them stay here. After that...

That Vicodin had kicked her butt.

She sat up, breath hissing between her teeth. It wasn't just the graze near her hip that hurt, but her entire body. She felt sore, like she'd worked out too hard—the after-effects of a major adrenaline surge, she supposed.

She glanced around, saw that she'd been sleeping in a massive king-sized bed with a rustic wooden headboard. A small electric clock on the nightstand told her it was seven-thirty. She took in the oriental carpets, the gleaming wooden floors, the closed blinds with sunlight streaking through. Her duffel bag sat next to a small desk, and there were photographs of horses on the walls.

Hadn't she heard that Jack West and his son bred horses?

She got to her feet only to realize she was still wearing the scrubs the nurse had given her. She wanted a shower, but that couldn't happen—not yet. She wasn't supposed to get her wounds wet for twenty-four hours. Still, she could wash most of herself. She'd gotten good at taking a bath out of her canteen in Iraq. She could manage this.

She lifted her duffel bag onto the bed, took out the plastic tote that held her toiletries, walked into the en-suite bathroom—and stared. The floors were stone tile. The shower was separate from the tub and enclosed by glass walls. The jetted bathtub was big enough for two. There were two sinks with rustic brass faucets, the cupboards beneath made of wood that matched the walls, ceiling, and floors.

A cabin with electricity, central heating, and a five-piece luxury bathroom.

When she'd heard "cabin," she'd been expecting a dark, chilly space with an outhouse, hunting trophies, and a smoky fireplace. But, hey, she wasn't complaining.

She found towels and washcloths hanging on a heated towel rack, filled the sink with hot water and undressed. She dipped a washcloth in the water—then caught sight of her reflection and stared. A dark bruise had spread beneath the bandage on her ribcage, and her hip was bruised, too. She looked down the front of her body, saw another bruise on her thigh—where had that come from?—and another on her shin.

She had never looked this beat-up in Iraq.

Somewhere in the back of her mind, dark thoughts

stirred. A man had tried to kill her yesterday, and he'd come close to succeeding. She shut those thoughts down. She'd fired back, and he'd run. She was fine.

She washed her face and body, careful to keep her bandages dry. Then she rubbed moisturizer into her skin, put on deodorant, and walked back to the bed to dress. Certain she wouldn't be able to handle jeans yet, she pulled out a pair of navy blue yoga pants and a purple fleece-lined pullover, her mind turning to that most important of things.

Coffee.

She opened the bedroom door—and found Joaquin still asleep on the sofa. She tiptoed over and stood there watching him, long lashes dark against his cheeks, bare shoulders peeking out from beneath the blanket. He'd slept here, giving her the bed, even though the sofa couldn't have been comfortable for a six-foot-tall man.

As if he felt her watching him, his eyes opened.

"Mia." He sat up, the blanket falling away to reveal his bare chest in all its heart-stopping glory. "How do you feel?"

"Better. Sore."

"I bet." He stretched, the sight almost more than Mia could take.

She cleared her throat. "Did you sleep well?"

"Yeah—once I was finally able to fall asleep."

"This is a nice place." She looked around, saw the woodstove, the blinds that covered a sliding glass door, the flat screen TV, the dining room, the kitchen with its stainless-steel appliances and walk-in pantry. "I can't believe they're just letting us stay here. If we're staying in their cabin, where are they?"

"This place?" Joaquin got to his feet, a big grin on his face, his body so close that she could feel his warmth. "It's nothing."

He moved past her, walked to the sliding glass door, and opened the blinds.

Mia followed him and found herself looking out onto a postcard. "Wow."

Through aspens, she could see a valley stretching out before them, ringed with high mountains. A mansion—she didn't know what else to call it—sat in the middle of that valley, stables and barns on one side of it, men going about their chores.

"They own all of this. See that big house, the place you called a hotel last night? *That* is where they live."

"I called it a hotel? I don't remember that."

"You were pretty out of it."

"This is just a guest cabin?"

"I think they rent it out to hunters. They stocked the kitchen for us, split and stacked firewood, and even left a shotgun and shells for us." Joaquin pointed to the Winchester 12-gauge leaning up against the wall. "They thought of everything. There's even a wine cellar—a wine pantry, really—and wine chilling in the fridge."

"Why would they do this?" Mia wasn't used to acts of generosity on this scale. "They don't even know me."

Joaquin turned to her, drew her into his arms. "Hunter is part of their family through his sister Megan's marriage to Nate. Nate and I are friends, and you're my friend. My group of friends—we help each other out. We take care of our own."

"I like that." She rested her head against his chest.

"The Wests are great people. I've been here before to ski and barbeque. They hold the best barbeques. They've let me ride around their property taking photographs in exchange for photos of their horses." He kissed the top of her head. "Why don't I get a fire going, and we can make breakfast?"

"As long as we start with coffee first."

He grinned. "*Sí, claro*. You think I'm loco?"

JOAQUIN SCROLLED through his text messages and emails, trying to catch up with everyone while Mia made more coffee. He had already called his mom and dad to tell them what had happened and let them know that he and Mia were okay. He'd left it to them to pass the word to Elena and everyone else via the family website and had promised to get in touch again when he had more news.

Matt had messaged him to let him know Tom was out for blood.

Sophie had sent a text urging him to be careful.

Kara McMillan, who had once worked with the I-Team but was now a freelance journalist, had texted him to ask what the hell was going on.

Tessa Darcangelo, Julian's wife and another former I-Team reporter, had also texted, saying that she'd heard what had happened from Julian and that she hoped the cops caught the bastard soon.

Holly Andris, another former co-worker who now worked for a private security firm, had told him to stay safe and offered to set up a consultation with her boss, Javier Corbray, to come up with a security plan.

STAY SAFE! ALSO, WHO IS THIS MIA???? I'M DYING TO MEET HER! IF SHE'S WOMAN ENOUGH TO INTEREST YOU, SHE MUST BE SPECIAL.

KISSES,

HOLLY

Her message made Joaquin smile, but that was Holly to a T—always looking at the light side of life.

Mia set a fresh mug of coffee down beside him. "A lot of people care about you."

"I'm lucky." He *was* lucky, but it bothered him that Mia didn't have what he had—a big family and a close circle of friends. He got to his feet, picked up his coffee. "It's time to face the music. I've got to call Tom."

She gave his arm a squeeze. "Good luck."

He walked out onto the deck so that Mia wouldn't have to hear his conversation with Tom and worry. Tom yelled at Joaquin for a solid two minutes about not returning texts, pages, and calls, and then asked him if he was okay. Then he asked Joaquin to tell him what the *hell* was going on between him and Mia.

So, Joaquin told him, leaving out his feelings for her or the fact that they had kissed. That was none of Tom's business.

"You ran into her at the cop shop, offered her a ride back to her vehicle, but took her to dinner instead."

"Yeah—and that's it. She and I have not slept together." It was true at the moment, so, hey, good enough.

"Are you telling me she was just stopping by for a casual visit last night?"

"Something like that. I didn't even know she was there." That was true, too, in a strictly literal sense. He'd known she was coming over, but he hadn't known she was there at that moment. "This asshole took a bunch of shots at her, fired a shot at me through my windshield, and made a mess of my truck. I would have called you back, but I was at the hospital with Ms. Starr."

Tom went quiet for a moment. "Chief Irving called me this morning."

"Yeah?" Joaquin tried to sound like he didn't have a guilty conscience.

"He said that the administrative assistant he fired is accusing Cate of asking her to steal documents."

*¡Carajo!*

It was legal for a reporter to take possession of stolen documents—as long as they had nothing to do with those documents being stolen. If Cate had *asked* Irving's assistant to steal that file, she had committed a crime.

"That's a serious allegation. What does Cate say?"

"She's off trying to get the service record of the most recent victim. When she gets back, she and I are going to talk."

"Is Irving going to press charges?"

"He said that if the paper had gotten a hold of those pages and published them, he would. He said the fact that he caught the source before that happened is the only thing stopping him. I assured him that no member of my staff would ask anyone to steal files. Then I asked him if you had tipped him off."

Joaquin's breath seemed to freeze in his chest.

"He said one of his detectives warned him. Apparently, this guy had been watching her, waited for her to make her move, and then told Irving."

*Thank you, Darcangelo and Irving.*

But Tom wasn't finished. "The question then is: Did

someone tip off the detective, or did he figure this out on his own?"

"I guess you'd have to know which detective it was and ask him—or her."

"You're good friends with some of those detectives." Tom had always had an uncanny sense of people. "But I am letting this go. In this instance, I'm glad they caught the source. I'd rather lose a story than see the paper up to its chin in legal bullshit. We don't need that kind of trouble. Something like that could destroy a reputation I've spent most of my career trying to build and protect."

"I hear that."

"HR has processed your leave. You've got a week, and then we'll re-evaluate. If Irving's boys would do their job and catch this bastard..."

"Don't I wish."

"See you in a week. And, hey, Ramirez, watch your ass."

"Will do."

As he walked back into the cabin, Joaquin realized it was the second day in a row that he'd dodged a bullet.

He found Mia finishing up the breakfast dishes. Her head came around the moment he stepped through the door, her eyes filled with anxiety for him.

"It's all good." He slipped off his boots. "I still have a job."

Relief blossomed on her face. "What did your boss say?"

He told her about his talk with Tom—leaving out the bit about Cate possibly breaking the law. "Then he asked Chief Irving point blank whether I had tipped him off, and Irving told him that he'd gotten word of it from one of his detectives."

Mia dried her hands. "I'm glad to hear that. I was afraid he was going to fire you."

"So was I." But there was something else. "Tom also said Cate is trying to get a hold of Jason's military record now."

Mia gave a little laugh. "She won't get much from that. The government won't release more than the basics without his family's permission. There's nothing about Tell al-Sharruken in the official records anyway—or mustard gas or looting."

Joaquin drew her into his arms, kissed her forehead. "I know this whole situation sucks. What happened yesterday —it must have shaken you up. I don't know how you're holding it together the way you are. Try to use the time we're up here to heal. Let go of the rest of it."

She rested her head against his chest, wrapped her arms around him, held him tight. "I wish it were that easy."

God, it felt good to hold her like this, to feel her alive in his arms, to know that she was safe. Yeah, yesterday had shaken her up. It had shaken him, too.

She drew back, looked up at him. "Jack called on the landline. He wanted to know if we'd like to go on a sleigh ride around the ranch and join them at the house for lunch. He says he's making his world-famous chili."

Under normal circumstances, Joaquin would have walked all the way to the ranch from Denver through a blizzard for Jack's chili. The man wasn't kidding when he said he it was good. But Joaquin wasn't sure Mia was up for meeting new people or going out in the cold. "How do you feel about that?"

Mia laughed. "I said yes. Hey, I grew up in Colorado, too. When someone boasts that their chili is world famous, I take that seriously. They need to put up or shut up."

～

MIA OPENED the cabin's front door, a smile coming over her face when she saw the sleigh and ... "Oh! What a beautiful horse."

Jack climbed down from the sleigh. "That's Buckwheat, my granddaughter Emily's favorite gelding. You can say hello if you like. He's as gentle as he is big, aren't you, Buckwheat, old boy?"

Buckwheat jerked his head and snorted, as if he understood.

Mia tromped through the snow and reached up to stroke the horse's forehead. "Hey, there, Buckwheat."

"Have you spent time with horses?" Jack asked.

Mia shook her head. "Not really. I went for some trail rides when I was in Girl Scouts, but I didn't know what I was doing."

"We'll have to do something about that." Jack reached into his pocket, pulled out a couple of carrots. "Want to give him a treat? Put the carrot in your palm and hold your hand out flat. Yep. Just like that."

Mia held out the carrot, Buckwheat's velvet muzzle tickling her palm as he took the carrot from her and munched.

She heard a click—and turned to see Joaquin taking photos. "Oh, no! You can photograph the horse, but don't take photos of me. I'm not photogenic."

"Is that so?" Joaquin turned his camera so she could see. "I don't believe you."

There was a digital image of a woman with red cheeks and a bright smile on her face, a horse eating from her hand. She seemed happy, alive, even ... pretty.

Mia looked up at Joaquin, surprised.

Joaquin grinned. "See?"

"Let's get this show on the road." Jack climbed into the

front of the sleigh. "We need to make tracks if we're going to get back to the house in time for lunch."

Joaquin helped Mia into the sleigh, the wound near her hip making her grit her teeth as she stepped up. "Be careful."

There were thick sheepskin blankets folded on red leather seats, a thermos and three insulated mugs tucked into a basket beside them.

"Just make yourselves comfortable back there. Those blankets ought to keep you warm." Jack climbed into the seat, took up the reins. "I brought hot chocolate, too."

"Thanks, West." Joaquin sat beside Mia, pulled one of the sheepskin blankets over the two of them, then took her hand. "You comfortable?"

"As toasty as a marshmallow."

Jack made a clicking sound with his tongue. "Let's go, boy."

The sleigh moved forward with a jerk and then began to glide through the snow, bells on Buckwheat's bridle jingling.

Mia couldn't wipe the smile off her face. She looked over at Joaquin, saw that he was watching her. "This feels like Christmas."

He kissed her temple. "Hang on, angel, because it only gets better."

He wasn't just saying that.

Jack took them behind the cabin and onto a path that led through stands of aspen and snowy pines, the valley opening off to their left, mountains all around them, their snowy summits hidden by clouds.

"God, it's beautiful here."

As they flew through forest, across meadows, around a frozen lake, and then down into the valley, Mia's tension began to melt away, her mind empty of everything but the beauty around her—and the man beside her. His body was warm, his breath mingling with hers in a cloud of white, his scent mixing with pine, snow, and fresh air.

Jack told them the story of the ranch—how his great-grandfather had bought this spread after World War I and raised his family here. "Nate is the fifth generation of Wests to work the ranch."

"That's amazing." Mia tried to imagine having such deep roots, having a place that told the story of one's family.

They stopped a few times so Joaquin could take photos. Apart from that, he sat beside her, holding her hand, asking her if she was warm, pouring hot chocolate for her, laughing with her when a startled squirrel jumped from one *Pinus ponderosa* bough to another and brought a shower of snow down on their heads.

She wasn't used to being treated like this by a man. She wasn't used to being the focus of such tenderness and concern. She wasn't used to someone putting her first, as he had done time and time again this past week.

*You're falling in love with him.*

Adrenaline hit her bloodstream, made her pulse spike.

Some part of her tried to deny it, but she knew it was true.

*Knock it off.*

What if she didn't want to knock it off?

"Look." He pointed, snowflakes on his eyelashes, his cheeks almost as red from the cold as hers. "There, through the trees."

A moose grazed on aspen shoots, its head coming up as they passed.

Yes, she was falling in love with him, and she wasn't sure she wanted to do a damned thing about it.

They came to a stop outside the great house at noon

sharp. A ranch hand took the reins from Jack as he climbed down. "I hope you're hungry."

Mia pushed aside the sheepskin blanket. "Starving."

Joaquin helped Mia to the ground. "I only hope you made enough chili so that the rest of you can have some."

Jack led them through a heated garage into a mudroom that was about the size of Mia's living room. "There's a restroom through here."

"Thanks." Mia went to the restroom, then washed her hands and followed delicious smells and the sound of voices into the kitchen.

Jack was washing his hands at the sink, and Joaquin was talking to two women and a man with a scarred face who must have been Nate, the Marine who'd been burned.

Joaquin saw her first. "This is Mia Starr."

Nate walked over to her, held out a scarred hand. "Welcome to the Cimarron."

The half of his face that hadn't been hurt was incredibly handsome, and she could see his resemblance to his father.

"Thanks for letting us stay here."

"You're welcome. We're happy to help out." Nate motioned toward one of the women. "This is my wife, Megan. Our daughter Emily is at school right now. The boy with the messy face—that's Jackson."

"You're Marc Hunter's sister," Mia said.

"Marc has told me so much about you. It's nice to meet you, Mia." Apart from being tall and having brown hair, Megan didn't resemble her brother. She struggled to take Jackson out of his high chair, but he didn't want to come. "He needs a nap."

A shorter woman with darker hair waved to Mia, a little girl in her lap. "I'm Janet, Jack's wife. This is our daughter, Lily. She needs a nap, too."

While Janet and Megan put the kids to bed, Nate gave Mia a tour of the house. There was the living room with its enormous fireplace of river rock. There was the two-story library with its own fireplace. There was the gym, the home theater, the sauna, and enough bedrooms for friends and extended family, all of it tastefully decorated.

"This is the most beautiful house I've ever seen." Mia was just being honest.

"Thanks," Nate said. "We've put a lot of love and hard work into it."

"Marc said you lived in a little cabin. I was expecting no heat, an outhouse, and spittoons."

Nate chuckled. "That joker."

By the time they returned to the kitchen, lunch was on the table, the scents making her mouth water. A pot of chili. Salad. Cornbread. Butter.

"This looks delicious." Mia caught Joaquin's gaze, shared her amazement with him in a glance, only to watch him smile.

He was used to this place. She wasn't.

"Have a seat, and help yourself," Jack said.

Mia did just that—and had to fight not to moan, flavors exploding across her tongue. Beef. Tangy tomato. Cumin. Onion. Black beans. Beer. "This is delicious."

"I told you he wasn't kidding," Joaquin said.

They talked through the meal, Nate and Joaquin ribbing each other the way men did when they were friends, Janet and Megan asking Mia questions about her job. Mia was surprised at how relaxed she felt. She'd met Joaquin just one week ago and Jack only last night, and still she felt like they were old friends.

Only after they'd finished their meal did Jack bring it up. "I hear you've had a hard time of it lately, Mia. I'm sorry about that. Hunter said he couldn't tell us everything, but I gather you witnessed some top-secret bullshit in Iraq and someone is trying to get back at you for that. He called you a hero, and that means a lot to us coming from him."

"It sure as hell does." Nate's expression went serious. "He's one of the most courageous men I know."

Heads nodded.

Jack went on. "You don't have to talk about what happened last night unless you want to. I just wanted you to know that you're safe here with us. We want you to heal and relax while you're here, so please let us know if there's anything we can do for you."

Mia's throat went tight. "Thank you. I don't know what to say."

"Say you left room for dessert." Jack got to his feet. "I baked a chocolate cake."

"He makes a mean chocolate cake, too," Joaquin said.

The cake was delicious, and soon it was Mia who needed a nap. She and Joaquin had just thanked Jack and the others for the meal and their hospitality when Jack's phone buzzed.

"What's up?" He scowled. "Huh. Well, hell. Let 'em in."

He ended the call, his blue eyes looking into Mia's. "There are a couple of FBI agents at the gate. They want to ask you some questions."

Mia's stomach dropped. Were they here about the case —or were they investigating her for divulging information?

Janet touched her hand to her husband's arm. "They're just doing their jobs."

Jack gave a noncommittal "hmph" and got to his feet.

Nate grinned. "My old man has no love for feds—except for the woman he married."

Mia stared at Janet. "You're a federal agent?"

Janet nodded, her lips curving into a smile, as if this were funny. "I'm a former FBI special agent. Jack once threw me off his property."

"She's exaggerating!" Jack shouted back to them.

Joaquin took Mia's hand. "It's going to be okay."

Mia wasn't so sure.

## 15

Joaquin sat on the sofa in the cabin, Mia leaning back against his chest, glasses of wine in their hands, a fire crackling in the woodstove.

"They thanked me," Mia said. "Then Shoals—he's the tall one—told me that I had been a big help and that I should contact them if anything else came up. Shoals said he thought I was a hero. I wish people would stop saying that."

Joaquin kissed the top of Mia's head. "Does that seem so strange to you?"

"I haven't done anything special. I reported people who were flagrantly breaking the law, and I fired a few shots at a guy who was trying to kill me—and missed."

"Oh, that's all."

But she didn't seem to get his sarcasm. "I should have been paying attention. I should have had my weapon out. I—"

He pressed his fingertips to her lips. "Shhh. Don't blame yourself. Nothing you did or didn't do is to blame here."

"But if I'd been paying attention..." Her words trailed off.

That reminded him. "Hey, what were those Spanish phrases you were trying to learn anyway?"

He glanced down, watched a blush creep into her cheeks.

"They were supposed to be a surprise."

"Yeah? Let's hear it."

She shook her head. "I don't think so."

"Oh, come on. I've seen you in your underwear. You can tell me anything now."

She craned her neck, looked up at him. "You're going to think I'm an idiot."

"I would never think that."

"Okay." She frowned as if trying to remember. "*Tócame*."

*Touch me?*

*¡Aye, bendito! Good God!*

Joaquin's night had just gotten a whole lot more interesting. He'd been expecting *buenas días* or *cómo estás or dónde esta el baño*, not something flirty or sexual. He found himself grinning like an idiot. "That was ... good. Anything else?"

"*Te deseo*." *I want you.*

He fought to rein in his reaction. This was a language lesson, nothing more. It didn't matter what his dick thought. "*Bien*. Well done."

She went on. "*Quiero arrancarte la ropa*."

*¡Carajo! Holy shit.*

"You *do* know what you're saying, right?"

She nodded, then hit him with another one. "*Eres el hombre más sexy que he cono... cono ...* I can't remember the last word."

"*Conocido*." Joaquin cleared his throat. "Yeah. That was ... uh... good."

A surge of tenderness washed over him. Mia had been distracted last night because she'd been thinking of *him*.

She'd been trying to do something sweet and sexy for *him* when that fucker had walked up behind her and opened fire.

Joaquin was struck again by how close it had been. Mia could so easily have been killed. Wu and the FBI needed to catch that son of a bitch—and soon. Had they even questioned Powell? Joaquin didn't want to think about that now, not when Mia had opened the evening to more interesting ideas.

"I'm touched that you did this for me." He took her wine glass and set it with his on the coffee table. "If you want a language lesson, *hermosa*, you only have to ask."

He sat up, and, careful not to bump her injuries, turned her in his arms, drawing her across his lap so that she straddled him.

She gave a little gasp, her arms going around his neck.

"*Sí*." He pressed his forehead to hers. "Right now, I want to kiss you. A kiss is *un beso*. If that's what you want, too, say *bésame*. Kiss me."

Her pupils dilated. "*Bésame*."

He brushed his lips over hers, contact igniting the desire he'd tried hard to ignore these past few days. He willed himself to go slowly, tasting her, testing her with his tongue, letting her anticipation build. She gave an impatient little whimper, slid her fingers into his hair, drew him closer. He answered by taking her mouth with his, her lips pliant, her body soft against him.

God, she tasted good. She felt good, too, her body so different from his, the feel of her sending blood to his groin.

Now she was kissing him back, challenging him, stealing control of the kiss, then melting in his arms when he stole it back. There was nothing cold or hard or aloof about Mia. She was soft and sweet and hot and eager.

"*Joaquin.*" She must have felt his hard-on, because she flexed her hips and pressed herself against him, moaning against his mouth.

His entire body tensed.

Joaquin broke the kiss, held her cheeks between his palms. "How far do you want to go with this, Mia? I don't want to rush you, and I don't want you to do anything you don't really *want* to do just to please me. I can wait."

"I can't. I want you, Joaquin. *Please* tell me you brought condoms."

Her words made his pulse skip.

He saw the longing in her eyes, felt it down to his bones. He reached for his camera bag and pulled out a small foil package. "I grabbed a fistful from the big bowl of free condoms they had at the hospital."

She laughed and took it from him, her lips curving in a sexy smile that hit Joaquin in the solar plexus. "Way to plan ahead."

SOME PART of Mia thought she must be dreaming as Joaquin got to his feet, scooped her into his arms, and carried her to the bedroom.

He set her on her feet beside the bed, ran his thumb along her lower lip. "I want to undress you."

She nodded, trying to ignore the voice in her head that told her that he would be disappointed, that she wasn't sexy.

"Relax." He slid his hands beneath her pullover, lifted it over her head, tossed it aside. "Oh, Mia."

His eyes went dark, his gaze moving over her. He reached out, cupped the bandage on her ribs, then he dropped to his knees and pressed a light kiss to the skin just above the bandage on her hip. "*Lo siento*, Mia. I'm sorry. I don't want to hurt you."

The tenderness of the gesture caught her off guard, made her chest constrict.

"I'll be okay."

"No." He looked up at her, his intensity taking her by surprise. "I don't want you to be *okay*. I want you to be happy. I want you to feel cherished. I want to make you scream."

Her breath caught, something fluttering deep in her belly. Did he want her permission for *that*? "Okay."

For some reason that made him chuckle. He caught the waistband of her yoga pants and drew them down her legs, wrapping a strong arm around her to help her keep her balance as she stepped out of them and kicked them aside.

He'd seen her like this yesterday. He'd seen her wearing nothing but panties and a bra, but that had been different. It hadn't been sexual.

He got to his feet again, slid his hand into her hair, and tilted her face upward for a kiss, speaking to her just before their lips touched. "You're beautiful, Mia."

His mouth closed over hers in a kiss that left her breathless and made her knees go weak. Seriously? A kiss could do that?

Somehow, she managed to tear her lips from his. "I want to undress you, too."

He was breathing as hard as she was, his lips wet and swollen. He released her, took a step backward, offering himself to her. "I'm all yours."

She unbuttoned his shirt with shaky hands and slipped it over his shoulders, leaving him to pull it down his arms while she indulged herself, exploring his chest, his pecs, his obliques, all that delicious muscle shifting beneath her palms, his skin like silk. "I love how you feel."

"Feel all you want."

She glanced up, a thrill shivering through her to find him watching her, a faint smile on his lips. Holding his gaze, she reached down, unzipped his fly and slid her hands between his underwear and his ass, pushing all that irritating fabric down his hips and freeing his erection. He took over from there, bending down to shuck his jeans and boxer briefs. And then he stood naked before her.

God, he was beautiful, his body so muscular and lean, his cock rising thick and hard from black curls, his testicles heavy and full. If she'd been an artist and someone had asked her to draw the perfect male nude, she would have drawn *this*.

She would have drawn Joaquin.

He took a step toward her, rested his hands on her waist, then brushed the knuckles of his right hand slowly up her left side, his touch turning her skin to gooseflesh. His hand found its way to her bra clasp in back, and her bra sprang free.

She caught it, held the lace cups to her breasts, a sudden rush of insecurity leaving her self-conscious.

He looked into her eyes, took hold of the bra, and pulled it slowly out of her hands, dropping it onto the floor. Then he caught her hands with his, his gaze burning over her, making her exposed nipples tighten. "Mia."

He pulled her against him and kissed her, their bodies pressed together, her breasts against his chest. His hands found their way beneath her panties to cup her bottom. He lifted her off her feet, turned with her in his arms, and laid her back on the bed, pulling off her panties with a single deft motion.

For a moment, he stood there, looking down at her, his smoky gaze moving over her body like a caress, the hunger on his face making her heart beat harder. He said something in Spanish that she didn't understand. Then he stretched out beside her and cupped her left breast, his thumb teasing its already tight nipple, sending jagged little bolts of arousal into her belly. "Does that feel good?"

"*Yes.*"

He kept it up until she was all but writhing beneath his touch. Then he lowered his mouth to her nipple—and suckled her.

Mia drew in a breath, her fingers sliding into his hair, nothing on her mind now but how Joaquin made her feel. The heat of his mouth. The sweet tug of his lips. The stroke of his tongue. She ached for him already, ached to have him inside her.

No man had ever made her feel like this—desperate, on edge, out of control.

Then he switched to her other breast, one of his hands sliding down her belly to cup her, nudging her thighs apart with his hand. "Let me in, angel."

She bent one knee, opening herself to him, her body humming with arousal, the anticipation almost killing her.

He explored her, finding and teasing her clit with slow strokes until Mia thought she would go out of her mind. Then he slid two fingers inside her, his thumb pressing circles to her clit as he stroked her inside and out.

Oh, it felt good. It felt so good.

"*Joaquin.*" She found herself moaning in time to his motions, her nails digging into his forearm. "God, don't stop."

She could come from this. She knew she could—if he just gave her time.

He chuckled. "I could do this forever."

He kept up the rhythm, his mouth moving from one nipple to the other and back again while she slowly unraveled, pleasure burning white hot inside her, stripping away her self-control, nothing in her heart or mind but Joaquin and what he was doing to her.

She came with a cry, climax washing through her like a tide of bliss. Joaquin stayed with her, prolonging her pleasure with clever fingers, keeping up the rhythm until she was spent. When she finally came back to herself, she found him watching her through eyes gone black.

JOAQUIN WATCHED the ecstasy on Mia's face relax into contentment, a knot in his chest. God, he loved her—loved her, wanted her, was out of his mind over her. He hadn't planned this, but here he was—head over heels with a woman he'd known for one week.

Then again, it had been one *hell* of a week.

He wasn't sure she would understand if he told her. She had such a skewed notion of herself and not much experience with close relationships. Maybe she'd spent too many years in uniform dealing with Powell's harassment to see how special she was. If only she could see herself the way Joaquin did.

He withdrew his hand from between her legs, his fingers drenched from her climax, and circled a still-puckered nipple with her juices, her musky scent filling his head. He lowered his mouth to her breast, flicked his tongue over that nipple, taking her taste into his mouth. Oh, he wanted more of that. "*Mmm.*"

She smiled up at him, a shy kind of smile, then twisted,

reaching for the condom. She tore it open, but he took it from her and set it aside on the bed.

"There's no hurry." He kissed her breastbone, licked her nipple again. "When I'm inside you, I want you to enjoy it as much as I do."

"I've never been able to come like that."

"There's a first time for everything."

*Watch it, amigo. Don't get cocky.*

He had learned long ago that the secret to satisfying women in bed was actually paying attention to them, seeing what they liked, and not assuming that their sun rose and set on his dick. Women were different than men when it came to sex. A guy could finish in two minutes and call it good. While there were probably women who got off like that, most would find it to be a major disappointment.

His Tío Danilo had once told him that women were like flowers. If given the proper attention, they would open and share their beauty in their own time, but without the right care, they would wilt while still buds and never bloom. They hadn't been talking about sex—Joaquin had been all of ten years old—but Danilo's words certainly applied in the bedroom.

"In Spanish, your name means *mine*. Isn't that convenient?" He kissed her breastbone, felt her heartbeat beneath his lips. "'Eres Mia' means 'You are Mia.' But lowercase with an accent on the 'i', *eres mía* could mean 'you are my woman.'"

She gave him a drowsy, sexy smile. "That's fun."

"I think so." He knew she would be hypersensitive, so he started small, nibbling the undersides of her breasts, tickling the sensitive skin of her inner thighs, skimming her puckered nipples with the flat of his palm.

She began to revive, her desire stirring again.

When she seemed ready, he reached between her thighs, using what he had learned about her to bring her to the brink once more, her nails digging into his arm, her eyes closed, her breathing rapid. "Joaquin, *please.*"

He took the condom out of its package, rolled it down his length, then settled himself between her thighs, mindful of her injuries. "Open your eyes, Mia. Look at me."

She did as he asked, her eyes looking into his as he entered her, penetrating her with a single, slow thrust that made them both moan.

Oh, she was heaven.

"God, Mia." He fought to rein in his need, giving her a moment to get used to him. Then he started to move in deep, slow strokes. "Does this feel good?"

She didn't answer, her eyes drifting shut, her lips parting.

He'd take that as an emphatic *yes.*

He kept his rhythm slow, willed himself to stay relaxed, wanting to make this last, to give her the time she needed. But she was so tight and hot, and it had been a long time since he'd been with a woman.

He might have tried to ride her high, rubbing his cock against her clit, but he was afraid that would put pressure on the wound near her hip. Instead, he withdrew from her, raised himself up and sat back on his heels, wrapping her legs around his waist.

Her eyes flew open. "What...?"

But her question turned into a moan as he entered her again, rocking into her with deep thrusts, his hands now free to play.

He saw that she was watching what was happening between her thighs, an expression of blatant hunger on her face. No, she was watching his abs contract and release as he drove into her.

Mia liked muscle? That was fine with him.

He glanced down, too, and almost came right then, the sight of his cock moving in and out of her, stretching her, filling her, almost too erotic to handle, her pussy bright pink beneath that thatch of red curls, her delicate inner lips like petals.

*Relájate. Relax.*

He reached down, toyed with her, stroking her clit *just* the way she liked it. It wasn't long before she was at the edge, her hands fisted in the sheets, her skin flushed, her knees bent and drawn back. *Dios mío*, she was beautiful like this—strung out on sex, not worried, not even thinking.

Her eyes flew open, went wide. "Oh, my God, *Joaquin*."

His name became a cry as a second orgasm took her, the bliss on her face straining his tattered self-control. He fought to stay with her, to drive her pleasure home, but he was too far gone now, her inner muscles contracting around his cock.

He shifted again, stretching himself over her, holding himself off her so as not to hurt her. Then he let himself go, driving himself into her until climax overtook him, shattering the world around him and turning everything to light.

For a time, he rested on his forearms, his cheek pressed to hers, his heart still pounding in his chest, her fingers tracing patterns over the skin of his back. Then he took hold of the condom and withdrew from her, tossing the condom in the bedside trash before taking her into his arms.

She ran her fingers through his chest hair. "I knew you'd be good in bed."

Joaquin was well on his way into a sex coma, but her words brought his eyes open. "What made you think that?"

"The way you dance. The way you kiss." She snuggled against him. "You're ... incredible. I'm afraid I'm going to end up addicted."

"Good." Joaquin drew her closer, taking her words with him into sleep.

## 16

Mia woke up to find herself in Joaquin's arms, her face pressed against his chest, one of his biceps pillowing her head, their legs tangled together. She inhaled the spice of his skin and smiled to herself, images from last night filling her mind.

*I want you to be happy. I want you to feel cherished. I want to make you scream.*

Joaquin had done all of that. Okay, maybe she hadn't *screamed* ...

"Good morning, *hermosa*." His voice was deep and husky. "Did you sleep well?"

"Oh, yes." She rolled onto her back and stretched, feeling as languid as a cat, her body purring.

He propped himself up on an elbow, ran his knuckles casually over her left breast, his dark hair adorably tousled. "Are you hungry?"

"I'm starving, but what I really want is a shower. I get to take these bandages off this morning."

He nuzzled her hair. "Want some help with that?"

"The bandages or my shower?"

"Either. Both."

Her pulse skipped. "I would like that."

They gave each other a minute alone in the bathroom. Mia had peed in front of guys in Iraq, but she really didn't want to go there with Joaquin. A little privacy preserved a lot of dignity as far as she was concerned.

After that was out of the way, they stood together near the counter to remove her bandages, Joaquin peeling off the dressing on her ribcage first. "I don't want to hurt you."

"Don't worry about it." It didn't hurt … much.

"That doesn't look too bad. You've got a nasty bruise, though."

At the sight of the graze with its tiny butterfly bandages, reality hit Mia in the face. This wasn't a luxury vacation. It wasn't a lover's retreat. She was here because she was hiding from a man who wanted to *kill* her and possibly also Joaquin, a man who had already killed two, possibly three, other people.

She fought back a pang of fear. "At least it's not infected."

The bandage on the wound on her hip was more painful to remove, the wound with its many stitches looking much angrier.

"Sorry." Joaquin's expression turned troubled. He tossed the bandages into the trash, drew her against him. "When I think how close he came…"

His words trailed off, as if he couldn't bring himself to finish the thought.

Mia rested her head against his chest. "It's like my world is breaking apart, and I can't seem to stop it."

"You stopped it. Your quick reaction saved your life. You made yourself a smaller target, and you fired back. You stopped him." Joaquin stroked her hair. "I won't let him hurt you again. *We* won't let him hurt you—you and I, the cops, the FBI. The bastard has the feds after him now. They'll find him. You're not in this alone, Mia."

This was new to Mia—knowing that someone was standing with her, that she didn't have to face this by herself. "I'm not used to this—being close to someone like this, trusting them."

"I know." He kissed her forehead.

For a moment, a long stretch of seconds, he held her, his skin warm, his heartbeat steady beneath her cheek. Then he let her go, walked to the shower, and started the water. "Is the temp good?"

She reached in, felt the spray. "Perfect."

They stepped into the shower together, taking turns washing each other, Joaquin's touch more tender than erotic.

Afterward, they dried off, and Joaquin helped her put on fresh bandages using the gauze and medical tape the nurse had given them. Then they dressed together, Mia pulling on another pair of yoga pants with a pastel blue top and a gray fleece vest, while Joaquin slipped into jeans and a black turtleneck.

Joaquin left the bedroom and built a fire in the woodstove, while Mia made the bed and tried to straighten out her own emotions. "I think I saw some potatoes in the pantry," he called to her. "How does scrambled eggs, home fries, and coffee sound?"

Mia's stomach growled. "Delicious."

Joaquin tried to keep the conversation light during breakfast. He'd known that all of this would catch up with Mia eventually. She was strong, but even the strongest person wouldn't be emotionally immune to someone trying to kill them.

As they were cleaning up, Mia's parents called. Joaquin finished the dishes, listening to her side of the conversation. What he heard made him want to take the phone and tell her parents to go fuck themselves.

"No, it's not like that. He and I are not living together. I met Joaquin through his work. He's a photojournalist. Yes, Dad, that's a real job. He's a Pulitzer Prize winner. The Pulitzer Prize?" Mia looked over at Joaquin, annoyance and disbelief on her face. "It's pretty much the biggest honor a news photographer in the United States can receive. It means he's among the best."

From what Joaquin could tell, neither of them had asked Mia how she was doing or expressed concern for her safety.

"No, no, we're not going through that again. There's a man out there who wants to kill me, and all you have to say is that I should've gotten married? Joaquin? Yes, he is—Mexican American. I don't know—Catholic, I suppose. I haven't asked. Good God, Mom! No, he's not here illegally. His family has lived in Colorado since before it was a state. You know what? I have to go now. I have to go. Bye."

She ended the call. "They drive me crazy. My dad said that I had no business going to college or joining ROTC and that I ought to have stayed home and gotten married instead. My mom wanted to know whether you're a US citizen, where you go to church, and whether you and I are sleeping together."

*Pendejos.*

"You should've said yes." Joaquin didn't mean it, of course. He was just pissed. He raised his voice and held an imaginary phone to his ear, pretending to be Mia. "'Yes,

Mom, we're sleeping together—and last night I came twice.'"

Mia gaped at him—and burst into laughter. "Oh, that's perfect. That's what I'll do next time."

Joaquin walked over to Mia, rested his hands on her hips. "How about I give Jack a call and ask about the two of us going to see the horses. Would you like that?"

Her face lit up. "Would we be getting in the way?"

"Getting in the way?" Joaquin handed her the receiver for the landline and punched the button that said *Ranch House*. "Why don't you ask Jack?"

Joaquin was putting her on the spot, he knew, but she still didn't get how things worked at the Cimarron.

"Hi, Janet. It's Mia. Good, thank you. Is Jack there?" Mia gave Joaquin an exasperated look, obviously uncomfortable about asking Jack for anything. "Jack, hi. It's Mia. Joaquin and I thought it might be nice to see the horses, but I don't want to bother you or get in your way."

An amused smile came over her face. "Okay. Thank you, sir. See you soon."

"What did he say?"

"He said, 'It's about damned time you asked.' He'll be here to get us in twenty minutes."

They put on warmer layers and were ready to go by the time Jack got there in his big extended cab pickup. On the drive down the mountain to the barns, he shared the history of the ranch's success breeding quarter horses.

"How do you know what a foal will look like?" Mia had no idea.

"You look at the dam—the mare. To some degree, it's genetic roulette, but that's what makes it interesting. Still, a champion mare and a stud with a long line of breeding successes like our Chinook are more than likely going to produce worthy offspring."

Jack parked behind the house and walked with them to the barn, joined by Nate and Megan's seven-year-old daughter Emily, who wore jeans, little cowboy boots, and a pink cowgirl hat, a sparkly butterfly painted on one little cheek.

Emily smiled shyly when Jack introduced her to Mia. "My daddy says you were a captain. Were you a pirate?"

Mia laughed. "Nope. I was in the Army like your grandpa. We don't have ships."

Emily looked disappointed.

"Miss Emily," Jack said, "would you like to show Mia the horses?"

Emily led the way inside the barn to the stalls where Jack and Nate housed the pregnant mares. "These are the mares that have foals inside them."

Joaquin had brought his camera and started shooting, his lens on Mia. Her amazement when she got her first glimpse of the palomino mares. The sweet smile on her face when one of the horses ate carrots from her hand. Her elation when Emily led her to a litter of week-old kittens in the straw.

"Can I have all of them?" Mia held two of them up to her cheek. "Aren't they adorable, Joaquin?"

"Yes," Joaquin said.

But all he could see was Mia.

Mia poured herself and Joaquin glasses of wine, while Joaquin built a fire. "Did you hear what Jack said about Chinook breeding three mares a day? Can you imagine having sex with three different women every day for months on end?"

She realized what she'd just asked him. "Don't answer that."

He chuckled. "I can imagine having sex with *you* three times a day. How's that, *hermosa*?"

Mia's heart seemed to skip a beat. "What does that mean —*hermosa*?"

He closed the iron door on the wood stove and walked over to her, taking his glass of wine from her and pressing a kiss to her lips. "It means *beautiful*."

Without thinking about it, she shook her head. "I thought it meant something like sweetheart or honey."

"What was that about? You just shook your head and rolled your eyes at me."

Heat crept into Mia's cheeks. "I'm a realist. I was always the tomboy, the girl who climbed trees and played softball. I'm much more at home in combat boots than dresses. I'm not very curvy—you know that now. My mom said—"

"She said you have your father's square jaw, and Powell called you the Iron Maiden." Joaquin shook his head. "Yeah, I've heard that. Now, hear me."

He leaned closer, looked into her eyes, the intensity of his gaze making her breath catch. "I know that your breasts fit perfectly in my hand. I know that your nipples are excruciatingly sensitive and pucker in my mouth. I know that your waist is narrow and your hips are round and your ass is nice and firm. I know the sweet look on your face when you come. I know the cry you make. I know how your nails feel when they dig into my skin. I know how you taste. You're beautiful, Mia."

Mia's throat went tight.

She swallowed, whatever emotion she'd been feeling

instantly transformed into irritation. She had a master's degree and a good job. She'd been a captain in the United States Army, for God's sake, and served two deployments. She had no debts. She was strong and healthy. Why did any of this matter?

Except that it did.

"What are you thinking?" He reached over, tucked a strand of hair behind her ear.

"I'm thinking how pathetic I am to want so desperately for what you just said to be true."

"Oh, Mia. I wish you could see yourself the way I see you." He frowned, as if remembering something. "Maybe you can."

Mia watched as he set his wine glass aside and went to retrieve his camera.

He scrolled through the images, shaking his head. "The light in the barn wasn't good. These are too dark."

He glanced around. "Wait just a minute."

He retrieved something from his camera bag—a light meter—and moved around the room with it. Late afternoon sunshine streamed through the sliding glass doors, making the wood floors gleam. But that apparently wasn't good enough.

Joaquin went from one room in the cabin to the next, grabbing every lamp that wasn't fixed to the wall, from big floor lamps to the tiny lamp from the nightstand.

"What exactly are you doing—or do I want to know?"

But he didn't seem to hear her. "I don't have a light kit with me. All I've got is one lousy bounce."

"A *bounce*?" She had no idea what that was.

He didn't seem to hear her, but moved lamps here and there, taking lampshades off, adjusting them, and using duct tape to hold them where he wanted them. "I think this will make a decent softbox."

Whatever that was.

She sipped her wine, feeling as if she were watching some strange reality TV show about home decorating with too many lamps.

He set a chair in the middle of his lamp forest.

"I'll put the bounce here." He took something out of his camera bag—a folding silver reflector—and set it across from the chair. Then he turned on all of the lamps and closed the blinds, shutting out the daylight. "Come sit here."

"You're taking my photo." Okay, fine. She would indulge him. "Shouldn't I put on some makeup or something?"

"You don't need it."

She sat on the chair, feeling incredibly self-conscious.

He held the light meter close to her face, adjusted a lampshade, then picked up his camera and fiddled with the settings.

"What should I do?" She looked at Joaquin, then realized she should probably be looking into the lens.

He started taking photos. "Do whatever feels natural."

She stuck out her tongue.

"Nice."

She smiled, then looked away. "Nothing really feels natural sitting here while you take pictures three feet from my face."

*That* was an understatement.

Mia had never felt more self-conscious in her life.

Joaquin lowered the camera, scrolled through the images, then knelt beside her. "Now, Ms. Realist, try to tell me the woman in this photograph isn't beautiful."

~

JOAQUIN WATCHED the play of emotions on Mia's face, watched her struggle to take in the photos of herself.

He broke it down for her. "Look at your big blue eyes, your delicate red eyebrows. You've got ridiculous cheekbones and a cute little nose. I love your mouth, that lower lip. Your face is a perfect oval—no square jaw here. Your skin is almost translucent. Your red hair is thick and shiny and feels like silk."

She lifted her gaze to his. "You didn't do anything to the images?"

"No. Nothing. Look." He scrolled to the next and the next. "You're cute even when your tongue is sticking out or you're nervous."

"Can we do that again?"

"Sure." He could shoot Mia all day.

After that, they played. Mia smiling, laughing, being silly. Mia with her hair drawn over her mouth like a mustache. Mia hugging her knees.

"Wait just a sec." She jumped up and ran into the bedroom, emerging a few minutes later wearing her bathrobe over a bra and panties. "Is this okay?"

She wanted him to photograph her barely dressed.

Joaquin swallowed—hard. "I'll get rid of the chair. Bring the sheepskin blanket that's on the top shelf in the bedroom closet."

They laid the sheepskin blanket on the floor, and Mia lay down on her uninjured side, looking somehow both sexy and innocent.

Joaquin moved the lights around, took a light reading, then got down on the floor beside her. "Just be yourself."

He clicked away, moving her hair, adjusting her robe.

Mia on her side, her head propped up on her hand. Mia with one creamy shoulder bared. Mia without the robe in her bra and panties. Mia on her back, arms above her head, red hair fanned across the white sheepskin.

Joaquin showed her the photos. "Do you see how sexy you are?"

She sat up, turned her back to him, her legs curled beneath her. "Undo the clasp."

"Are you sure?"

She nodded.

He did as she'd asked, some part of him wondering how he was going to get through this without spontaneously combusting.

She looked at him over her shoulder, the trust on her face putting a hitch in his chest. Then she turned to face him—and let her bra fall to the floor.

*Madre de Dios.*

She was shy at first, covering her breasts with her arm, then letting her hair fall over her breasts, one pink nipple peeking through her strands.

*Damn.*

"Beautiful." He showed her those photos, saw the impact they had on her, the change in her expression.

Mia's sense of herself was changing before his eyes. His camera was showing her a part of herself she hadn't seen before, a part of herself she hadn't known existed.

She grew bolder, leaving her breasts bared to him, pulling her hair over one shoulder, even lifting the weight of her breasts with her hands.

*Click. Click. Click.*

Joaquin couldn't help the way his body responded, blood rushing to his groin, his mouth going dry, his pulse picking up. But he wasn't doing this for his benefit. He was doing this for Mia.

He shared those with her, too. "This one—where your nipple is peeking out of your hair—is so fucking sexy."

Then she slipped off her panties.

Joaquin had only himself to blame. He had started this, and now he had no choice but to see it through—even if it killed him. "Lie down on your belly if you can."

She did as he asked, the soft mounds of her delicious ass making him want to set his camera aside to kiss them.

"God, Mia, you have no idea what you're doing to me."

Or maybe she did.

She smiled, raised her bottom just a little, giving him a glimpse of the treasures that were hiding between her thighs.

*Click. Click. Click.*

She rolled onto her side, bent one leg, showing him a bit more of her hidden beauty—red curls, those sweet inner folds, a hint of clit. Oh, how he wanted to bury his mouth there, to taste her, to feel her come against his mouth.

"Mia."

*Click. Click.*

The room must have been too hot, because Joaquin was sweating now, his cock threatening to split his jeans.

He showed Mia the images. "No Ice Maiden here."

Then she lay back on the blanket and played with a pink nipple, one knee raised, and that delicious female anatomy *right there.*

"To hell with this." He set his camera aside, grabbed her ankles, and drew her across the blanket toward him. "I need to taste you."

## 17

Mia's heart tripped, wetness pooling between her thighs, Joaquin's forcefulness and his use of strength striking unexpected sparks inside her. She hadn't known she would like that. "Okay, that was hot. You can skip the foreplay."

"Why would I want to do that?" He bent her knees back, settled himself so that his face rested between her thighs, his gaze fixed on that part of her.

Mia shivered at the blatant male hunger on his face, anticipation making her ache. Out of nowhere, the lyrics of the song he'd sung to her popped into her mind.

*I want to kiss you everywhere, to taste your sacred places.*

He parted her and then tasted her with a single, slow lick.

She sucked in a breath and then another as he repeated that motion, the sensation sweet, a hint of what to come.

He licked her again. "I love how you taste—natural, like woman, like sex."

Then his mouth closed over her.

He explored her most sensitive places with his tongue, tugged on her with his lips, then suckled her, moaning as he drew her clit into the heat of his mouth.

Mia gasped at the shock of it, her hips giving an involuntary jerk, her fingers sliding into his hair. "*Joaquin.*"

She'd never felt anything like this, the pleasure ... *so* ... *intense*. What was he doing now? His tongue ... *Oh, my God*.

She couldn't think, couldn't talk, could barely breathe, pleasure staggering through her. Begging, panting, sweating, she fought to hold herself together, the heat inside her like a backdraft. She wanted him to put out the blaze, to stop this sweet torment. But Joaquin was relentless, sliding two fingers inside her, stoking the flames, making her burn hotter, giving her no choice but to surrender to him.

Her moans were cries now, every thrust of his fingers and the sucking motion of his mouth taking her closer to that bright edge, climax already building inside her. Oh, but he didn't let her go easy. For what seemed an eternity, he held her there, suspended on the iridescent brink of an orgasm, pleasure driving her out of her mind.

"Oh ... *Joaquin* ... I ... *oh, my God* ... you ... *aaah* ... fuck!" Nonsense, moans, and word fragments mixed in a sexual train-of-consciousness plea for release.

She shattered with a cry, her body shaking apart in a rush of white-hot bliss that left her to float somewhere between heaven and earth.

She opened her eyes, found Joaquin watching her, his lips wet, his pupils dilated, the heat in his gaze sending a frisson of excitement through her.

He sat back on his heels, yanked off his turtleneck and jerked down his fly, shoving his jeans down his hips. Then, gaze locked with hers, he kissed his way up her body, stopping to taste her nipples before raising himself up and reaching for something.

A condom.

He unwrapped it, rolled it onto his cock, then settled himself between her thighs, entering her with a slow, deep thrust. "Mia."

It felt incredible—the stretch, the deep caress, his steel hardness.

He moved slowly, deliberately, his cock grazing her clit. She would have told him not to worry about her—she'd just had the orgasm of her life—but what he was doing felt so incredibly good. Burning again, she slid her hands up his arms, over his shoulders, and down his back, eager for the feel of him.

He was moving faster now, his eyes closed, his breathing rough.

She clung to him, wrapping her legs around him, orgasm building inside her again with such speed and intensity that it startled her. It had *never* been this easy for her.

Faster, harder.

Joaquin drove into her now, every thrust filling her, rocking her, inching her closer and closer.

"Oh ... my ... *God*."

He caught her cry with his lips, his kiss filling her mouth with her musky taste, strong thrusts drawing out her climax. But he wasn't far behind her, groaning out her name as bliss carried him away, too.

∾

MIA'S HEAD rested on Joaquin's chest, her body replete, the

warmth of his skin and the heat from the fire warding off any chill. "Joaquin?"

"*¿Sí, mi amor?*"

"It's never been like this for me before."

He drew her closer, kissed her hair. "Me neither."

J OAQUIN PUT ALL the lights back where they belonged. Then the two of them made a dinner of pasta and salad together, Joaquin in his boxer briefs, Mia looking distractingly sexy in her bathrobe. He told her about his cousins—the forty she hadn't yet met—sharing the good and the bad of having such a big family.

Mia listened, laughed at his stories of getting into trouble as a kid, and did a pretty good job of keeping all the names straight. There was something different in the way she looked at him now, a vulnerability on her face that hadn't been there before, a softness and gentleness in her gaze he'd never seen. He hoped it meant what he thought it did.

He hoped she was falling in love with him, too.

Joaquin had never felt more naked, more exposed. He'd thought he was in love a couple of times before, and he'd had some hard crushes. But he'd never felt like this, his heart wide open, every part of him from his brain to his balls unguarded. It left him feeling like he was flying—and scared the shit out of him.

Love had to be a two-way street, and he couldn't be sure how Mia felt about him. Her life had been thrown into chaos by a killer. The fact that she had turned to him was gratifying, but it didn't necessarily mean that she cared for him the way he cared for her.

On top of that, she didn't have much experience with relationships, not just with men, but also close family relationships. She'd spent her life fending for herself. He had no idea how she'd react if he told her how he felt. He didn't want to overwhelm her or freak her out, which meant he needed to let her set the pace.

*If it's meant to be, it will work out.*

That's what his *abuelita* had always told him. But then, as now, her words didn't make him feel better.

Mia lit candles and poured glasses of white wine while Joaquin got dinner on the table. The meal was perfect, but Joaquin barely noticed what he was eating. All he could think about was Mia.

*You have it bad, cabrón.*

Yes, he did.

"What should we do with those photos?" Mia asked as they cleared dishes away.

"We'll do whatever you want. They're yours." Joaquin had never intended to keep them. "I could give you the memory card. You could tell me which ones you want to save, or I could erase all of them by reformatting the disk."

They ended up on the sofa together, scrolling through the images one by one, giving Mia a chance to see them again before Joaquin deleted them.

"I can't believe that's me."

"That is one hundred percent you—no retouching, no makeup, *nada*. I wasn't even coaching you. You came up with all of those sexy poses yourself."

"I guess that's true."

"You know it's true."

They were down to the last few shots when a noise on the deck brought the conversation to a halt.

"Someone's out there," Mia whispered, getting to her feet.

A sound like quiet footsteps, snow squeaking.

Joaquin set the camera aside, ran for his holster and weapon. "Grab the shotgun, and go into the bedroom. Lock the door."

"But *I'm* the soldier. I'm not helpless."

"I know you're not helpless, but he wants you not me. I'm not letting this bastard get another shot at you."

She ran on bare feet to where the shotgun stood propped against the wall, grabbed it and the box of shells, and disappeared into the bedroom.

Weapon drawn and loaded, Joaquin walked over to the closed blinds, peeked outside, then let out a relieved breath. "Come see our intruder."

He set the pistol down on the table and picked up his camera, then opened the blinds so that Mia could see.

She stepped out of the bedroom carrying the shotgun, her expression transforming from fear to delight. "Oh, it's beautiful!"

The mountain lion—a big male—stood outside on the deck, looking at them with what could only be feline horror on its face.

Cougars were notoriously shy around people.

"I wonder if he's cold." Mia ditched the weapon and knelt down on the opposite side of the glass. "Look how long his tail is."

The mountain lion hissed, scratched at the glass, then took a few backward steps, clearly unsettled to find himself this close to humans and outnumbered.

Joaquin got a couple of shots of the cougar before it turned tail and vanished into the night.

"Wow." Mia stared after the mountain lion, a big smile on her face. "I've never seen one in person before."

Joaquin sent a text message to Nate just to let him know the mountain lion was in the neighborhood and got a quick thank you in reply. Then Joaquin and Mia picked up where they'd left off, deleting the last of the nude photos and checking out the shots he'd just taken of the mountain lion.

Mia slid a hand up Joaquin's thigh, cupping him through his boxer briefs. "You know what I found in the bathroom?"

"Uh..." His brain had gone blank.

"There's a giant tub."

"A giant tub, huh?" He set aside his camera. "Is it big enough for two?"

MIA HELD onto the edge of the tub, her knuckles white, Joaquin pounding into her from behind, one clever hand busy with her clit. "Oh... my... *God!*"

She came fast and hard, pleasure swamping her in a wave of perfect bliss.

Joaquin let himself go, his fingers digging into her hips as he came. He sagged against her, breathing hard, pressing kisses to her spine. "I thought you said you couldn't come like this."

Mia laughed, only too happy to be proven wrong. "You make me into a liar."

"You should make a list of all the ways you think you can't come so that we can work our way through them."

"You are very sure of yourself." She loved that about him. Somehow, he managed to be confident without all the macho bullshit.

He grinned. "I really am."

He got rid of the condom, and they sank back in the tub together, Mia resting against Joaquin's chest, neither of them speaking, silence stretching between them, warm and golden in the afterglow.

She hadn't known it was possible to feel this close to another person—or to feel so at ease in her own body. Images drifted through her mind. Joaquin with his camera focused entirely on her. A photograph of a pretty woman stretched out naked, a teasing expression on her face. Joaquin looking up at her while his mouth devoured her.

That pretty woman was Mia. Joaquin had used his camera to show her a side of herself that she hadn't known was there. She still didn't know how to feel about it. Everything was so new—her ability to come so easily and have multiple orgasms, her sense of self, her feelings for Joaquin.

It was as if a missing piece of her life's puzzle had fallen into place.

She ought to feel elated, and yet...

Was this even real? When they left this place, would he still care about her, or would their lives go back to the way they'd been before?

She forced her doubts aside, not wanting to sour the sweetness of the moment.

He broke the silence. "Are you cold, *mi amor*?"

The water was only lukewarm now.

"A little."

They climbed out, dried each other, then crawled naked into bed.

"Come here." He slid an arm around her. "Thank you for trusting me today. I know it took a lot for you to pose for me like that. It meant a lot to me. It's the most erotic thing I've ever done with my camera."

Mia raised herself up to look into his eyes. "Thank you,

Joaquin. What you did for me this afternoon ... I didn't know men like you existed."

He tucked a strand of hair behind her ear. "I'm glad I found you, too."

⁓

MIA WALKED toward the elevator wearing ACUs and combat boots, her footsteps echoing through the parking garage. Out of the corner of her eye, she saw movement. Her head jerked around, her gaze seeking the source.

Nothing.

Unable to shake the feeling that someone was watching her, she kept going, sand churning beneath her feet, making it hard to hurry. She saw the security door, the small room in front of the elevators glowing with fluorescent light.

A man's voice. "Mia."

She turned, heart thudding, but again saw no one. Driven by a growing sense of panic, she ran for the security door and locked it behind her, shutting out the blowing sand and the darkness.

She turned toward the elevator, saw her own reflection in the mirrors on its doors. Why was she in uniform? She'd resigned her commission, left the Army behind. She shouldn't be wearing ACUs. She didn't even own any.

"Mia." He was there, behind her, the mirror reflecting his black hoodie—and the pistol in his hand.

He was going to kill her.

She reached for her weapon as he opened fire, panic like ice in her blood, but her pistol wasn't there.

*BAM! BAM! BAM!*

"Who are you?" she shouted, bullets tearing into her, her

blood spilling in the sand, making rivulets, tiny rivers of red. "Who are you?"

All she could see was his feet walking away.

"Mia! Wake up!" Joaquin's voice pierced her nightmare.

Awake now, Mia found herself sitting up in bed, confused and covered in cold sweat, her heart racing. "He was behind me. I couldn't see his face."

Joaquin turned on the bedside lamp, light chasing away the shadows. He drew her into his arms. "You're safe. It was just a dream."

"It felt *real*."

Joaquin stroked her hair. "Do you want to tell me about it?"

She described the nightmare to him, the details quickly slipping away, while the fear it had caused lingered. "I reached for my weapon but couldn't find it. I asked him who he was, but he didn't say. Then he opened fire, and I knew I was dead."

"That's not how it went in real life." Joaquin's voice was deep and soothing. "When he showed up, you were ready. You shot back, and he ran."

"He said my name."

"Did you recognize his voice?"

She shook her head. "I wish."

"*Pobrecita*. You're shaking like a leaf. Come."

Mia got out of bed and slipped into her bathrobe, while Joaquin put on a pair of boxer briefs and a T-shirt. She followed him out to the living room and sat on the sofa, watching while he stoked the fire and poured her a whiskey.

He sat beside her. "Did you have nightmares after your deployments?"

She took a drink, shuddered at the taste. Why did people like this? "After our convoy got hit by that IED, I had nightmares for a while, mostly about LeBron Walker bleeding out."

Blood in the sand. Rivulets. Tiny rivers.

"Did he make it?"

She took another drink. "He lost that leg, but he survived. He's got a wife and kids now. They seem happy."

"That's good."

Mia swirled what was left of her whiskey in the glass. "Have you ever done something you regret, something you'd give almost anything to change?"

"Regrets?" He pondered that for a moment. "Nah, not really. Nothing useful comes from looking backward."

She supposed he was right about that. "There are times I wish I'd never reported Powell for sexual harassment or looting, that I'd been one of those people who knew what was going on and said nothing. Things might have been so much different."

"What did he do to you, Mia? Can you tell me?"

They were talking about nightmares, so Mia might as well tell him. "He was friendly at first. Then he started saying inappropriate things like, 'Your lips would look so hot wrapped around my dick' or, 'I bet you're one of those chicks who loves anal.' Which, by the way, I am not."

"*Hijo de perra.*" Bastard.

"One day, he grabbed my butt. When I smacked his hand away, he squeezed my breast and told me that he only supported women in the military because it kept a fresh supply of pussy close by and that women in uniform were useless otherwise"

Joaquin's expression had gone hard. "That's not just sexual harassment. That's sexual assault."

She nodded. "After I reported him, Powell took his anger out on me, trying to turn every man in the company against me with his Iron Maiden stuff. I guess I shut down. I figured if my chain of command didn't care that he'd harassed and assaulted me, they wouldn't care about a little name-calling. Then I found out he was looting with the others, and I reported him. They didn't care about that, either."

Joaquin reached out to cup her cheek. "You did the right thing. You're the only person in that whole clusterfuck who has nothing to regret. The truth is important, Mia. Without it, we're all lost."

"That's what I've always believed, too, but will it be worth it in the end if he kills me? What if he kills you?"

Joaquin took her free hand, determination turning his gaze to steel. "That's *not* going to happen."

The conversation shifted to lighter topics after that—Mia's desire to get a house with a big yard so she could plant things and dig in the dirt, Joaquin's wish that he could transition away from photojournalism to doing more nature and wildlife photography. And then the whiskey was gone, and Mia was buzzed and sleepy.

They went back to bed, Joaquin holding Mia close.

This time, she didn't dream at all.

## 18

Joaquin and Mia spent Sunday cocooned together, Joaquin doing all he could to make Mia forget. He made her breakfast and strong coffee, talked with her, made love to her in the shower, on the sofa, in bed. They went for a hike in the bright sunshine with the snowshoes Joaquin had found in the closet, then warmed themselves by the fire with cups of hot chocolate.

They talked about everything and nothing. Their childhoods growing up in Colorado. What they liked to do on their days off. Their favorite places to hike and ski. Then Joaquin told her about his friends, sharing war stories from the newsroom with her, leaving out the scary stuff, like last month's terrorist attack, and focusing on the good memories, the things he thought might make her laugh.

"Holly worked for the CIA?" Mia stared at him, open-mouthed.

Joaquin chuckled. "That look on your face right now— that was all of us when we heard. None of us had a clue."

"I feel like I know them now."

"Hang with me long enough, and you'll meet them. You've already met Darcangelo and Hunter."

After that, he showed her his family's private website with its birthday tracker, events calendar, and message board. "There's a spot for family recipes here. This is where my mom and dad updated everyone yesterday to let them know I was okay."

It took him a moment to remember that it was all in Spanish.

"What's your middle name?" Mia's cheeks were flushed from sex and sun.

"My middle name? Um... " All this fucking must have shorted out his brain because he had to think. "I have two. Joaquín Cristián Delgado Ramírez."

"Wow. That's pretty."

"Spanish is a pretty language. What's yours?"

"Mine is nothing that fancy. Just Rose. Mia Rose."

"I like it. It fits you. No wonder you like flowers."

After sunset, snow started to fall. Joaquin and Mia accepted an invitation to join the West family for Sunday dinner and a movie, good food, good wine, and good company putting a perfect end on a perfect day—or a day that might have been perfect had the threat of a killer not been hanging over Mia.

"I'm afraid to fall asleep," Mia said as they crawled into bed. "I'm afraid real life is going to catch up with us."

Joaquin drew her close. He knew exactly how she felt, but he didn't say that. She didn't need empathy right now. She needed someone to be strong for her. "Whatever happens, Mia, I'll be right here."

Real life caught up with them at eight in the morning, when Joaquin's cell phone buzzed. He fumbled for it in the darkened room. "Ramirez."

"You're still asleep? Must be nice."

"Darcangelo." He sat up, saw that Mia was awake now, too. "I *was* still asleep. What's going on?"

"I wanted to give you a heads up. Wu is going to call you two soon with an update. Right now, he and the two special agents are in one of the interrogation rooms with that asshole Powell. He's saying some offensive stuff about Mia—dark, hateful stuff. He says he hasn't had anything to do with the murders or the attempt on Mia's life, but he's cheering on whoever is behind this. He says he can't wait to read about her murder in the paper."

"*Hijo de puta*. Put *me* in an interrogation room with that son of a whore. I'll take the bastard apart."

"Hey, if I were running this show and it weren't against the law, I just might give you that chance."

"Do they have any real evidence against him?"

"Not yet, but Wu says everything in this investigation is pointing to him right now. He has clear motive, at least where Mia is concerned, and he lives within easy driving distance of all the victims. They're trying to get something out of him that will justify a search warrant. I expect you'll be hearing from Wu or Shoals the moment they're done questioning the bastard."

"Okay."

"Also, speaking of papers, that reporter is sniffing around the building again, sidling up to people."

"I'm not surprised." Joaquin had known Cate wouldn't give up.

"Old Man Irving would ban her from the building, but he doesn't want to have to deal with your dickhead boss."

"I can't blame him for that. Hey, thanks for the heads up."

"*De nada*." Darcangelo ended the call.

Joaquin turned around to find Mia standing in the doorway to the bedroom, barefoot and in her bathrobe, worry plain on her face. "That was Darcangelo. He says Wu and the FBI guys brought Powell in for questioning. They don't have any real evidence yet, but everything else seems to point to him."

He refused to tell her the rest of it. That son of a bitch had hurt her enough with his vile bullshit. She didn't need to hear more.

"Was there anything else? You two talked for a few minutes."

"He said Wu and Shoals will probably be getting in touch with you this morning to give you an update on the case. He didn't say why. He also said Cate is hanging around the cop shop again, asking questions."

"Great." Mia walked into the kitchen and started making coffee, as if they hadn't just been talking about a man who wanted her dead. "What do we want for breakfast?"

MIA WATCHED the Black Hawk land, snow swirling in the rotor wash. Special Agent Shoals had called her a little more than an hour ago to let her know that he and Wu were on their way out to the ranch with news. She had expected them to drive, not fly in. "Isn't this a bit dramatic?"

"Your taxpayer dollars at work," Jack muttered.

"Oh, Jack." Janet shook her head. "They don't want to risk driving up and giving away Mia's location. Flying is also a lot faster."

"I hope they arrested that bastard," Joaquin said.

"So do I." Mia desperately wanted this to be over.

Jack sent his foreman to pick Shoals and Wu up and headed back inside with Janet, Mia, and Joaquin. "Coffee? Hot chocolate? Something stronger?"

"Coffee, please." Mia never turned down caffeine.

"Nothing for me," Joaquin said.

Jack made his office available to Mia and Joaquin, leading Wu and Shoals their way when the men arrived.

Shoals shook Mia's and Joaquin's hands and then started telling Mia how a firearm leaves marks on brass shell casings and bullets that help law enforcement connect both brass and projectiles to a specific firearm. "When the firing pin strikes the primer—"

"I know how firearms work." Mia didn't mean to be rude, but she didn't feel like sitting through an hour-long lecture on something she already understood.

Wu looked like he was fighting back a grin. "The shell casings left in the shooting and disappearance of Mr. Meyer, the two murders, and the attempt on your life came from the same firearm."

Shoals gave Wu an irritated sidelong glance, as if Wu had stolen his big news, then went on. "We worked with CGIC—the Crime Gun Intelligence Center here in Denver, also known as Operation Hot Brass—and have been able to confirm that the same shooter is behind all of this."

That was it? They'd flown up in a freaking Black Hawk to tell her that?

"Didn't we already know this?" Joaquin was under-whelmed, too.

"We suspected it, certainly," Shoals said. "But now we know for a fact that the shell casings at these crime scenes came from the same firearm. This is now evidence that is admissible in court."

Okay, admissible evidence. That was something.

"What about Powell?" Mia had to know.

"We questioned him and let him go—for now."

"He has alibis," Wu said. "He said he was home with his wife at the time all four crimes were committed, and she corroborated that. We'll be checking into that further. We're also looking into everyone else involved in the looting."

"The big reason we flew out here was to get a sample of DNA from both of you."

Mia couldn't have heard him right. "DNA? Why do you need that?"

"We now assess that when you fired back, you hit him, Mia."

"I hit him?" Mia felt a stab of savage satisfaction.

"Good." Joaquin gave her hand a squeeze.

"It was probably just a minor graze, but it was enough that he dripped blood where he was standing. It wasn't much—just a couple of drops. The initial forensic sweep missed it. A team from the Colorado Bureau of Investigation found it. We just need to make sure that it's not *your* blood, given that your blood was at that same crime scene. Mr. Ramirez, you weren't cut or grazed, were you? No. Okay, well, even so, you were at the scene, so we'd like DNA."

Mia met Joaquin's gaze, saw that it made sense to him, too. "What do we do?"

Shoals picked up his briefcase, set it on Jack's desk, and opened it, taking out two small boxes, kits of some kind. "We can do that by buccal swab. It has to be done by the book, of course, because it's evidence, so I'll need to handle the swab. It needs to be done at least thirty minutes after you've last had something to eat or drink."

So much for finishing her coffee.

They walked back out to the living room, where Nate

had a big fire going in the fireplace. Shoals and Janet got into a conversation about the different people they both knew and had worked with, while Wu seemed impatient, the scowl that was a permanent part of his face deeper today.

"Is this taking you away from your other work?" Mia asked him. "I know this isn't your only case."

"There are never enough hours in the day." When he looked at her, there wasn't anger in his gaze, just weariness.

After thirty minutes had passed, they went into the kitchen, where Shoals washed his hands, put on Nitrile gloves, and took out a small swab. "Open wide."

He scraped the inside of Mia's cheeks, first one and then the other, and then stuck the swab into a tube that held a small amount of liquid. Then he took off his gloves and started from the beginning again. Clean hands. New gloves. Buccal swab on Joaquin's inner cheeks. "That's it."

"What happens now?"

"We'll take this straight to the CBI lab and put a rush on it. We ought to have results within forty-eight hours."

"What if he's not in the system?"

"Then he's not in the system," Wu said. "But when we find him, we'll already have the tool we need to convict him."

"Every piece of evidence is a dot on the page, a piece of the puzzle," Shoals said. "Connect the dots, put the pieces into place, and the picture comes together. That's what we're doing right now—getting dots on the page, collecting pieces of the puzzle."

Joaquin turned to Mia, his dark eyes searching hers. He lowered his voice, spoke to her alone. "This is more than we've had so far."

For the first time since this nightmare started, Mia felt they were making progress.

A WINTER STORM was moving in fast, with at least a foot of accumulation in the forecast, so Joaquin chopped firewood. He wanted to make certain they'd be warm in case the power went out, as Nate said it sometimes did in big storms. Already, the wind had picked up, and the temperature had dropped.

Joaquin didn't mind the snow. He didn't mind the physical work either, as it gave him an excuse to hit something. In a rhythm now, he swung the ax, venting his rage on the wood, which flew apart into two pieces. He tossed them on his pile, then set another log on the stump, and swung again.

*Crack.*

If Mia's chain of command had done their job, she might not be in this situation, and people might not be dying. Instead, they'd covered up for Powell, burying Mia's accusations against him, forcing her to work with a bastard who obviously had no respect for women, not even his fellow officers. They'd ignored her report about his looting, too, until they'd had no choice but to act. Their failure to do their duty had put lives in danger in Iraq and had almost gotten Mia killed in Denver.

*Crack.*

The cops were onto Powell now. They had DNA. If it belonged to Powell, they would lock him up and throw away the key. If it didn't, then the cops had next to nothing, and the killer was still out there. No one had been murdered these past few days. Wu had pointed that out. He'd said that

Mia was likely the killer's primary target—and that he had saved her for last like dessert or some shit.

Fuck him. He wasn't going to get her.

*Crack.*

Joaquin stacked wood on the deck, then carried a few armloads inside, where Mia sat at the table, studying the images Shoals had left her—images of the man who wanted to kill her. Mia had mentioned a few times that something about him seemed familiar. They were hoping that seeing the images might help her recognize him. But Joaquin could tell by the troubled frown on her face that it wasn't working.

He stepped out of his boots, took off his gloves, hat, and parka, then added wood to the fire, warming his fingers. "You know you don't have to keep looking at those. If it's not sparking anything, you should stop."

One of the images had been taken from the security camera in the elevator and showed Mia pistol raised, determination and terror on her face. It had made Joaquin's stomach knot to see it. He couldn't imagine how it affected Mia.

"I suppose this could be Powell. Shoals said the height and weight were right. The images are so dark and grainy. Why have surveillance cameras if they're useless?"

"Good question."

"I just don't understand why he would kill Andy or Jason." She had a pencil in her hand, and Joaquin could see she'd drawn something. "Why would he take their money and phones? His family is wealthy."

He shut the wood stove's iron door and went to sit beside her. "What are you drawing?"

She gave an irritated little shake of her head. "It's me being stupid and literal. Shoals called the evidence dots, so I made dots. So far, all I have is dots."

Joaquin looked at the page, saw dots labeled with the names of the killer's victims and a dot for Mia. "It might work if you knew how to arrange them."

"What do you mean?"

"You'd have to know why he's doing this, understand what each victim represents to him, right? Then you'd know how to arrange the dots, and you'd get your picture—metaphorically speaking."

"That's what I'm trying to do. I just can't figure out what Powell would have against Andy and Jason." She closed her eyes, pressed her fingers to her temple. "I wish Shoals hadn't given these to me. I don't want to look at them, and yet I can't stop myself. Can you get rid of them for me?"

"Are you sure?"

She nodded. "If I keep staring at them..."

She didn't need to say more.

He took the printouts and walked over to the woodstove, then opened the door and fed them to the fire.

HE STOOD JUST inside the alley, huddled against the snow, his head feeling as if it were about to explode. Where was that asshole?

He should have waited till spring or summer to do this. It was too fucking cold to be out like this in winter.

*Cold. Cold. Cold.*

He saw his d-boy hurrying down the street and stepped back into the shadows, taking the bills he'd lifted from Frank out of his pocket. It had been nice of the bastard to come loaded with cash. He'd probably been planning to pay his hooker, but he hadn't been that lucky. No last fuck for him.

The Doctor looked over his shoulder, then stepped into the alley and walked over to him, hands in his coat pockets. He probably had a piece hidden there. "You got cash?"

"You're late. My head is fucking killing me. What you got?"

"Sixty Oxy—ten mgs each and ten bucks a shot."

He didn't have six hundred bucks. "I got them for a fiver each last time. I'll give you three hundred."

The Doctor shook his stupid head. "Costs go up. Expenses go up. Hey, I'm a businessman."

He got in the dude's face. "You think I'm just another fucking junky? I'm a veteran, man. I was injured in Iraq. Mustard gas. Doesn't that mean anything to you?"

"Why are you wasting time with Oxy, man? You should be using the *real* stuff. It's easier to get, and it will take away your pain." Doc smiled.

"Heroin." He shook his head. "No way. That shit is expensive."

Doc shrugged. "You get what you pay for. Do needles scare you?"

"Needles? Fuck, no." He lived with them—needles in his brain, in his eyes.

*Stabbing, stabbing, stabbing.*

Would heroin do a better job of helping him than Oxy?

It's not like he had to worry about getting addicted—not when he planned to blow his own head off.

"How 'bout this—twenty-five Oxy for two hundred, and another hundred for five good doses of smack."

That would only get him through a couple of days.

"Just give me the Oxy for three hundred."

"For three hundred, you can have forty."

*You stupid son of a bitch.*

He was sick of this, sick of pain, sick of talking. With

sixty pills, he could make it a good few days, maybe long enough to finish this.

He drew out his pistol, put a bullet in the middle of Doc's surprised face, then grabbed everything he could—bottles of pills, heroin, a bag of weed, a syringe—and ran.

## 19

Mia stared into her coffee, mind and body exhausted. She'd had the nightmare again last night, jerking awake to find herself shaking and sick in the pit of her stomach. *Three times* she'd dreamed she was standing in front of the elevator. Three times she'd seen him in the mirrors and grabbed for a firearm that wasn't there. Three times, he'd opened fire, bullets hitting her, her blood running in rivulets—

"Mia?"

She jumped, realized Joaquin was talking to her. "Sorry. What did you say?"

He reached out, tucked a strand of hair behind her ear. "I asked Nate if he could come get us and give us some riding lessons this morning. As soon as he's back from driving hay out to their herd, he'll come get us."

Mia didn't want to go riding. She didn't want to move. She wanted to shut her brain off so she could sleep without dreaming.

She pushed a smile onto her face. "That sounds fun."

"Nice try, *mi amor*. I know you're not really into the idea, but I think you'll feel better if you get out of here, get some fresh air, and spend some time with Buckwheat."

Okay, maybe Joaquin had a point.

"Isn't it awful snowy for riding?"

"They have a riding barn."

"A ... what?"

"A big-ass barn with nothing but sand for riding indoors. It's heated, but it's not very warm. Fair warning."

"Wear layers. Got it." She got up from the breakfast table and went to dress.

While Joaquin caught up with his family on their message board, she put the breakfast dishes in the dishwasher and decided to wash a load of laundry, too, tossing her things in with Joaquin's. It gave her something to do and kept her mind busy.

Nate drove up in a big pickup with a snowplow attached to the front just after ten and gave them a ride down to the riding barn, which was exactly as Joaquin had described it —big, full of sand, and cold as a well-digger's ass.

Buckwheat was waiting for them, saddled by one of the ranch hands, who gave Nate the gelding's reins and tipped his cowboy hat at Mia. "Ma'am."

"Hey, Mia." Nate motioned to the horse. "Why don't you go first?"

Mia greeted Buckwheat, petting the velvet of his forehead. "Hey, big guy."

The gelding returned her affection with a low whicker, as if he knew she'd had a shitty night and needed a break.

Mia climbed onto the mounting block. "I don't have much experience at this."

"That's why I'm here." Nate checked the saddle. "Put your right foot in the stirrup and swing your left leg over his back. Good job."

From nearby came a clicking sound—Joaquin with his camera.

"It looks like you brought the paparazzi, Mia."

Mia laughed. "He follows me everywhere."

"Listen to you two. Aren't you funny?" Joaquin said.

Nate handed Mia the reins. "Sit up relaxed and straight in the saddle so that your shoulder, hip and foot are aligned. Hold the reins loosely in your hands. Now make a little cluck and squeeze lightly with your heels."

Mia did as Nate told her and felt a thrill when Buckwheat began to walk, more than a thousand pounds of animal moving beneath her. She went around the barn three or four times, aware she must be smiling like an idiot.

"You're doing great," Nate called to her. "Now bring him to a trot. Squeeze with your legs."

Mia did what Nate said and felt Buckwheat's gait change and pick up speed. But now she was bouncing up and down in the saddle. "This is ... painful."

"Try to let your hips and behind absorb the motion. That's better."

Mia made a couple of trips around the barn. "Can I make him run?"

"How about a canter?" Nate talked her through that, Buckwheat instantly responding to the messages she sent with her body.

When she'd done that for a few minutes, Nate talked her through bringing Buckwheat to a gallop. And then Mia was flying. She heard herself laugh, felt the powerful animal shifting beneath her, a sense of freedom coming over her.

All too soon, it was over.

Nate had her bring the gelding to a walk and then caught Buckwheat's bridle. "Am I really supposed to believe you've never had riding lessons?"

Mia couldn't stop smiling. "I don't think it's me. I think it's Buckwheat."

Joaquin appeared near the mounting block, camera hanging from a thick strap around his neck, a big grin on his face. "You did great. How was that?"

"It was amazing." She climbed off the horse's back, walked around to kiss his muzzle. "I love you, Buckwheat."

She didn't see the glance Joaquin shared with Nate.

"Okay, caballero." Nate handed the reins to Joaquin. "It's your turn."

Joaquin handed Mia his camera. "Can you take this for me?"

"Show me how to shoot."

He adjusted some settings and took off the lens cap. "It's on automatic now. You point the lens and push this button."

"Got it." She adjusted her grip and stepped back.

Joaquin mounted Buckwheat and urged him to a walk and then to a canter, riding with the ease of someone born in the saddle.

"I didn't know he could ride horses."

Nate chuckled. "His grandparents had a farm near San Luis, so he's been riding horses since he was little."

It struck Mia as she watched and snapped photos that there were probably lots of things she still didn't know about Joaquin.

Joaquin stood back while Mia brushed Buckwheat down, relieved to see her smiling again after last night. He'd felt so helpless, watching nightmares shred her sleep and savage her emotions. He hadn't been able to do anything but hold her, talk to her, comfort her. It hadn't seemed like enough.

Nate came to stand beside him, speaking quietly so as not to be overheard. "I've seen horses work miracles with people. She's welcome to ride every day while she's here. If there's anything else we can do ..."

"Just pray they catch this bastard."

"You got it."

JOAQUIN LOOKED at the photo Mia had just taken and burst into laughter. "From this angle, my dick looks bigger than my forearm. The magic of perspective. Maybe I should use this for my online dating profile photo."

Mia had taken his camera and turned it on him while he'd been riding. She hadn't given it back when Nate had dropped them off at the cabin. She had asked him to undress, snapping photos of his naked body, though without his expertise or good light. The results were more comedic than sexy, at least in Joaquin's opinion. Still, it turned him on to be the object of her gaze—as the hard-on in these last few shots proved.

"You'd get a lot of hookups. A gorgeous face, abs, pecs, and a dick the size of a baseball bat—you'd be Mr. Popular."

"The only woman I want is right here." He was taking a risk saying this, but he wanted her to know that what he felt for her was real.

She set the camera aside, pushed him onto his back, and began to undress. "I had fun playing cowgirl today. I don't want to stop."

"You want to ride me, *hermosa*? I'm all yours." He reached between her thighs to tease her to readiness, but discovered she was already wet. Maybe taking nude photos of him had turned her on, too. He handed her a condom, held himself while she rolled it onto his erection, then helped her straddle him. "Saddle up."

She lowered herself onto his length, taking all of him inside her, her palms splayed on his chest for balance.

He reached up to cup her breasts and tease her nipples, loving the fact that both of his hands were free to touch her.

She began to move, sliding up and down his length.

She felt so good, her tightness gripping him, but he couldn't see how she was going to get a whole lot from that.

He caught her hips, stilled her, his cock deep inside her. "This is for *you*. Make it feel good for you."

She moved again, this time making slow circles with her hips, then canting them so that her clit pressed against his pubic bone. Her eyes drifted shut, her body tensing, her head falling back on a moan.

*¡Ay, Dios mío!* Good God, she made him burn.

"That's right, Mia. Use my body. Take what you need." He resisted the urge to thrust into her, holding his hips motionless, letting her set the pace, his hands still busy with her breasts, teasing her nipples into tight points.

He watched her pleasure build, her muscles gradually going rigid, the look on her face shifting from enjoyment to sexual distress, her hips grinding against him faster and faster until her lips were parted and she was moaning and her nails were biting into his pecs and he was close to coming, too.

"*Mi amor. Mi alma.*" My love. My soul.

He had to fight to keep his hips still, his balls drawing tight, every instinct he had telling him to pound into her. Then her pleasure peaked—and broke. The cry she made and the bliss on her face—so precious, so beautiful —undid him.

He grasped her hips, his cock still inside her, and let

himself go, bucking into her, riding her from below until pleasure claimed him, too.

Afterward, they lay together in bed, daylight streaming through the windows.

She trailed her fingertips along the groove in the middle of his belly. "A part of me can't wait for this to end so life can go back to normal. It feels like everything is on hold. But a part of me wants to stay here with you forever. I care about you so much that it almost scares me. What happens to us after this is over?"

Her words touched him, took him by surprise.

He held her closer, kissed her hair. "I'm not going anywhere. I want you in my life, Mia. You are everything to me."

She relaxed, her body going languid in his embrace, her voice sleepy. "By the way—what we just did? I've never come that way before either."

Joaquin drifted off to sleep, a grin on his face.

Mia had just done her first perfect *enchufa* when her cell phone rang. She laughed. "Not fair! I had it."

"That was *fantástico*." Joaquin went to turn down the music. "You're really starting to get this."

Mia hurried to the kitchen counter, where she'd left her phone. The display read "No caller ID."

She hesitated for a moment, then answered. "This is Mia."

"Ms. Starr? This is Catherine Warner from the Denver Independent. Please don't hang up on me. I need a quote from you. Please just give me some kind of reaction."

"Reaction?" Mia didn't understand. "Reaction to what?"

"You haven't heard?"

Mia's pulse tripped. "Heard what?"

"They got him. They arrested Bennett Powell about ten minutes ago."

"Wh-what?" The blood rushed from Mia's head, leaving her almost dizzy. "They arrested him?"

Joaquin stood beside her. "What's going on?"

"They arrested Powell," Mia told him.

"You mean you don't know?" said the voice in Mia's ear.

"No. I had no idea." What had happened? The last she'd heard, they'd had no evidence and Powell had alibis.

"Can you please give me a quote for my story?"

Mia took a deep breath to clear her head. "I'm grateful to the Denver Police Department, the Colorado Bureau of Investigation, the FBI and all of the experts who were involved in this case. It's a relief to know it's over."

"How does it feel knowing that a man who sexually harassed you—"

"How do you know about that?" Mia couldn't deal with this—not now. "I need to go. Sorry, Ms. Warner, but I don't want to answer more questions right now."

She ended the call, her hands shaking. "Can you call Julian or Marc or Wu and find out if this is true?"

But Joaquin was already on it. "Hey, D, I'm putting you on speaker phone. Mia's here with me. What the hell is going on? Cate just called from the paper to say DPD arrested Powell."

Mia sat at the table, her pulse still racing.

"Hey, Mia," Julian said. "Hunter's team just brought Powell in. His alibis turned out to be bogus."

"It's over." Mia closed her eyes, let out a relieved sigh.

"Looks that way," Julian said.

Joaquin rested a reassuring hand on her shoulder. "Bogus? What does that mean?"

"He coerced his wife into lying to cover for him. Wu discovered she was at work during the time each murder occurred and confronted her. Great detective work on his part. Wu pulled a warrant based on that, and Hunter's SWAT boys helped him execute with an assist from FBI SWAT. I don't have all the details, but I know they found heroin and some other street drugs, along with a metric shit ton of firearms and ammo. He didn't come easy. Hunter had to play rough."

"I'm jealous," Joaquin said.

"I think Shoals or Hunter planned to call you as soon as they finished putting out fires here. They've got to process him and go through a debriefing. You'll be hearing from someone soon. I'll make sure Hunter and Wu know you called."

"Thanks, man. We're grateful."

"I can't take the credit. That goes to Wu. Talk to you later." Julian ended the call.

Mia stood, walked into Joaquin's embrace. "I can't believe it's over."

He stroked her hair, held her tight. "You'll be repotting orchids again in no time."

She raised her gaze to his. "I don't know how I would have gotten through this without you, Joaquin. You came into my life and changed everything."

He kissed her. "That's what I was going to say about you. As for getting through this—I'm glad I was here. But you're one of the strongest people I know. You would have been fine without me."

Mia wasn't so sure about that.

AN HOUR LATER, they got a call from Jack letting them know that Shoals was on his way to the ranch—this time by car. Once again, Jack gave them the use of his office, where Joaquin and Mia listened to Shoals' version of the story.

"Powell resisted, and we had no choice but to escalate our response."

Joaquin wanted the gory details. Had Hunter punched him in his fucking face? Had he struck him upside the head with his nightstick? Had he kicked him in the balls?

Joaquin hoped it was all three.

But Shoals had already moved on. "We found a large amount of heroin in his possession, along with other illegal drugs and an arsenal that includes several nine-millimeter firearms. One of those was found in his vehicle."

This was good, but was it enough?

Joaquin wanted rock-solid proof. He wanted to *hear* that prison door clang shut and the key turn. "Did you find anything concrete that ties him to the murders—the black hoodie, Frank's wallet, Garcia's credit cards?"

"We found a black hoodie in the wash. Powell is too smart to keep the other stuff in his house. We figure he took what he needed and threw the rest in some dumpster in an alley. We will keep looking, of course. Just because we've affected an arrest doesn't mean we stop investigating. Our case against him doesn't hinge on those items. We have surveillance footage showing a man of his height and weight. More than that, we have DNA from the scene. We put a rush on the DNA we took from the two of you, as well as the DNA left at the crime scene by the shooter. Testing revealed three distinctly different sources. We'll take a sample from Powell tomorrow."

"What if he refuses?" Mia asked.

Shoals shook his head. "He is now under arrest, so he doesn't have a choice. The police can compel him to give evidence."

"Good." Joaquin was happy to hear it.

"Also—I can let you in on this—a known drug dealer was murdered in Denver last night, shot in an alley at point-blank range. Witnesses saw a man in a black hoodie running away. Preliminary testing on the casings we picked up at the scene tied that shooting to Powell, too."

"So much killing." Mia rubbed her temples. "What are the charges against him?"

"He's looking at three counts of capital homicide, one count of attempted homicide and assault with deadly intent for his attack on you, along with a bunch of drug charges. We can't charge him with anything where Mr. Meyer is concerned because we haven't found a body yet. I hope he'll realize the situation is hopeless and do what many of these psychopaths do—start bragging about who he killed and how and where. He must have wanted us to catch him because he never picked up his brass. Someone who doesn't want to get caught removes all ballistic evidence from the scene."

"Maybe he's an idiot," Joaquin said.

Shoals grinned. "That's a possibility, too."

"He's not," Mia said. "What happens now?"

"He has lawyered up—a big criminal attorney. We'll do our best to question him. He's got an arraignment tomorrow morning. We'll put our case together and, depending on how much he cooperates, the DA will either make a plea deal or take the case to trial."

"Will I have to testify?"

"Try not to worry about that." That was easy for Shoals to say. "If there is a trial, it won't happen for months."

"Can I go home?"

The expression on Shoals' face told Joaquin he thought this was a silly question. "The killer is in custody, so, yes."

Joaquin asked another. "Is there any chance he could get out?"

"Escape? I seriously—"

"That's not what I meant. Could the judge let him out on bail or some shit?"

"The man is accused of killing three people, including a brigadier general. I doubt any judge would grant bail." Shoals got to his feet, handed Mia a business card. "If you have any other questions, feel free to call my office. We're grateful to you for helping us bring this together, Ms. Starr."

Joaquin knew those last words were Shoals' way of acknowledging the risk Mia took in sharing classified information with his agency.

Mia stood, shook Shoals' hand. "Thanks for everything."

After Shoals left the room, Joaquin pulled Mia into his arms. "Are you okay?"

She nodded. "I couldn't believe it was real when it started, and now that it's over, I can't believe that's real either."

They found the Wests waiting for them in the living room.

"What's the word?" Jack asked.

Mia told them the good news, including the part about Hunter hitting Powell.

"Good," Nate said. "I'm sure he enjoyed that."

Joaquin's gaze met Nate's. "I know I would have."

"When is the arraignment?" Janet asked.

"Tomorrow. Shoals says he doubts the judge will grant bail."

"Three counts of capital murder?" Megan said. "Not a chance."

"That's great news, Mia. We're so happy for you." Janet hugged her.

"Thank you all for everything." Mia hugged her back. "I guess you'll want us out of the guest cabin."

Jack frowned. "Did anyone say that? You stay as long as you like. You're among friends here, Mia. Feel free to come visit us anytime."

Mia's smile lit up the room. "Thank you."

Nate headed toward the back of the house. "I don't know about the rest of you, but I feel like celebrating. Got any good champagne in the wine cellar, old man?"

"Damn straight, I do." Jack walked up to Joaquin and Mia. "I hope you'll join us for supper because I'm grilling steaks in your honor."

Mia kissed Jack's cheek. "How could we say no to that?"

## 20

Saying goodbye to the cabin was harder than Mia had imagined it would be. Drained by another night of bad dreams, she found herself close to tears as she packed her things and got ready to leave. The five happiest days of her life had been lived here. The cabin had been their sanctuary, their refuge, their little love nest.

Joaquin must have sensed her sadness because he pulled her aside while Nate loaded her bag into his truck. "Nothing is changing between us, *mi amor*. I was hoping you'd let me stay at your place tonight."

Some of the tension she was carrying faded. "I would love that. I don't think I could survive going cold-turkey off you just now. I warned you I'd get addicted."

He kissed her, grinned. "I'm happy to be your fix."

Fingers laced, they sat side by side in the front of Nate's pickup, Mia doing her best to ignore the lingering anxiety that gnawed at her.

Powell was locked up. The FBI was sure he was the killer. It was over.

She drew in a breath, released it, willing herself to let go.

But a sick feeling stuck with her through the day, playing in her head like a wrong note, niggling at her, and she couldn't shake it. Not when they unpacked, went shopping for groceries, and made lunch together. Not when they went to Joaquin's gym to work out. Not when she drove Joaquin to the police impound yard so he could get his truck out of evidence and towed to a garage. Not even when they had dinner with Joaquin's mom and dad, who treated Mia as if she were a long-lost daughter.

She thought she was doing a pretty good job of hiding her anxiety—until they got back to her condo and Joaquin brought it up.

"Hey, you don't have to pretend with me. You've been troubled by something all day. Don't keep it to yourself."

So much for hiding *anything* from him.

"Do you have emotional radar or something?"

He drew her into his arms, chuckling. "I don't need radar to read your emotions. I know you well enough to see when you're upset. It's in your eyes, *hermosa*. Everything you feel is in your eyes."

She sank into the comfort of his embrace. "I've got this feeling that something is wrong, that something terrible is about to happen, and I can't shake it."

"You've been through a lot this past couple of weeks. I think anyone in your shoes would feel the way you do right now." He didn't use the term post-traumatic stress, but she knew that's what he meant.

"I suppose that makes sense." But it didn't. Not really. "I served in a combat zone with a man who hated me and tried to make my life hell, and I didn't feel like this. When I close my eyes, I'm there at the elevator again. When I'm awake, I keep seeing him standing up there on that balcony looking at me and then walking away."

She pulled away from Joaquin and walked to the window, feeling too itchy to sit still. "It's like I'm forgetting something—something important. I can't put my finger on it. Sorry. I'm not much fun tonight."

Joaquin got to his feet, came up behind her, rested his hands on her shoulders. "Don't apologize. I don't expect you to entertain me. What you're going through—this is real life. I told you I wasn't going anywhere, and I meant it. Tell me, Mia—what are you feeling?"

"Powell's arrest—something doesn't fit."

"You're not sure the cops have the right guy."

She turned, stared up at him, his words hitting the nail on the head, unleashing a wave of panic. "I'm not. I can't say why. I'm being stupid. It's probably just stress, right? If the cops and the FBI say Powell did it..."

"Do you want to talk it through?"

A part of her just wanted to forget, but she couldn't think about anything else at the moment. "I'll get paper and pencils."

Joaquin headed for the kitchen. "I'll pour the wine."

Joaquin looked at his blank sheet of paper. "Okay, what am I doing?"

Mia shook her head, frustration and anxiety lining her face. "Hell if I know."

"Why don't you list the things that make you feel uneasy?"

She did that, naming them as she went. "Why would

Powell want to kill Andy and Jason? He thought Andy was funny—the company idiot, always getting himself into trouble. Everyone liked Jason."

Joaquin grabbed at a straw. "Did either of them give away anything during the investigation into the looting that might have upset him or made him look bad?"

Mia thought about this for a moment, then shook her head. "I don't know. I doubt Andy would have said anything. He was involved himself. Jason was the one who figured out that they'd been exposed to mustard agent. I remember him asking again and again how they'd been exposed, and no one would tell him."

She made a note next to Jason's name, then wrote down her next couple of questions. "Powell isn't an idiot. Why would he leave shell casings and slugs? Why would he start killing people now all these years later?"

"Sometimes people grow more bitter over time. His life went to shit after Iraq, didn't it? He went from being an Army officer to a disgraced asshole and a junky. Maybe he's spent these past few years growing angry and vengeful."

Mia wrote that down, too. "Why did he try to frame me if he planned to kill me?"

That made no sense to Joaquin either. "Yeah, I got nothing there—unless he's half out of his mind on drugs or some shit."

Mia hadn't touched her wine, the distress on her face making Joaquin's chest ache. "This isn't helping."

Joaquin reached over, pushed her wine closer. "Try to relax."

She picked up the glass, sipped, set it down again. "Okay, I'm relaxed."

He bit back a grin. "Right."

"We're getting nowhere."

"We're just getting started." Joaquin had an idea. "Shoals talked about this being a puzzle. What are the missing pieces? There are questions about why he framed you. There's Powell's motivation for killing Andy and Jason. There are the questions you've already written down. There's physical stuff, too, like Frank's wallet and Jason's wallet. There's Andy's body. He was the first to be killed, but..."

Chills skittered down Joaquin's spine.

He looked up to find Mia staring at him through wide eyes.

She shot to her feet again, paced the length of her small dining room. "That afternoon when I saw Andy, he was angry. He felt betrayed by the Army. He blamed me for the fact that he didn't get an honorable discharge and lost his disability benefits. Mustard agent left him with constant headaches, and he thought the VA owed him treatment. He didn't understand that many service members exposed to mustard agent have been denied disability benefits. It has nothing to do with anything I reported and everything to do with mustard agent. In other words, it's political."

"What about Jason and Frank? Did he have any reason to want to kill them?"

Mia picked up her wine, sipped, then sat again, a thoughtful frown on her face. "I was there with Andy in medical. He was terrified. He had inhaled the gas and gotten liquid agent on his skin and in his eyes. He shouted at Jason to help him, but Jason had a half-dozen others there, too. He was angry that Jason didn't know what to do for them. Jason did eventually speak with investigators."

"What about Frank?"

"Frank was the brigade commander and oversaw the

initial investigation. He couldn't stand Andy. He shouted at Andy in front of the entire company that Andy was a waste of a uniform. He probably played a role in Andy's discharge."

"What was Andy's rank? What was Jason's?"

"Their rank? Andy was an E2—private second class. Jason was young. I think he was a first lieutenant at the time."

Joaquin took up his pencil, wrote down the men's names again—and Mia's—in order of rank. Andy was at the bottom, and everyone else involved was above him. "If it's Andy, he's taking out his chain of command."

"Jason wasn't in his chain of command."

"But he was an officer, right?"

Mia stood, looked over at him, her face going pale. "The police have been through all of this, right? They must have eliminated Andy as a suspect somehow."

"There's only one way to find out. I'm calling Wu."

MIA DID her best to explain everything to Wu on speaker phone, telling him about her growing sense that something was wrong and walking him through the details of what she and Joaquin had discussed. "I can't find any reason why Powell would kill Andy and Jason. It just doesn't make sense until you flip it around. Andy blamed all of us for the fact that his life was a mess."

Wu didn't sound particularly impressed. "Ms. Starr, I see why you're concerned, and I understand why you've reached this conclusion. But we've kept a close eye on Meyer—his credit cards, his bank account, his cell phone and even his car. It's gotten us nowhere. If he's alive out there, he has turned his back on everything he owned. He has no hope of returning without giving himself away."

Mia hadn't realized that. "What about the bloody towels and bath mat that ended up in the wood chipper? Was the blood his?"

"We did take hairs and a semen sample from his sheets so that we'd have something in case we found a body. I don't know if they've processed it yet. We didn't put a rush on it or the DNA in the towels, just the samples you two gave us and the blood from the crime scene. I can check on the other stuff in the morning."

"Why can't you check on it now?" Joaquin asked.

"Because, Mr. Ramirez, even people who work at the CBI lab need sleep." Wu softened his tone. "How about you two come to the station tomorrow morning and we go through this then? We should have DNA back on Powell. We'll know definitively whether he was in that parking garage or not. I suspect we'll find that he's our doer. He fits the height and weight of the individual in the security footage."

"He and Andy were close in height," Mia said.

Wu went on as if he hadn't heard her. "The son of a bitch lied about his whereabouts and didn't want to give DNA. We had to strap him down and take blood, because he wouldn't open his mouth. Why would he do that unless he knows DNA will incriminate him? On more than one occasion, he told law enforcement how much he'd like to see you dead."

Joaquin glared at the phone, muttered something in Spanish, his gaze softening when he looked at Mia. "What about Mia's safety? You confiscated her firearm. Can you at least put a patrol on her house?"

"I can do that. I'll do my best to get your piece back to you quickly."

That was something.

"Goodnight," Wu said. "I'll see you in the morning."

Joaquin pulled out his cell. "I'm calling Darcangelo."

They went through the whole conversation again, telling Julian about Mia's misgivings and their suspicions about Andy.

"I asked Wu if he could check on the DNA from the towels and bath mat. He said he'd do it in the morning. Mia would sleep a lot easier if we knew definitively that the blood belonged to Meyer."

Julian must have been taking notes because he repeated what they'd told him. "I can call the lab, see if anyone's there. If they haven't processed it yet—you said Wu didn't put a rush on it—then it's not going to help you at all. You said Wu is putting in for extra patrols on your street?"

"Yes. I'm not sure Wu will follow through, but that's what he said."

"Wu is a good guy. If he said he'll do it, he will. I'll check to make sure the order has gone through. What's your address, Mia?"

Mia gave him the information, then thanked him. "I'm sure I sound crazy."

"You don't sound crazy at all. You sound scared, and I don't blame you. Let me check on this, and I'll call you back. You still got your Glock, Ramirez?"

"Yeah, and Mia has a shotgun upstairs."

"Good. Keep the firearms close by and ready."

"Will do. Thanks, man. I owe you."

"No, you don't." Julian ended the call.

Mia let out a relieved breath. "I know this will sound nuts, but I feel better. Just knowing they'll look into this makes me feel safer."

He took her hands, kissed them. "If you feel safer, then it was time well spent."

They settled on the sofa, Mia's shotgun propped against the wall nearby, and turned on the TV news, waiting for Julian to call them back. Wall Street down three hundred points. A school shooting in Alabama. More turmoil in Syria.

"This war—I feel like it's never going to end," Mia said.

Joaquin's phone rang, making Mia jump.

"It's Darcangelo." He answered. "Hey, what did you—"

Joaquin's eyes went hard, his jaw tight, making Mia's pulse ratchet. "Got it. Yeah. Will do. Thanks, man."

He ended the call, got to his feet. "The lab started the DNA test on the towels this morning. The blood on the towels and bath mat isn't human blood at all. They don't know what it is yet, but it's not human."

Mia's mouth went dry.

JOAQUIN RAN up the stairs behind Mia. "Darcangelo has a unit on the way. They'll escort us to the police station and from there, Darcangelo will take us up to the Cimarron. He woke up Wu, who put a BOLO out on Meyer."

Mia stopped so suddenly that Joaquin bumped into her, a stunned expression on her face. "Powell's leg. His shrapnel wound. He has a limp. The man at the nightclub, the man who shot at me—he didn't. That's it. *That's* what's been eating at me."

*¡Carajo!* That *right there* settled it.

The killer wasn't Powell. It had never been Powell.

It was Andrew Meyer.

"That's what your nightmares have been trying to tell you." Joaquin texted that information to Darcangelo, then followed Mia the rest of the way up the stairs.

He hadn't yet unpacked, so he grabbed his toiletries out of her bathroom, shoved them into his backpack and was ready to go. Mia had put everything away, so he helped her pack panties, toiletries, and a few changes of clothes into her duffel bag. They walked downstairs together and put their bags by the door.

Then there was nothing to do but wait.

Joaquin pulled Mia away from the windows, not sure who might be out there. He was taking no chances where her life was concerned. He drew her into his arms. "You are incredible."

"Not so incredible. If I had remembered the limp sooner, the police might have Meyer in custody instead of Powell."

"Don't be so hard on yourself. You haven't seen Powell in, what, five years?"

"I guess. You did your part tonight, too."

"I supposed I helped—a little."

She gave him a sardonic look. "You think?"

They sat on the couch, Joaquin glancing compulsively at his watch. "Darcangelo said the officer ought to be here in ten to fifteen minutes."

It seemed like an eternity with Mia's life potentially on the line.

While Mia ran upstairs to use the restroom, Joaquin checked his pistol again, tempted to keep it in hand. Using what he'd learned at the gun range with Hunter and Darcangelo, he found himself evaluating her condo in terms of security. Sliding glass door. Lots of windows. Open floor plan. Poor cover.

Yeah, not ideal.

He glanced at his watch again, saw that fifteen minutes had already passed. Where was this cop?

Mia hurried down the stairs. "The police car just pulled into the parking lot."

"We'll stay inside until he comes to the door."

"Right. Okay." Mia sat, her gaze moving over the windows.

A few seconds passed and then...

Red, blue, white. Red, blue, white.

The colors of police overheads flashed against her drawn curtains.

They got to their feet, Mia heading for the door.

Joaquin drew her back. "Wait. He'll knock."

"Okay. Have it your way, Mr. Protective."

"Damn straight."

Footsteps on the stairs. The chatter of a police pack set.

The doorbell rang.

Pistol in hand, Joaquin looked out the peep hole and recognized Petersen. "Oh, hey, we're going to have a nice little reunion. Remember Petersen?"

"How could I forget the cop who patted me down, cuffed me, and shoved me in the back of his car?" She picked up her duffel, slung it over her shoulder.

Joaquin opened the door. "Hey, Petersen."

"Ramirez. You two ready to go?"

Joaquin turned to pick up his bag.

It happened all at once. Gunshots. Mia's scream. The stunned look in Petersen's eyes as he toppled down the stairs.

Joaquin raised his pistol just as something hit him hard in center mass. His legs seemed to disappear beneath him, the world fading around him.

He'd been shot.

*Mia.*

She grabbed him, tried to pull him out of the doorway

just as a man in a black hoodie stepped out from behind her car.

*Meyer.*

Vision fading, Joaquin pushed Mia away. "*Run.*"

That's all he managed to say before pain and darkness took him.

## 21

"Joaquin!" Mia's heart seemed to explode in her chest. *Dear God, no!*

She couldn't get to him, couldn't help him, couldn't even reach his pistol.

Andy was running for her, pistol raised.

She started toward the shotgun, then realized that going after it would put her in the line of fire, Andy's heavy footfalls already sounding on her front steps.

She bolted for the stairs just as the son of a bitch cleared the front door and opened fire again.

*BAM! BAM! BAM! BAM! BAM!*

Her right arm went numb, drywall exploding in front of her face, bullets ripping into her walls, her own blood splattering the white paint.

*Shit!*

She reached the landing, ran into her bedroom and locked the door, using her left arm to block it with a chair. She backed away, ran for her phone, dialed 9-1-1. She gave dispatch her name and address. "Officer Petersen has been shot. He's down. He shot Joaquin Ramirez, too. They may be dying. We need help—SWAT and medical. Andrew Meyer is the killer. He's here."

*BAM! BAM! BAM!*

Andy put a few bullets through her door to blast away the lock. "Mia, you fucking bitch! You can't win. You might as well give up."

She ignored him, interrupting the dispatcher. "He's going to kill me if he gets through my bedroom door. Hurry for fuck's sake!"

*Please, God, no. Not Joaquin. Not my Joaquin.*

Knowing she had only moments, she set the receiver down, keeping dispatch on the line, and went to her closet, looking for something, anything, that she could use as a weapon.

Ski poles. They would bend. She threw them aside.

A baseball bat. It was too heavy for her to wield with one arm.

Bear spray! She had a small canister in her backpack somewhere. She searched the pockets, found it, and used her teeth to peel off the plastic safety tab.

Andy roared in rage, kicking at the door now, trying to dislodge the chair.

Mia looked down, saw blood dripping from her fingers. *Damn it.* She didn't have time to make a tourniquet. If Andy got through that door, her arm would be the least of her problems.

*Joaquin!*

She took cover as best she could inside her closet. She wouldn't give Andy a clear or easy target. If that fucker wanted her, he was going to have to fight.

She took a deep breath, tried to focus her mind and calm the pounding of her heart. If she wanted to help Joaquin, she had to stay alive. She *had* to stay alive. She'd passed combatives training, but she hadn't drilled in more than three years, and she'd never fought anyone hand-to-hand in real life.

Her bedroom door was coming apart, bits of foam and chipboard flying free.

Andy raged, kicked, slammed his body against it. "Open this fucking door!"

She got the pepper spray ready, tried to guess his height. She'd have only a second or two to keep him from blowing her away. If she could blind him, get the pistol away from him...

In the distance, she heard sirens.

"Do you hear that, Andy? They're coming for you. They know it's you. They're onto your little trick with the animal blood. They know you killed Garcia and Frank. They have your DNA from when I shot you."

That only enraged him more, the sounds coming from outside her bedroom more animal now than human.

The door splintered with a *crack*.

Andy kicked his way through the remaining pieces, shoving the chair aside.

Mia reached out of the closet with her left arm, aimed the bear spray at his face, hitting him dead in the eyes.

He screamed in pain, dropping his weapon and clutching at his face. "Cunt!"

She jumped out, lunged for the pistol, gripped it with her left hand, her right arm completely useless. He kicked at her, catching her in the sternum, knocking her back, crushing pain driving the breath from her lungs. The pistol skittered across her bedroom floor. She tried to reach it, pain almost making her sick.

Andy grabbed her by her hair, yanking her to her feet and throwing her back onto her bed. "You ruined my life!"

"You ruined your own life, you sad piece of shit!" She kicked him as hard as she could, hitting his face and throat, the pain in her chest making it hard to breathe.

Broken ribs?

Eyes red and watering, he fell on her, wrapped his hands around her throat and squeezed, trying to strangle her.

"I think I'd like killing you with my bare hands better."

*Oh, no you don't, you asshole.*

She took hold of a ski pole with her left hand and jammed its pointed tip into his temple. He shrieked and released her, blood flowing from a wound on his head now.

She sucked in air, pain shooting through her chest. "How's your headache now?"

He drew back his fist and struck her hard on the cheek, pain exploding inside her skull, lights dancing before her eyes, darkness dragging her down.

*Stay awake!*

If she didn't, she would die.

She fought the darkness, opened her eyes, saw Andy retrieve the pistol.

It was over.

Mia fought to hang on, pain and blood loss sucking her down. "I held your hand. When you were in medical, I held your hand. I helped you."

"Then you went and told Frank *everything!*"

The sirens were getting closer.

"You need to go, Andy. You need to run. They're almost here."

"I don't care." He took a few steps backward, pistol aimed at her. "When you're dead, I'm going to put a bullet in my head. You have no idea how hard it was to see this through, to live with this pain every day. I've wanted to end it for so long, but I held on so that I could watch you die first."

*BAM!*

Meyer howled, fell to the floor, looking in shock toward the doorway.

*Joaquin!*

He lay on his belly on the landing, pistol raised with one hand. "Stay... down..."

Whether Joaquin was talking to her or Meyer, Mia couldn't be sure. She rolled off the bed, taking what cover she could, just as Meyer raised his pistol again.

This time it was pointed at Joaquin.

Mia heard herself scream. "No!"

*BAM! BAM! BAM!*

Meyer fell to the floor and didn't move.

Mia struggled to her feet, kicked the pistol out of the bastard's grasp, and picked it up, tucking it into her waistband before hurrying over to Joaquin.

She pulled him onto his back, the physical act making the pain in her chest unbearable. She knelt down, touched his face. He was pale and cold and shaking from shock and blood loss. His parka and T-shirt were soaked with blood, a trail of red leading from the wide-open front door across the living room and up the stairs.

He looked up at her, pain lining his face. "You're ... safe?"

"Yes. I need to get something to stop the bleeding."

She dashed into the bathroom, grabbed a handful of washcloths, and ran back to kneel beside him, the pain in her chest making her work for every breath. She tore open his shirt, saw a bullet wound in his upper right abdomen, and pressed a folded washcloth against it, applying as much pressure as she could with one hand.

He grimaced, moaned, his jaw tight.

"I'm so sorry, Joaquin. I'm so sorry."

Worry came over his face. "You're ... hurt. You're ... bleeding."

Her arm throbbed now, blood dripping out from beneath the sleeve of her parka, staining her hand red. But he was much worse off, blood quickly soaking the washcloth.

She grabbed another, placed it over the first, and pressed harder. "Don't worry about me. I'm going to take care of you."

He reached up, cupped her cheek. "I don't think... it matters—"

"No! Don't say that." She tried to act like she wasn't scared to death. "You'll be fine. They're almost here. Just hang on."

"You're ... crying."

She was?

"I've never ... seen you cry before."

"I've never been afraid that you were fucking dying before!"

His lips quirked in a smile. "You ... are incredible."

"Stay with me, Joaquin." Tears ran down her cheeks. "Please, stay with me. I love you, Joaquin. I love you. Please don't leave me."

Why hadn't she told him sooner?

He seemed to fight for every word, his brown eyes looking into hers, his love for her shining through his pain. "*Te amo,* Mia. I love you, too."

Then his eyes closed again.

"No! Joaquin, please." But Mia was struggling now, every breath painful.

Darkness coiled around her, tightening its grip on her chest, making her dizzy.

She had to stay conscious, had to stay awake. If she didn't, she wouldn't be able to maintain pressure, and he would bleed out here outside her bedroom.

"Stay with me... I love you, Joaquin... I love ..."

Spots took over her vision, and then there was nothing.

MIA HEARD HERSELF CRY OUT, gentle hands pulling her from Joaquin and turning her onto her back, pain like a weight on her chest.

"Mia, can you hear me?" A familiar voice spoke to her, hands moving over her. "Shit. Some of this blood is hers. She's hit. Eight-twenty-five."

A burst of static. "Eight-twenty-five, go ahead."

"We need another ambulance. Female victim with GSW to her right arm. It looks like she's lost a lot of blood. I think she must have a collapsed lung or some kind of chest injury, too. She's having trouble breathing."

Someone put pressure on her arm, pain bringing her eyes open.

Julian's face loomed above her. "I know it hurts, Mia, but I've got to slow your bleeding."

"No. Help ... Joaquin."

"Just rest, Mia. He's in good hands."

"Jesus! Did Ramirez drag himself this entire way?" That was Marc.

"It looks like it." Julian's voice again. "He took the guy out from here in four shots—one to the pelvis and three to center mass. Her bedroom looks like a war zone."

"God! That fucker beat the shit out of her."

"You should see what she did to him."

She must have passed out again because when she

opened her eyes next, she was crying out in pain, EMTs with blue gloves touching fingers to her bare chest.

"There's no pneumothorax. I think we're looking at a fractured sternum."

Motion. Bright lights.

She was cold. So cold.

Snatches of conversation drifted around her.

"It looks like she put up one hell of a fight."

"We need to make sure her trachea doesn't swell."

"They tried to save him, but he was pronounced dead at the ER."

*Joaquin?* He was … dead?

Pain filled her, her heart seeming to shatter. She couldn't find the strength to speak, tears rolling down her temples.

"It sounds like he deserved it. I heard one of the cops saying he's killed three people, including a brigadier general."

No, not Joaquin. Andy.

Andy was dead.

Sirens. People rushing. A nurse putting an IV in her arm.

"Mia, we're going to give you some oxygen and something for pain, okay? Then we're going to get a CT scan of your chest."

"Joaquin?" she managed to say.

Then her pain faded along with all awareness.

Mia heard herself moan.

"Mia, you're in the recovery room. It's Doctor Aito. We took that slug out of your arm and put your humerus back together with some hardware. We also repaired the damaged nerve. How do you feel?"

"My chest ... hurts. My arm ... feels like you cut it off."

"Luckily, we didn't have to do that. We'll try to get your pain under control."

But Mia had to know. "Joaquin. How is Joaquin? Please ... tell me."

"Your friend and the police officer are still in surgery."

In surgery.

That meant they were both still alive.

*Thank God.*

Joaquin was alive, but his life was still on the line.

MIA WOKE to see daylight outside her hospital room window, her thoughts fuzzy from morphine.

"You're awake." Isabel, Joaquin's mother, stood beside her bed, a comforting hand resting on her left arm. "How do you feel?"

"Joaquin—is he...?" Oh, it hurt to breathe, the pain in her chest still sharp.

Isabel smiled, lines of fatigue on her face. "The bullet struck his liver. He made it through surgery. The doctor said they had to give him forty units of blood. They kept him in ICU overnight, but he's stable now."

*Thank God!*

Relief washed over Mia, bringing tears to her eyes. "I was afraid I'd lost him."

Isabel gave her a tissue. "So was I. I've been worried about you, too, *hijita*. You're hurt, too. Tell me what about you so I can tell Quino."

"I have a broken sternum where Andy kicked me, but no

heart damage. A bullet broke my arm, but they put it back together. They think I have a concussion, too."

Isabel stroked her hair. "You poor thing! Can I get you anything?"

Mia shook her head. "I just want to see him."

"We'll make that happen soon, but for now, you need to rest." She patted Mia's arm. "I can see why my son fell in love with you. You're very courageous."

An image of Joaquin lying on his belly at the top of the stairs, pistol raised, flashed into her mind. Bleeding, in pain, and weak, he had dragged himself across the living room and up the stairs to save her.

"I don't understand why you're being so kind to me. Joaquin was almost killed trying to keep me safe. He held me back and opened the door and …"

*BAM! BAM! BAM!*

Mia squeezed her eyes, shut out the memory of gunshots. "He saved my life."

Isabel took her hand. "The only person to blame is the murdering bastard who shot him, and he's dead. I'm proud of the man my son has become. If he loves you so much that he is willing to give his life for yours, then I love you, too. You're a part of our family now."

Mia found herself blinking back tears again. "Thank you."

"Elena's here. She wants to see you. Is that okay?"

"Elena's here?"

"Most of the family has been here." Isabel smiled. "They set up a special room for us last night because we were taking up most of the surgery waiting area."

That made Mia smile, too—and put an ache in her heart. She knew the police department had contacted her parents. Apparently, they'd just set off on a cruise and were somewhere in the Gulf of Mexico. They had sent her flowers and a card, but they hadn't gotten off the ship and flown back to the US to see her.

"Rest, *hijita*. We're just down the hall. I'll send Elena in."

Mia caught her hand, stopped her. "Tell Joaquin I love him."

Isabel gave her fingers a squeeze. "I will, but he knows, Mia. He knows."

JOAQUIN SAT PROPPED up on pillows and surrounded by friends, drifting in and out, trying to keep up with the conversation, his mind in a morphine haze.

"You're one hell of a shot, Ramirez," Hunter said. "You fired one-handed, right?"

"Yeah." A memory of Meyer raising his pistol and pointing it at Mia cut through the morphine, putting a knot in Joaquin's stomach. "I was afraid I wouldn't hit him."

"You got him—four times," Darcangelo said.

"I guess shooting at the police range paid off," Matt added.

Hunter slapped Matt on the back. "You're welcome anytime, Harker."

"I heard they just moved Petersen out of ICU. I guess the bullet ripped a hole through his lung. He came close to bleeding out."

"I'm glad he made it." Joaquin knew he could tell his friends anything, but the admission he was about to make wasn't easy. "I know it's wrong, but when I heard that fucker Meyer was dead, I was glad I was the one who'd killed him."

"If you're hoping one of us will tell you that you should feel sorry for that, you're barking up the wrong tree." Tessa

Darcangelo had a sweet Georgia drawl that made everything she said sound polite. "I'm glad you killed him, too."

"It was either him or you and Mia," Kara said. "I'm glad it was him."

"He killed himself," Zach McBride stood near the foot of Joaquin's bed, arm around Natalie's shoulders. "The moment he murdered that medic, he started down a path that put him in front of your bullet. All you did was pull the trigger."

"I'm so sorry, Joaquin." Sophie looked pale and upset. "It must have been terrifying for both of you."

Joaquin knew that hearing about what had happened to him and Mia couldn't have been good for Sophie, who had just been diagnosed with post-traumatic stress disorder thanks to the holiday party from hell. "Don't worry about me. You just take care of yourself."

She nodded, Hunter's fingers twining with hers.

"I'm going to be meeting the agencies involved to debrief this investigation," Reece said. "There was some good police work, but there were some oversights. I need to understand what happened and make sure our state law enforcement agencies are working together the way they're supposed to."

"Thanks, man." Joaquin reached out to fist bump Sheridan.

Cate stepped into the room. "Hey. I thought you might want this."

She set a copy of the paper on his lap, the words *"Deadly Shooting: Disgraced soldier murders two, wounds three in quest for revenge"* across the top of the front page.

"Good job, Cate."

"I'm glad you're okay." She gave him a tight smile, clearly still angry. "See you back at work soon."

Then she turned and left the room.

"Bless her heart. What was that about?" Tessa asked.

"She's the one who fucked up," Alex said. "She needs to get over it."

Joaquin drifted off, dozing while Alex told what he knew about Cate and the source she'd asked to steal documents.

A knock brought Joaquin awake again, and Holly stepped inside, walked over, and kissed him on the cheek. "Oh, my God, look at you! You're all tubes and wires. I hear you blew the bastard away. Good for you. Nick is still in Istanbul, but he told me to tell you to get better. I brought someone else who wanted to see you."

Holly stepped outside the door and came back in pushing a wheelchair.

"*Mia.*" Joaquin's heart skipped a beat at the sight of her.

One of her cheeks was bruised and swollen, her right arm bandaged and in a sling, a couple of IVs in her left arm. His mother had told him what Meyer had done to her—the fractured sternum, a gunshot wound that had broken her arm, a concussion. But apart from the bruises and the IV, she looked ... gorgeous.

Was she wearing *lipstick*?

"She said she wanted to see you, and the nurses were busy. I figured they wouldn't mind if I borrowed their patient—well, and a wheelchair."

"You went to her room?"

Holly gave him a look. "You didn't seriously think we'd let you keep her to yourself now, did you? After hearing what happened, I *had* to meet her."

Holly made introductions, going around the room.

Mia smiled. "I feel like I know all of you already. Joaquin has told me so much about you and your adventures."

"I'm sure it was all lies," Matt said.

Mia started to laugh, then grimaced, pressing a hand to

her chest. "Please don't be funny. It hurts too much to laugh."

"All right. Time to go." Hunter motioned toward the door. "Let's give these battered love birds some time alone. They probably have a lot to talk about."

Joaquin's friends filed out the door.

"See you later, Ramirez."

"Nice to meet you, Mia."

"But I just got here," Holly whined.

"You can talk to them later," Hunter said.

"Okay." Holly kissed Joaquin on the cheek again, then moved Mia closer to his bed. "Get better, okay? Mia, it was lovely chatting with you. We'll talk again soon."

And then Joaquin and Mia were alone.

"Holly came to your room?"

Mia reached out with her left hand, laced her fingers through his. "I knew who she was the moment she stepped inside. I told her what had happened and how you saved my life. I told her I had been waiting for a nurse to bring a wheelchair so I could visit you. She pulled a makeup kit out of her handbag, did my face and combed my hair, and then went off after a wheelchair."

"That's Holly."

"Your mother stayed with me for a while—Elena and Mateo, too."

Joaquin was happy to hear it. He'd asked his mother to look in on her, angry that she was alone with no family to watch over her. "You're one of us now."

"That's what she said. Do I get a page on your website?"

Did Mia know what she was asking? "We'll have to see about that."

"I want to kiss you, but I can't bend over."

"I'd love to kiss you, but I can't sit up higher without lots of cussing."

Mia gave a little laugh. "We're quite the pair."

Then her expression crumpled.

She raised his hand to her uninjured cheek, turned her face into his palm, kissed it. "I was so afraid, Joaquin. Those shots rang out, and you fell, and I thought I'd lost you. I don't know what I would have done."

"God, Mia, I'm so sorry. If I'd only seen him..."

"How could you? It was nighttime. He was wearing black and hiding behind my black car. No one saw him. Officer Petersen walked past him to the door and didn't see him. Please don't blame yourself."

"I heard him beating down your door. I wanted to get to you, but when I tried to stand, everything went black again. I had to crawl. I thought he was going to tear you to pieces before I could reach you. You fought so hard, but I could hear he was hurting you. When I looked up and saw him aiming that pistol at you... *Madre de Dios*."

"You saved my life."

Joaquin cupped her chin. "You *are* my life, Mia."

## 22

Joaquin was reading Cate's article about the shooting with Mia the next morning when Detective Wu knocked on the door and stepped into his hospital room. He asked to take their statements so he could close out the case.

"If you'd like we can wait until you're discharged and arrange for a victim advocate to be present."

"I'm okay," Mia said, though Joaquin could see in her eyes that the last thing she wanted to do right now was relive fighting for her life.

"No." Joaquin was done with this bullshit. He had a bone to pick with Wu anyway. The man had blown him off, and he and Mia had nearly been killed. "You want to talk to either of us, make an appointment after we're out of here."

Mia gaped at him, but Joaquin could see that she was relieved.

Wu nodded. "Just to let you know, the blood we found by the elevator at your condo did belong to Meyer. The DNA on the towels and the bath mat belonged to a cat. We're guessing Meyer came up with the idea of framing you just to be malicious. We spotted him in the background of security footage from the Botanic Gardens making his way toward the mulch yard with a backpack. We couldn't see his face, but he was wearing that damned hoodie."

"Did you release Powell?" Joaquin had to know. If that son of a bitch was on the street, Joaquin would make damned sure he went nowhere near Mia.

Wu shook his head. "He's still in custody. He was found in possession of several illegal drugs, and his DNA matches that associated with three unsolved sexual assaults. The judge denied bail, and the DA is certain we'll get convictions. Powell is up to his ears in his own shit now, so he'll be behind bars for a long time."

Joaquin was happy to hear that. "A rapist, huh? I'm not surprised."

"That must be why he resisted when you tried to sample his DNA," Mia said.

Wu nodded, then frowned. "I want to apologize to both of you, but especially to you, Ms. Starr. If I had put a rush on the DNA from those towels at the same time we rushed all the other DNA we collected for this case, we would have known to look for Meyer. When you called the other night, I ought to have listened. Your exemplary service record and your truthfulness during this investigation merited a better response from me. I was so certain that Powell was our guy. I was blinded by that."

"You weren't the only one who made those decisions." That was Mia. With her big heart, she was letting Wu off the hook. "What about Shoals and the FBI? They thought Powell was the one, too."

"They did, true, but it was my case." Wu turned to go. "Oh, one last thing. I never really thought you were the killer, Ms. Starr, but at the time you were all I had. If it were up to me, every head that failed you during your time in uniform would roll."

"Thank you." Mia watched him walk away.

Joaquin took Mia's hand. "Are you okay?"

"I was just thinking how hard that must have been for him to apologize."

Yeah, well, Joaquin was less impressed. "What do you know? Powell is a rapist."

"I'm not surprised. He was always *cruel*."

"It's not you that Powell hates, Mia. It was never you. He hates women. You were a target in his eyes the moment he saw you were female."

"I'm sorry for his victims, but I'm glad they're finally going to get justice."

"He assaulted you, too. He didn't rape you, but he assaulted you. It's justice for you, too, in a way." Joaquin hoped it would make a difference for her.

"I suppose you're right."

"He's going to discover that prison isn't a friendly place for rapists, not even West Point grads with rich daddies."

For a moment, there was silence, Wu's news a lot to think through.

"That poor cat," Mia said.

Joaquin caressed her hand with his thumb. "I wish we'd had that news sooner."

"I don't think I can ever set foot in my condo again."

Joaquin couldn't blame her for that. "You don't have to. Sell it. Put your stuff in storage until we're both healed and have time to decide what comes next."

"Someone has to clean up all the blood. I have to pack and move my furniture. It's going to be a long time before I can do any of that. The doctor said it could be three months before I can lift anything, not because of my arm, but because of my chest."

Joaquin had the solution to this. "We can hire a crime-scene cleanup crew to clean the place. My cousin José Luis —that's Elena's older brother—has a moving company. He would be only too happy to show up with his crew, pack your stuff, and move it all to my Uncle Danilo's U-Store-It. We can call my brother Antonio. He can bring his construction crew in to repair your place. You can put your condo up for sale without setting foot there again, spending a fortune, or doing any of the work."

"Really?"

"Really." He watched relief dawn on her face and lifted a strand of hair from her bruised and swollen cheek. "Big families come with benefits, and you're part of that family now, remember?"

And there was that smile—the smile that lit up his world.

MIA WAS RELEASED from the hospital two days later. She wasn't ever going back to her place, and she wasn't capable of doing much of anything with a broken arm and a fractured breastbone. She couldn't drive or lift more than a few pounds with her good arm. Even brushing her hair hurt.

Holly invited her to stay at her place. "We've got a lot of space and top-of-the-line security. Nick won't be back from his current job for a few weeks. I'm free to drive you to the hospital to visit Joaquin every day, and we can get to know each other."

"I would like that."

The four-bedroom condo Holly shared with her

husband was posh and luxurious with a fantastic view of Cheesman Park and the city beyond. Holly moved a recliner into one of their guest bedrooms so that Mia could sleep sitting up—the only way she was able to sleep at all. Holly also went to Mia's condo, packed up her toiletries, clothes, and shoes, and brought them to her place.

"My place is a mess, isn't it?" Mia asked.

Holly was deadly serious for once. "It looked like a massacre happened there. I'm so grateful that you and Joaquin are alive. I don't know how he was able to crawl all that way. He must love you very much."

Mia's mind flashed to the memory of him lying there, pistol raised. "Yes."

"But, hey, I need to take you shopping when you're better," Holly said. "Did you know that you have *three* pairs of hiking boots but only one pair of heels?"

Mia had planned to spend all day every day with Joaquin, but the Percocet they'd given her knocked her out. If she didn't take it, she was in too much pain from both her arm and her chest to function. She was only able to spend a few hours with Joaquin each day, holding his hand and savoring the fact that they were alive and together. The rest of the time, she was at Holly's place, talking with Holly or trying to sleep.

Holly was exactly as Joaquin had described her—beautiful, blond, and brilliant with a big heart. She had dinner delivered for the two of them each evening and made sure Mia was comfortable. She also taught Mia things she'd never learned, like how to apply makeup. Most of all, she made Mia laugh—even when laughing hurt like hell.

"You have the most beautiful skin, gorgeous eyes, and lips and cheekbones that make me jealous." Holly gently dabbed concealer on Mia's bruised cheek. "You don't need much makeup. In your case, less is definitely more—unless a bad guy has recently punched you in the face, and then more is more."

Three days after Mia's discharge they sat by the gas fireplace eating Mexican food that Mateo had delivered in person. He had wanted to let Mia know that he and his wife had started a fundraising drive for Joaquin and Mia to cover any medical expenses that weren't paid by their health insurance.

"It's so incredibly kind of you to include me." Mia hadn't even thought about medical costs—deductibles and copays and all of that.

Mateo took her hand, kissed it. "I knew from the first night Joaquin brought you to my place that you were the one—even if he tried to play it cool."

"That sounds like a story," Holly said after Mateo left, sitting down beside Mia, a glass of wine in her hand.

Mia told Holly how she and Joaquin had met, starting from the beginning. "I was rude to him. I'm surprised he spoke to me again."

"In his version of the story, he fell in love at first sight, so I don't think you have to worry." Holly smiled, as if remembering something funny. "When Nick and I met, we almost killed each other."

"Really?"

Holly told her how Nick had been sent after her, misled by his corrupt supervisor into believing that Holly had betrayed her country. "His boss thought I knew something I didn't know and wanted me dead. Nick didn't know at first that I was with the Agency, too. He kidnapped me, interrogated me, and had orders to kill me. Thankfully, he had a conscience. To his surprise, not only was I with the Agency, but I had higher security clearance than he had."

"And you both got over that?"

"Strange things happen when bullets start flying."

Mia knew that was true. Then something Holly said sparked a thought. "Do you still have high-level security clearance?"

Holly nodded. "I need it for the work I do."

"What kind of work is that?"

Holly gave her a sweet smile. "The kind I can't discuss, not even with kick-ass former Army officers."

"I figured." Relieved to have someone she could safely talk to, Mia shared the entire story of Tell al-Sharruken with Holly from the first time she'd reported Powell for looting to the night Meyer had caught up with her and Joaquin.

"And they buried it—the looting, the mustard agent?"

Mia nodded. "It's all classified confidential. Frank told me I couldn't speak about Tell al-Sharruken with anyone. When I realized the murders probably had something to do with what had happened there, I told the police—Marc and Julian and Detective Wu—and then the FBI. Lives were on the line. I couldn't take care of myself and let others die. But Meyer is dead. Powell is going to prison. Frank is dead. I guess it's over now."

Holly gave her a mysterious smile. "We'll see about that."

NINE DAYS AFTER THE SHOOTING, Joaquin came home from the hospital. His brother Antonio picked him up and drove him and Mia to Joaquin's condo, carrying Joaquin's shit for him as they made their way through the parking garage toward the elevator. The glass in the security door had been replaced. From a distance, it looked as if nothing terrible had happened there.

Joaquin slid his key into the lock. "Are you okay?"

Mia nodded, her gaze on the concrete floor.

He'd known this wasn't going to be easy for her. Her nightmares—even the ones she'd had since the night of the shooting—all started right here with her standing in front of these elevators.

Antonio held the door for the two of them. "Is this where...?"

Joaquin shot him a look that shut his mouth, but Mia's attention was focused on the elevator doors, where indentations from bullets pocked the steel. The wall hadn't yet been repaired, either. He reached over, took her hand.

"I'm fine." The tight lines on her face and her rigid posture said otherwise.

Antonio got them settled, then went down to open the security door for José-Luis and one of his crew, who carried up Mia's things—her clothes from Holly and Nick's place and the new recliner she'd bought to sleep in until her chest healed. They put her clothes in Joaquin's closet, set the recliner up next to Joaquin's bed, and then moved Joaquin's flat-screen TV and DVD player into the bedroom, speaking to one another in Spanish until Joaquin reminded them that Mia couldn't understand.

"Mom has been here with Aunt Aleta, so your fridge should be full. Dad and I are going to pick up your truck tomorrow. Anything else, brother?"

Joaquin had to sit, the small amount of walking he'd just done exhausting him. "I think we're good, man. Thanks. Thanks to you, too, *primo*."

"*De nada* ... er... You're welcome," José-Luis said. "Call if you need anything."

Joaquin glanced around. "God, it's good to be home."

Mia sat beside him. "The realtor just texted to tell me that my condo is going to be up on their website this afternoon. She thinks it will sell quickly."

"That's good news." Joaquin's family had pulled together and taken care of her place in a matter of days, all of her things now in storage. If her condo sold quickly, she'd soon be free to move somewhere new. He had ideas about that.

Joaquin took her hand. "I was hoping you'd stay here with me."

Her face brightened. "Are you asking me to live with you?"

He raised her hand to his lips. "I suppose that seems kind of sudden—"

"No. No, it doesn't." She turned so that she could face him. "It's just..."

"What is it?"

"I love your place. It's where you kissed me for the first time. The view is incredible. But the parking garage, the elevators ... Maybe I'm just weak, but it's going to take time to get over that."

He wanted to put an arm around her shoulder and draw her against him, but it would have been excruciating for her. "You're not weak, Mia. I think anyone who had lived through what you've lived through would feel that way. Let's see how it goes. If it's too hard for you, we'll come up with another plan. The important thing isn't this apartment. It's that the two of us are together."

For lunch, they heated some tamale casserole—just one dish in the lifetime supply of meals his mother and Tía Aleta had left in his fridge—then made their way to the table.

Joaquin sat, pressing a hand against his incision. "Getting shot sucks."

Mia sat across from him, careful to keep her upper body still, a little smile on her lips. "Is this what it will be like when we're old—both of us moaning and groaning?"

"Are you saying you want to grow old with me?"

Mia looked into Joaquin's eyes, smiled. "Maybe."

THE NEXT SIX weeks were among the best Mia could remember. No, the exercises she had to do for her arm every day weren't fun, and she still had to sleep in the recliner rather than in bed with Joaquin. There were nightmares, and there was pain. Still, every day felt like a treasure to Mia.

They were alive, and they were together.

They spent their time talking, playing video games on Joaquin's Xbox, watching entire series on Netflix, and going for short walks in the park. After a couple of weeks of involuntary abstinence, they figured out that if they were careful and Mia was on top, they could have sex again. With all the time in the world, they did a lot of that, too, though the condoms were growing old.

A month to the day after the shooting, they paid a visit to the women's clinic, where they both got tested and where Mia had an IUD inserted.

"In twenty-four hours, we won't have to use condoms again," she said as Joaquin drove the two of them home.

The sheer lust on his face made her laugh. "I can't remember what that feels like."

"I have a vagina handy if you'd like to find out."

"God, yes—but I'll probably come in a minute flat."

To their mutual delight, he lasted much longer than that.

They were able to handle longer walks now, so one morning Mia took him on a tour of the Botanic Gardens, showing him her favorite garden beds, which, she had to admit, weren't much to see right now.

Mia waved to one of her co-workers. "You have to use your imagination."

"Okay." Joaquin glanced around at bare ground, which was punctuated with tufts of dried grass and bare shrubs.

"This is *Bouteloua gracilis*—my favorite grass."

"You have a favorite grass?" He seemed to find this funny.

"Its flowers—what you might call tufts or seed pods—look like eyelashes. See?"

Joaquin bent down. "They do."

"One day when I have a yard of my own, I'm going to have tufts of *Bouteloua gracilis* growing here and there."

"You want a big yard?"

"One day when I can afford it."

In the evening, they often had visitors—family or friends who came by to check on them. One evening, Officer Petersen stopped by in a T-shirt and jeans. He wanted to apologize, but neither Mia nor Joaquin would let him. He surprised them with the news that he was leaving the police force.

"My wife couldn't take it if I went back out onto the streets."

Mia couldn't blame her. "Thank you, sir, for all you did to try to keep us safe."

"I wish I had succeeded."

Their last two weeks of leave seemed to fly by, the precious time slipping through Mia's fingers.

"I'm selling my condo," Joaquin said over breakfast one morning.

"What?" Mia hadn't been expecting this.

"Every time we come up the elevator, I see what it does to you. I don't want you to live someplace that reminds you of Meyer. I think it's time to start over, pool our money, and find a place that we own together, a place with no bad memories."

"But this place is so you."

"It's who I was before I met you. Let's find a place that is *us*."

The following Monday, they both went back to work, Joaquin at the newspaper and Mia at the Botanic Gardens, where she was placed on light duty, her arm still in a sling and her chest not yet fully healed. The staff welcomed her back with cake and a beautiful arrangement of living orchids to take home.

"Thanks, everyone. I'm so happy to be back."

"You're a valued member of the staff, and we're so glad you're here with us again," Kevin said, speaking for the group.

Michael, the head of security, pulled her aside to tell her they had changed their security protocols in light of what had happened and now checked any large bags or backpacks that guests wanted to bring into the gardens. "If we had done that, maybe we would have caught that bastard long before he had the chance to aim a weapon at you."

"Thanks, Michael. That means a lot to me."

Then all the men's heads turned, their jaws dropping, even Michael's.

Holly crossed the room, wearing a black leather biker jacket with a gray beaded skirt and crazy leather boots. "Hey, Mia, do you have a second?"

"Sure." Mia stepped outside with her. "What's up?"

"Cobra International Solutions—that's where I work—has close ties to the Pentagon going all the way up the flagpole. I told my boss what you shared with me, and our organization went to work on it. We had a few conversations with key people in the Department of Defense. Frank lied to you. Army brass buried what happened at Tell al-Sharruken, but the documents were never classified. Frank just wanted to silence you. There's some talk of congressional hearings, so it's going to come out sooner or later."

Mia stared at her, stunned. "Not classified?"

She handed Mia a heavy manila envelope. "I want you to have these. The story should be *yours* to tell."

## 23

Joaquin sat with Mia and Cate in the conference room, Mia's folder of documents in her hands.

"You two are living together now?" Cate asked the question with a smile, but there was an undertone of acid to her sweetness.

"We're house hunting," Joaquin answered.

"Nice." Cate gave him a fake smile.

Tom stepped into the conference room and closed the door, notepad and pencil in hand, another pencil behind his ear. He shook Mia's hand. "Ms. Starr. I'm glad to see you've recovered.

He sat, glanced around at them. "What's this about?"

Mia pushed the folder, which held copies of the originals, across the table to Tom. "Everything I'm going to tell you is included in these documents, which are files dating to 2013. I was told they were classified, but that was a lie. Now that I know the truth, I can share them with you."

Tom opened the folder, glanced through the pages, then looked up at Mia again, a hint of surprise on his face. "I'm listening."

Mia told Tom what had happened, starting with Powell's sexual harassment and verbal abuse and continuing through events at Tell al-Sharruken and the subsequent cover-up. "Andrew Meyer blamed me for the fact that he couldn't get disability benefits, even though I had nothing to do with that decision. He wanted to kill everyone he thought had played a role in his discharge and lack of benefits, and then he planned to kill himself."

"Did the cops know all of this?"

"Of course, they did," Cate blurted. "This must be what my source had heard. It's why they fired her. You knew, didn't you?"

Joaquin nodded. "Yes—but I wasn't going to land Mia in legal trouble by giving away supposedly classified information she had shared with me in confidence, not even to my own newspaper."

"Irving's guys knew, and I assume the FBI and other alphabet soup agencies knew as well."

"Yes, sir, but they thought Powell was the perpetrator. They believed what I believed, at least until the end—that Andrew Meyer was missing."

It was time for Joaquin to tell Tom the truth. "I did tip off a police detective to warn him that someone on staff was going to steal the files that Chief Irving was getting from the Pentagon."

Cate glared at him. "I *knew* it!"

"I had promised Mia that if she told law enforcement what had happened, she wouldn't have to worry about facing charges. She trusted me. I wasn't going to let you land her in hot water—or prison."

"You cost me a story."

"Now, I'm dropping that same story in your lap."

Cate turned to Tom, her face red with rage. "Aren't you going to fire him?"

"I didn't fire you, and you broke the fucking law."

"He betrayed this newspaper—and me."

"Your ambition betrayed you," Joaquin fired back. "You would have burned an innocent woman. All you wanted was a byline and a—"

"Fuck you!" Cate got to her feet, started toward the door.

Joaquin reached under the table, took Mia's hand in his to reassure her.

"Ms. Warner!" Tom's voice boomed through the room. "If you walk out that door, you're off the I-Team."

Cate stopped for a moment, then opened the door and disappeared.

Tom drew a breath, then glanced through the pages and asked a few questions. "You're saying Powell, the alleged rapist, was the looting ringleader?"

"Yes."

Tom closed the folder. "May I keep these?"

"Yes. Those are copies." Mia's chin went up. "I haven't talked to any other newspapers. I wanted Joaquin's paper to have the story first. But I did tape an interview with Laura Nilsson that is scheduled to air tomorrow night. She has all the same information that you have."

"How is Nilsson?"

Laura had worked on the I-Team until Tom's firing of Holly had prompted her to walk off the job. She was now one of the most beloved news anchors in the nation with a weekly news hour watched by millions around the world.

"She's great. Her husband, Javier Corbray, helped uncover the truth about these files so that I could tell this story."

Tom nodded. "The interview airs tomorrow night? Fair

enough. That gives us until deadline tomorrow to pull together a story. Thank you, Ms. Starr. We'll do our best to tell this story right and nail these bastards to the wall."

He stood. "Ramirez, we need to talk."

Mia's gaze met Joaquin's, and he saw that she was worried.

He leaned down, kissed her cheek. "I'll be right out."

Tom waited until she was gone. "I thought you weren't sleeping with her."

"I wasn't—at the time."

Tom rubbed a hand over the back of his neck. "I'm not sure what to say. I trusted you. We all did."

"Mia trusted me, too. If Cate had gotten those files, it would have been *my* fault because I convinced Mia to trust the police. I was forced to choose between the woman I love and my job. I made my choice."

Tom nodded, his blue eyes seeming to measure Joaquin. "In the end, it was for the best. Cate would have landed the paper and herself in a lot of hot water. What bothers me most is that you didn't trust *me*. If you'd told me what was going on, I would have reined Cate in. Have I ever thrown an innocent person under the bus for a headline?"

"If you want to write me up, fine. If you want to fire me—"

"Stop!" Tom rolled his eyes. "I'm not going to fire you, Ramirez. I could never replace you. You're the best photo-journalist this paper has ever had."

In that case...

Joaquin decided to take a chance. "I'm sick to fucking death of working on-call and doing bullshit news assign-ments. I want more challenging work."

Tom nodded. "Okay. Fine. I'll have Syd take you off the

on-call schedule, and you and I can talk about the kind of assignments you'd like."

This had turned out better than Joaquin had imagined.

"Tell Hughes to get in here. I'm giving her Cate's seat—and this story."

Anna was finally getting her spot on the I-Team.

"You got it."

MIA SAT in the living room of the great house up at the Cimarron, children of all ages running everywhere, people talking and laughing. All of Joaquin's I-Team friends were here with their families. Marc and Sophie. Julian and Tessa. Reece and Kara. Zach and Natalie. Alex Carmichael. Matt. Anna Hughes, who had interviewed Mia for the story that was in today's Denver Independent. They'd come together to catch up with Laura and Javier—and to watch Laura's interview with Mia on the big screen in the Wests' home theater.

Jack and Janet had laid out a spread for them, as always —everything from bacon-wrapped figs to a dozen varieties of cheeses with baguette slices to olives and charcuterie. There was even popcorn, tortilla chips, and salsa.

It felt like a party.

"Are you nervous?" Laura, with her pale blond hair and Swedish beauty, managed to look glamorous in blue jeans and a Nordic sweater.

"I'm not nervous about the interview. I am a little worried about the aftermath."

Laura reached over, gave her hand a squeeze. "I understand."

Mia knew she wasn't just saying that. Laura had told Mia

before their interview how she'd been kidnapped, held captive, and repeatedly raped by the leader of an al-Qaida splinter group until Javier, who had been a Navy SEAL at the time, had rescued her and helped her start her life over again. She had wanted Mia to understand that she wouldn't exploit her situation. She just wanted to tell Mia's story.

"Based on my interviews for a follow-up story, I think you can expect a lot of support from the military community. You're what an Army officer *should* be, and everyone in uniform knows that."

"I hope you're right."

"More wine?" Jack asked.

Mia shook her head. "No, thank you. It's a good thing you have a big house."

Jack glanced around, grinning. "Chaos. I love it. There was a time after the death of my first wife when this house felt too big, when I was the only one here. Then Nate came home, badly wounded. Those were hard times."

Mia could understand that kind of loneliness. Oh, yes, she could.

"My son met Megan, and she brought him back to life. She brought this motley crew with her. There isn't a day when I'm not grateful."

Janet must have overheard. She leaned down. "He loves having friends over—the more, the merrier. Nate and Javier served together. Did you know that?"

"Joaquin told me on the way up."

The doorbell rang.

"I've got it." Megan went to answer.

She returned with Kat, whom Mia had met at the newspaper, and her husband Gabe, together with their two preschoolers and their three-month-old baby girl, who had been born during the holiday party hostage crisis.

"She's tiny!" Mia peeked at the precious face poking out of the blanket. "What's her name?"

"Noelle Yanaha. We call her Yana. *Yanaha* means brave in Navajo. Everyone was very brave for us the night she was born. Joaquin stayed beside me and held my hand the whole time. He tried to get me out, tried to get the terrorists to release me. I couldn't have gotten through that night without him."

Then Kat introduced Mia to her husband, Gabe Rossiter. A tall, dark-haired man with the raccoon tan of a skier, he kissed Mia on the cheek. "It's good to meet you, Mia. I've heard so much about you. Hunter and Darcangelo won't shut up about you."

Mia recognized Gabe from the series of photos Joaquin had taken of the cartel shootout. He'd been giving Zach CPR. "I'm a member of their fan club, too."

Gabe turned to Joaquin. "So, I leave for eight weeks, and you go and get yourself shot? What the hell?"

"Did you miss the part where I took out the bad guy?"

"I heard that. Thank God." Gabe hugged Joaquin. "I'm just glad you're okay, man. It saves me having to kick your ass."

Mia could tell Gabe was moved by what had happened to Joaquin, even if he tried to hide his feelings behind humor.

"I'm glad those two clowns were able to help." Gabe motioned with a jerk of his head toward Julian and Marc. "I think they're having a marital spat."

The two stood out on the deck drinking beer and pretending to argue about something. The door was closed, so she couldn't hear, but they looked angry as hell, and yet she knew they were enjoying themselves.

*Men.*

"It's about to start," Javier said, beer in hand. "Mia, you're the guest of honor."

Tessa went to get Julian and Marc, while Mia followed the others down the hallway. Kat and Sophie took the children into the playroom, while the adults found seats down the hall in the home theater.

"Sophie just can't handle this right now," Marc said for Mia's ears alone.

"You don't need to explain. I understand." Since meeting Joaquin, Mia had read about the terrorist attack on the Palace Hotel and knew what Sophie had gone through. If that had been Mia, and terrorists had taken Joaquin out to execute him…

Mia sat between Laura and Joaquin, her pulse picking up.

Joaquin took her hand, whispered in her ear. "Relax. It's going to be okay."

A car commercial. A beer commercial. A soft drink commercial.

The program started, the introductory music quite dramatic.

Laura leaned over. "I've asked them to remake that, to make it more newsy and less like the Olympics, but no. They want trumpets and fanfare."

Then Laura appeared on the screen, looking polished and beautiful. "Tonight, we bring you the disturbing story of a military officer who was harassed, abused, and almost murdered for daring to report crimes committed by members of her own company, including her commanding officer. This is the first time Mia Starr has shared her story in its entirety, and what she told us will shock you. This story includes graphic images of injury and violence. Viewers are urged to exercise discretion."

Mia watched, listening to herself speak, seeing the photographs of stolen artifacts and skin blistered by mustard agent, watching some of the worst memories of her life unfold on the screen. Images of shattered glass and bloodshed. Footage of Powell's arraignment. Andy's sister standing at his graveside, in tears.

As the program came to a close, Joaquin beside her, her new friends surrounding her, Mia realized those memories no longer owned her. They were the past. Joaquin and his big family and his crazy group of friends—they were her life now.

In the second week of April, Joaquin and Mia closed on their new home—part of the urban redevelopment of Denver's old airport. Antonio and his crew had built the house and let Joaquin know about it so that he and Mia could put an offer on it before anyone else did. The place had four bedrooms, an unfinished basement, a study, a big kitchen, a wrap-around front porch, and lots of room for friends and family. Joaquin loved the modern feel of it and all the space. But Mia loved the yard—if you could call a half-acre of mud and weeds a yard.

They pulled into their driveway, he in his truck, she in her Mazda, and met on the front steps. Joaquin unlocked the door, then scooped Mia into his arms, laughing at her surprised shriek as he carried her across the threshold.

"Welcome home, *mi amor.*" He kissed her on that luscious mouth, then glanced at his watch. "José-Luis will be here in about thirty minutes with the moving van."

That didn't give him much time.

They went off together to explore, peeking into all of the

rooms, their voices echoing through the empty space, midday sunlight spilling through the windows onto golden wood floors, graceful arched entryways, and gray granite countertops.

"It's beautiful, Joaquin. I love it. It's so bright and cheery and peaceful."

Best of all for both of them, it came without bullet holes and bad memories.

She'd gained some peace and healing from going public with her story, which had made international headlines. She'd received many requests for interviews and had also gotten a phone call from a three-star general who had apologized to her on behalf of the Army—and promised they would do better on sexual harassment.

She seemed so much happier now, more confident, more outgoing in bed and out. She believed in more than her intellectual abilities now. She believed in herself as a red-blooded woman. And, yeah, that hadn't hurt their sex life.

*Santa María Madre de Dios*, she amazed him.

No woman could do to him what Mia did.

His family and friends adored her. Now Joaquin wanted to make it official. He was pretty sure she'd say yes, but, shit, what if she surprised him?

Mia made her way toward the sliding glass door that led to the big concrete patio in back. She was impatient to look at the mud and the weeds, of course. He'd known she'd head in that direction sooner rather than later. In fact, he'd worked it into his plans.

They stepped outside into the warm spring air.

"Isn't it beautiful?"

Joaquin could only see her face. "Yes."

She started telling him about the trees she wanted to plant. "I think a bigtooth maple over there for fall color. I really want some pines in the front yard and back here so we can decorate them with Christmas lights. Won't that be pretty?"

"Yeah. That sounds good." He wondered when she would notice it, some part of him excited and some part of him scared out of his mind.

"I'm torn between mugo pines and some kind of Swiss stone pine. Mugos do really well in Colorado because they're well adapted for our climate and fairly xeric, but the stone pines do well, too. I want to avoid arborvitae. They just don't thrive here."

Trees, trees, trees.

It was adorable, really, but he needed her to *see* before José-Luis and his crew arrived and started lugging boxes everywhere.

"What about over there?" Joaquin pointed.

She turned her head—and gave a little gasp. "*Bouteloua gracilis.*"

She walked over to the little pot, picked it up, lovingly ran her fingers over the grass blades. "You got me my favorite grass. You know me so well."

This wasn't going the way he'd planned. She still hadn't seen.

"Are you sure this is the kind of grass you want?" *¡Carajo!* What would he do if she flat-out didn't notice?

She gave him a look. "I know my grasses."

Desperate now, he took the pot of *Bouteloua* grassy stuff, and dropped to one knee, hoping this would make his intentions obvious. "*Look* at it, *mi amor.*"

"Why are you on your knee?" She gaped at him as if he were a lunatic—which maybe he was—then peeked down among the grass blades. "What am I supposed—oh, my God! Oh, Joaquin!"

Her eyes went wide, and she reached inside the clump of grass with careful fingers and pulled out the ring—a single oval-cut diamond encircled by diamonds and set in an antique band of white gold. "It's *beautiful!*"

"Mia Rose, my love, my soul, will you marry me?" The words were out now, his heart beating naked on his sleeve.

She didn't make him wait for an answer. "Are you kidding? Yes! ¡*Sí!*"

He got to his feet, took the ring from her, and slid it onto her finger, relieved to see that it fit.

She sniffed, tears spilling down her cheeks. "I love it."

"You're crying. I've never seen you cry when you were happy."

She laughed, sniffed, smiled up at him. "I've never been *this* happy before."

He drew her close, held her, kissed the top of her head. "This is just the beginning, Mia."

There would be so many happy days to come.

# EPILOGUE

*June 2*

Mia looked into the mirror, her heart swelling. Her reflection smiled back at her, excitement on her face, long red curls hanging around her shoulders. "Wow."

"You look stunning." Holly stood beside her, beaming, makeup brushes in hand.

"You look beautiful—like a bride." Isabel adjusted the lace veil attached to the barrette that held Mia's curls back from her face. "My son is a lucky man."

"Oh, Mia." Elena, Mia's maid of honor, blinked back tears. "I *knew* you and Quino would be right for each other."

Mia reached out, took Elena's hand. "I will always love you for that."

Mia glanced around the room. "Thanks for your help. I couldn't have pulled this together so quickly without you."

Elena had worked with the Cousin Mafia—that's what Mia called them now—to help Mia order flowers, print and mail invitations, and pull together a reception.

Isabel had loaned Mia her veil—the same antique lace

veil she had worn at her own wedding and her mother before her.

Holly, who had become Mia's closest friend, had done Mia's hair and makeup. She had also helped Mia choose her dress—a white sleeveless gown with an illusion neckline and sweetheart bust that made the most of Mia's chest, and a full skirt of silk taffeta that emphasized her narrow waist. The delicate lace details on the neckline were a close match for the lace in Isabel's veil. But the best part about the gown was the skirt.

It came with a surprise, and only Mia and Holly knew what that was.

Mia turned so that her mother, who stood near the bedroom door, could see, too. "What do you think?"

Her mother gave her a tight smile, her puffy eyes proof that she'd been crying. "You look very pretty."

Mia knew her mother believed that the lack of sleeves was immodest, but Mia's choice of gown was the least of her objections. What troubled her parents far more was the fact that Joaquin had been raised Catholic—and that he had brown skin. They'd never come right out and said it, but she knew it was true.

"Forget them," Holly had said after the rehearsal dinner yesterday. "You enjoy your day."

Mia's parents had offered to drive her to the dinner, but had taken the scenic route to Mateo's restaurant, making Mia late. They'd spent the entire drive trying to talk her into calling off the wedding. She'd thought they had warmed up to Joaquin. After all, he had almost died trying to save her life. But what they'd said on that drive had proved to Mia that they'd been pretending to care about him.

"This is your last chance, Mia," her father had said as

they'd pulled into Aztlán's parking lot. "End this before it becomes another regret."

"I don't have any regrets, Dad. I'm proud of the choices I've made. This is *your* last chance. Either accept that I love Joaquin and that I'm going to marry him, or go home and stay out of my life."

Mia had been furious.

Determined not to let her parents steal her joy, she took her bouquet—a confection of pink cabbage roses—from Elena, while Holly and Isabel adjusted her skirt and veil.

"The limo's here," Mia's father called from downstairs.

"Let Elena carry your bouquet so you can hold your skirt," Isabel said.

Mia's mother stepped away from the door. "I'd like a moment alone with my daughter."

Isabel and Holly looked at Mia, who nodded.

Mia's mother waited until the door had closed. "I wanted to give you this. It used to belong to my mother."

She handed Mia a rectangular box. Inside lay a sapphire and diamond tennis bracelet set in white gold. "Oh, Mom. It's beautiful. Can you help me put it on?"

Her mother lifted the bracelet from the box and clipped it onto her wrist. "I want you to keep it. You remind me of your grandmother. You have her passion for life."

"Thank you."

A troubled expression came over her mother's face. "I'm sorry for the way we behaved the other night. I have nothing against Joaquin. I just worry about your soul."

"You should have a long talk with Joaquin's grandmother. She's worried, too, because I'm not converting and we're not getting married in the Catholic Church."

Her mother stared at Mia—then smiled. "I suppose she and I *do* have something in common there."

"Don't you think it was God who brought Joaquin into my life?" Mia wasn't a religious person, but the words felt true to her. "He saved me, Mom. He literally put himself between me and a bullet, and then he crawled across my condo, close to dying, to kill the man who was trying to murder me."

Did her mother not understand?

"He is very brave—and so are you."

"Apology accepted. I don't suppose Dad knows about this little talk."

"You just enjoy your day. I will deal with your father." Her mother smoothed a hand over Mia's curls. "You are a beautiful bride. Let's not keep Joaquin waiting."

JOAQUIN STOOD with Matt in the Rose Pavilion at the Botanic Gardens, which had been closed off to all but members of the wedding party and their guests. The roses were in full bloom, their scent filling the air. No wonder Mia loved it.

Chairs had been set up, and most of the seats were filled, family and friends mixing on both sides, some coming up to congratulate Joaquin. The string quartet they had hired sat in the shade, tuning their instruments.

It was all coming together.

"Did the judge get his payment?" Joaquin had found a Spanish-speaking judge who was willing to marry them outside of his courtroom—for an extra fee.

"Yes." Matt, Joaquin's best man, fidgeted with Joaquin's rosebud boutonniere. "Would you relax?"

"Weren't you nervous at your wedding?"

Matt shook his head. "I was drunk. That's *why* there was a wedding."

That explained a few things—such as why Matt was now divorced.

Matt glanced around. "You saved a fortune on flowers by having the wedding here, man. Look at this place."

"This is Mia's favorite part of the gardens."

"It's strange that she works here and she's getting married here. I sure as hell wouldn't want to get married in the newsroom."

Joaquin laughed. "She loves roses."

Most of the guests had arrived, his relatives mingling with their I-Team friends and Mia's co-workers, talking and laughing with one another. Jack and Nate made their way through the crowd with Janet and Megan, Jack in an Army dress uniform and Nate in his Marine dress blues. Zach, too, had come in dress uniform, complete with his Medal of Honor. They'd worn their uniforms to honor Mia.

Everyone was smiling—including his long-suffering *abuelita*. She sat up front with his parents, holding the *lazo* in her lap. It was the only element of a traditional Mexican wedding that he and Mia had preserved. *Padrinos*—godparents or mentors—draped it around the bride and groom in a figure eight before they made their vows as an added blessing and a sign of the unity of marriage. If they'd had a church wedding, the *lazo* would have been an extra-long rosary, but Joaquin and Mia had opted for orange blossoms, which were also traditional.

The judge made his way up the aisle, dressed in black robes. He shook Joaquin's and Matt's hands. "The big day is finally here. This place is lovely."

Joaquin was in the middle of telling him that this is where Mia worked and that the roses were her favorite part of the gardens when Matt interrupted him.

"Here comes Mia's mom," Matt said.

That meant Mia was here—and that the ceremony was about to begin.

A hush fell over the gathering as Mia's mother took her seat.

"Are you ready for this, man?" Matt asked.

Joaquin was more than ready.

The quartet began to play—Bach's Air on a G String.

Elena appeared, looking incredible in a mermaid gown of pastel pink, her gaze meeting Joaquin's, a bright smile on her face. She walked up the center aisle, which was already strewn with rose petals, bouquet in hand.

"Whoa," Matt whispered. "She's—"

"My cousin," Joaquin finished for him.

"Right."

*Mia.*

Everyone stood as she stepped into the pavilion on her father's arm.

It seemed to Joaquin that his heart had stopped. She looked like a dream in her white gown, her hair curling at her shoulders, a big bouquet of roses in her hands. She looked straight at him, her smile bright enough to shame the sunshine.

Joaquin found himself blinking back tears. He had waited a lifetime for this woman, for Mia. So many lonely nights. So many empty days. There were times when he'd wondered whether he'd ever find her—a woman to share his life with, someone special he could cherish for the rest of his life. Now, here she was, walking toward him.

Mia's father placed her hand in Joaquin's, but all Joaquin could see was Mia. "You are so beautiful."

He bent down, kissed her.

Quiet laughter.

The judge welcomed everyone to the ceremony in

English and Spanish, his words drifting over Joaquin like a breeze. Then Joaquin's godparents stood and came to drape the *lazo* around them, the scent of orange blossoms mingling with roses.

It was time for their vows.

Joaquin looked into Mia's eyes. "I, Joaquín Cristián, vow to love you, Mia, and to forsake all others for as long as I live. What I possess in this world, I give to you. I will keep and hold you, comfort and care for you, protect and shelter you, in good times and in hard times, for all the days of my life."

Now there were tears in Mia's eyes. "I, Mia Rose, vow to love you, Joaquín, and to forsake all others for as long as I live. What I possess in this world, I give to you. I will keep and hold you, comfort and care for you, protect and shelter you, in good times and in hard times, for all the days of my life."

Matt handed Joaquin Mia's wedding band, which Joaquin slipped onto her finger. "I give you this ring as a sign of my love and faithfulness and commit myself, body and soul, to you."

Mia repeated those words as she slid a band of white gold onto his finger.

"*Te amo, Mia.*"

As the judge began to pronounce them husband and wife, Joaquin drew her into his arms and kissed her.

"You may kiss ... er... well."

Cheers.

MIA TOOK a sip of the champagne she and Joaquin had opened in the limo, looking around at the reception hall.

The Cousin Mafia had rented the place and decorated it. She hadn't been sure what to expect, but they had come through again. Sheer pink and white fabric panels were draped across the walls. Bouquets of flowers sat on every table. There was a sound system, too, and a long table weighted down with food from the caterers.

Joaquin nuzzled her ear. "It's almost time for our dance."

They had been working on this—their first dance—since the day Joaquin had proposed. They'd practiced until Mia had mastered it and felt comfortable on the dance floor. Elena had helped Mia learn some of the sexier elements of salsa—that sensual, undulating motion, all that hip action.

Alejandro, another cousin of Joaquin's and their DJ for the afternoon, took the stage, welcoming everyone in English and Spanish. "We have a surprise for the newest member of the family. Mia, *prima*, are you watching?"

Joaquin's male cousins lined up on the floor in front of the stage. To a man, they shed their suit jackets, tossing them to friends, wives, and girlfriends.

"You better not be planning to take anything else off!" Joaquin shouted.

Laughter.

"Mia, we are so grateful to have you in our family," Alejandro said, as they all began to unbutton their dress shirts. "We are *your* cousins, too, now. We are your own personal ..."

"Cousin Mafia!" they all shouted in unison, shedding their shirts to reveal T-shirts with the words COUSIN MAFIA spelled out in big, red letters across the front.

Cheers. Applause. Laughter.

Mia laughed, too. Never had her life been so full of people who loved her as it was today. She blew them a kiss. "*¡Gracias!*"

Joaquin kissed her. "See? They love you, too."

"Now, we'd like to ask Quino and his beautiful bride to take the floor and kick off this party with the traditional first dance."

"Are you ready for this?" Joaquin took off his tux jacket and rolled up his sleeves.

"Are you?" *Poor man.* Mia was about to blow his mind.

She walked out onto the dance floor with him, people cheering and clapping for them, Holly standing nearby as she and Mia had planned.

Joaquin would have drawn her into his arms, but she gave him a playful push and stepped away from him. Then she reached down, unfastened the clasp, and removed the full skirt, revealing the beaded, white mini-dress beneath.

Whistles. Cheers. Applause.

"¡*Ay, carajo!*" Joaquin's jaw dropped, his gaze sliding over her.

Holly came and took the skirt from Mia, a conspiratorial smile on her lips.

"We'll give the groom a moment to recover," Alejandro said into the microphone, chuckling. "Quino, are you okay, man? Give us a sign."

Joaquin took a step toward Mia, drew her forcefully into his arms, his gaze never leaving hers. "Start the music!"

They danced it the way they'd practiced it—sexy and raw. All the love Mia felt for Joaquin, all the passion she'd found with him, seemed to flow through her as they moved, Joaquin spinning her in his arms, her hips in sync with his, their bodies sharing a single rhythm. Joaquin arched her backward, bending over her, lowering his face to the space between her breasts, kissing her there as the music ended.

The room exploded in cheers.

"I didn't know Ramirez could dance like that," Mia heard Marc say.

"You're kidding, right?" That was Julian. "When he talked about salsa, did you think he was talking about hot sauce? You did."

Joaquin slowly raised Mia up again, the intensity in his eyes making her pulse skip, their lips almost touching, their hearts beating together. "*Eres mía—para siempre.*"

*You are mine—forever.*

"*Y tú eres mío, Joaquín.*"

*And you are mine.*

# ALSO BY PAMELA CLARE

*Falling Hard* (Book 3)

*Tempting Fate* (Book 4)

*Close to Heaven* (Book 5)

*Holding On* (Book 6)

*Chasing Fire* (Book 7)

## Historical Romance:

**Kenleigh-Blakewell Family Saga**

*Sweet Release* (Book 1)

*Carnal Gift* (Book 2)

*Ride the Fire* (Book 3)

**MacKinnon's Rangers series**

*Surrender* (Book I)

*Untamed* (Book 2)

*Defiant* (Book 3)

*Upon A Winter's Night: A MacKinnon's Rangers Christmas* (Book 3.5)

# ABOUT THE AUTHOR

USA Today best-selling author Pamela Clare began her writing career as a columnist and investigative reporter and eventually became the first woman editor-in-chief of two different newspapers. Along the way, she and her team won numerous state and national honors, including the National Journalism Award for Public Service. In 2011, Clare was awarded the Keeper of the Flame Lifetime Achievement Award for her body of work. A single mother with two sons, she writes historical romance and contemporary romantic suspense at the foot of the beautiful Rocky Mountains. Follow her on Facebook, Twitter, and Goodreads, or visit her website and join her mailing list to never miss a new release!

www.pamelaclare.com